THE MYSTERY OF THE
MARTELLO TOWER

THE MYSTERY OF THE
MARTELLO TOWER

A HAZEL FRUMP ADVENTURE

JENNIFER LANTHIER

Harper*Trophy*Canada™
An imprint of HarperCollins*PublishersLtd*

The Mystery of the Martello Tower
© 2006 by Jennifer Lanthier. All rights
reserved.

Published by Harper*Trophy*Canada™,
an imprint of HarperCollins
Publishers Ltd

Harper*Trophy*Canada™ is a trademark
of HarperCollins Publishers.

First edition

HarperCollins books may be pur-
chased for educational, business, or
sales promotional use through our
Special Markets Department.

HarperCollins Publishers Ltd
2 Bloor Street East, 20th Floor
Toronto, Ontario, Canada
M4W 1A8

www.harpercollins.ca

Library and Archives Canada
Cataloguing in Publication

Lanthier, Jennifer
The mystery of the Martello Tower :
a Hazel Frump adventure / Jennifer
Lanthier. — 1st ed.

ISBN-13: 978-0-00-639523-2
ISBN-10: 0-00-639523-6

I. Title.

PS8623.A555M98 2007   jC813'.6
C2006-905831-8

hc 9 8 7 6 5 4 3 2 1

Printed and bound in the United States
Set in Berling

For Jane and Jim Lanthier

PROLOGUE

Hazel Frump opened her mouth to cry out, but her voice had disappeared. She tried to spit, to get the dust and cobwebs out of her mouth, but her throat was too dry and her tongue too swollen. She longed to get up, to run away, but she couldn't move her arms or legs. She couldn't even feel them.

Hazel could only lie still, listening to the ragged sound of her own breathing. The stone of the flagged floor was cool and rough beneath her cheek, the curved walls of the old tower room faintly illuminated by the stars that shone through the tall arched windows. This was crazy. She had to get out of here before they found her.

Get up, get up, *get up*, she urged herself.

Nothing happened. She stared at her legs, willing them to move. Nothing. If only she could at least crawl to that window, maybe she could climb out and escape. Why couldn't she move?

What am I doing here? she cried silently. No, that was the wrong question.

What am I doing here *again*?

CHAPTER ONE

"Hazel!"

Hazel awoke with a jolt, certain she had heard her father call her name. She opened her eyes and instantly snapped them shut again. The light streaming through her windows was strong enough to blind her. Where was she? And what time was it?

With one hand shading her face, Hazel squinted cautiously around the room. It *was* her room, she noted with relief. She was back at home, in the apartment in the city; not in her dormitory at boarding school, and definitely not in some musty old tower from a dream.

There were her posters of dunking basketball players from the NBA and the Women's National Basketball Association. There was the ball autographed by her favourite player who had made it all the way from New York City's fabled Rucker playground to the Olympics. There was her computer, with its basketball screen saver. There, against the far wall, was the hoop set to NCAA height, and there, a short distance away, was the window she'd cracked last night when she'd failed to grab a rebound. There was—

"Hazel! Helloooo? Hazel? Earth calling Hazel!"

A small boy with ruler-straight brown hair stood at the side of her bed, polishing his glasses. It was something her brother did when he was nervous or excited.

Now that he finally had her attention, Ned placed the gleaming spectacles on his nose and peered owlishly at her.

"You were having that dream again," he accused. "Weren't you?"

Hazel glared at her brother. Her thick hair was plastered to her neck with sweat and her forehead felt clammy. Her skin was probably flushed as red as her hair, and she seemed to be tangled up in her quilt. Her father always said the only thing a nightmare meant was that your dinner had been too rich, or your room was too hot. Hazel felt pretty darn hot and cranky now.

She decided not to answer Ned.

"What are *you* doing in *my* room?" Hazel demanded instead.

Ned could ignore questions, too. He ploughed ahead, as if she hadn't spoken.

"Have you ever noticed that every time you have that dream, something bad happens?" he asked.

Hazel groaned. Why had she ever told Ned about the dream she'd had since she was small? She had done it in a moment of weakness after she'd tried to talk to their father about it. A strange look had appeared in Colin Frump's eyes and he had changed the subject. Now Hazel wished *she* could change the subject.

"Not that I have any interest in having this conversation with you—especially before breakfast—but I think if you ask around, you'll find that *most* people associate nightmares with bad things happening," Hazel replied. Her tone dripped condescension. "It's called stress, Squirt. When you're older, you'll understand."

"Actually, I think if *you* ask around, you'll find that *most* people have nightmares *after* something bad happens. You have them *before*," Ned observed, mimicking her tone. "Specifically, you have this one particular dream. And then something bad happens."

Hazel slumped against the pillows and contemplated the vast difference in age, experience, and intellect that separated her from her kid brother. (Well, maybe not intellect. Ned was widely regarded as brilliant.) But still, they had so little in common, they practically spoke a different language. He was a boy. A nine-and-a-half-year-old boy. She was almost twelve.

Practically a teenager.

"Look, I just had the stupid dream because I . . . I was attacked by my duvet," she explained.

Ned raised one eyebrow. He did it because he knew it drove her crazy. Their father could raise one eyebrow, too. But try as she might, Hazel could only raise both eyebrows at the same time. It was frustrating being the only one who couldn't do it. She suspected her mother hadn't been able to do it either, but Jane Frump had died before Hazel's fourth birthday and Hazel couldn't remember much about her. She didn't like to ask their father—he always looked so sad whenever her mother was mentioned.

"Ned, nothing's wrong and nothing bad is going to happen," Hazel insisted. She began ticking off points on her fingers: "Look, it's the first day of summer vacation . . . school is, like, a hundred miles away, and by the smell of things, I'd say Dad is cooking bacon and eggs for a Welcome Home breakfast."

Hazel kicked at her covers. She had managed to get one leg free, but the other seemed to have a sheet wound round it so tightly it was a miracle her circulation wasn't cut off. Was it actually knotted?

"Except for me being attacked by killer sheets, there's no bad here," she concluded. "It's all good—I'll bet you a month's allowance."

"You can pay me anytime," Ned answered. His voice sounded odd, as if his throat had tightened.

Hazel stopped tugging at her sheets and stared. The siblings didn't look much alike. It wasn't just their hair. Hazel was as tall for her age as Ned was short for his. Her eyes were green; his were brown. And while her skin was the colour of milk, Ned looked tanned all year long. But not right now. Right now, Ned's face looked almost as white as Hazel's.

It wasn't a good look for him, Hazel thought.

"Frankie's the one in the kitchen, and if you actually want to be able to *eat* the bacon she's cooking, you better get out there and take over," Ned said.

"*Frankie's* in the kitchen?"

Hazel was stunned. Frankie couldn't cook. She was an artist. Not that the two things couldn't go together. Hazel and Ned knew plenty of artists who could cook. The apartment they lived in was part of an old warehouse that their father had converted into lofts, and he only rented to artists. Frankie herself lived just across the hall. But she helped their father run his gallery. She *never* helped him cook.

"Where's Dad?" asked Hazel.

"Gone," answered Ned.

Gone?

Before Hazel could ask where their father had gone, Ned had put his head down and turned away. As he slipped silently out of the room, Hazel could see he was, once again, polishing his spotless glasses.

· · · ·

"All I can tell you, honey, is that he called me late last night and said something important had come up and he had to catch an overseas flight quite early this morning."

Frankie's voice was bemused rather than worried. "He was

supposed to knock on my door *before* he called the taxi, but he must have been running late because by the time I opened my door he was already in the elevator."

Frankie slid a plate of charred meat and leathery eggs in front of Hazel. The slender blonde woman frowned, as if seeing the food for the first time.

"I can't understand why my cooking never looks the same as other people's," Frankie observed.

"Or tastes the same," Ned said, pouring the remains of a box of cereal into a bowl.

"Oh, what a sweet thing to say," Frankie replied, sounding pleased.

"Not really," Ned muttered.

"Frankie, thanks for making this, but really, I'm not hungry," Hazel said, trying to avoid looking at the eggs, which were sort of grey and lumpy. "I'm too . . . uh, too confused to eat. Where *exactly* did Dad say he was going, and when did he say he'd be back?"

"Well, he didn't, dear, that's the thing," Frankie replied. She threw her hands in the air in an all too familiar why-ask-me? gesture. "I'm assuming he'll be back in time for your birthday. But you know your father. Colin Frump is not a chatty man."

"Yes, but he's not . . . I mean, he's not the sort of person who just goes running off into the night—"

"Or the morning," Ned interrupted.

"—without an explanation," Hazel continued. "He's not . . . what's the word I want?"

"Impulsive," Ned said.

"Yeah," Hazel agreed. "He's careful and—"

"Secretive," Ned added.

"I was going to say cautious," Hazel said, raising her eyebrows. "But yeah, I guess you could say he's . . . well, not secretive exactly . . . more like guarded. Reserved. The sort of person who studies all the angles before he makes a move. The sort of—"

"Well, right now he's the sort of person who's left *me* responsible for keeping his gallery open *and* calling all his clients to cancel his appointments *and* looking after you two—just when I'm trying to get my next show ready," Frankie said.

Anyone else would have been cross, Hazel reflected, but Frankie just sounded lost. Organizing stuff wasn't really her thing. Still, she'd always been a good friend to Hazel and Ned. That incident with the food poisoning last Christmas wasn't even her fault, really. Everyone knew you couldn't eat Frankie's cooking. Everyone except Frankie.

A twinge of guilt pricked at Hazel's conscience. It hadn't occurred to her that they might be messing up Frankie's life. Hazel jumped up and ran over to rub her neighbour's shoulder.

"Don't worry, Frankie. Ned and I don't need any looking after," Hazel said, trying to make her voice sound older and more reassuring. "In fact, we can even help out."

"We can definitely take over the meals," Ned said, his mouth full of cereal.

"And we can help at the gallery too," Hazel added, shooting her brother a warning glance.

"Oh, the gallery!" Frankie said. "I've got to get over there. Listen, would you kids mind awfully . . . no, I can't ask you that. You've just returned home, back to your own beds . . ."

"Ask us what?" Hazel enquired.

"Well, I have lots of work to do to get ready for my show, and since I'm going to be in the gallery most of the day, I was thinking . . ."

"You were thinking if we slept across the hall at your place instead of here, you could paint all night." Hazel guessed. She shrugged and glanced at Ned.

"We don't mind," Ned said, "so long as we can use our rooms during the day, whenever we want."

Frankie nodded. Hazel and Ned had grown up treating Frankie's apartment almost like an extension of theirs. When their father had renovated the warehouse, he had created only two apartments for each floor. The elevator wouldn't stop at any floor unless you had the proper key. And since no one but Frankie and the Frumps had keys to their floor, they hardly ever locked either door during the day. When they were younger, Colin Frump had tried to discourage his children from wandering in and out of Frankie's apartment, fearful they might disturb her work. But Frankie had never objected; it was clear she adored both of them. Besides, if Frankie was in the middle of painting, you could walk in with a wheelbarrow and walk out with everything she owned, except for her paint and brushes. She would never notice.

"That's settled then," Frankie said, sounding relieved. "I'll go open the gallery. Why don't you two drop by around lunchtime and we can all go to Café Gentil?"

Ned looked at the clock. It was already noon. He opened his mouth as if it to point out this fact, then closed it again and shrugged. He looked at Hazel.

"It sounds like you have a lot to do at the gallery," she said. "What if Ned and I come by around closing, and we'll have dinner at the café?"

"Sure, sweetie," Frankie agreed. "Whatever you say."

"It's settled then," Ned announced. "Now if you'll excuse me, I've got to go email my chemistry club."

"I didn't know nine-year-olds did chemistry," Frankie marvelled, as Ned padded down the hall toward his room. "Although, I suppose he will be ten soon . . ."

"Even twelve-year-olds don't do chemistry," Hazel told her. "But Ned's started doing a lot of stuff online this year. I'll bet the other members of this club don't have a clue who they're dealing with—they probably think he's twenty-one or something."

Frankie nodded thoughtfully. "It can't be easy always being the smartest one in the room," she observed, "especially at his age."

"Hey! Standing right here beside you, Frankie," Hazel said.

"Oh, sweetheart, you're smart too," Frankie said soothingly. "But you know what I mean."

Hazel rolled her eyes. But she did know what Frankie meant.

Hazel waited until she heard the door close behind Frankie before making her way to the garbage can to dump the cold, alien substance that had congealed on her plate. The eggs sounded oddly heavy as they landed at the bottom of the bin.

"Hazel!"

Hazel jumped, dropping her plate in the sink.

Frankie was standing in the doorway.

"Whoa, Frankie, you startled me," said Hazel, moving away from the garbage bin.

"I did? Oh, honey, maybe it's really not such a good idea—you guys hanging out here on your own. You seem nervous."

"No, I'm fine," Hazel replied. "Uh, did you need something?"

"I just forgot to tell you that your dad mentioned he would try to email you, so you should check your computer later."

"Okay." That gave Hazel an idea. "Frankie, does he have his cell phone with him?"

"Umm . . . I think so. But he warned me he wouldn't have it on very much. Anyway, I'm sure he'll be in touch soon. See you later!"

This time, Hazel saw Frankie to the door and watched as she entered the elevator.

After she had gone, the apartment seemed very quiet. Hazel stood for a moment, listening to the distant sounds of plumbing upstairs and traffic in the street below. She couldn't have said why, exactly, but when she closed the heavy oak door, she bolted it behind her.

The afternoon crawled by more slowly than a math class on a warm September afternoon. Hazel tried dialing her father's cell phone once, just to see what would happen. A recorded voice told her the customer was "not in service."

After showering, dressing, and checking her computer for email about two hundred useless times, Hazel decided it was time for some fresh air. Grabbing a basketball from the stash in her closet, she dribbled it down the hall toward Ned's room.

"Hey, Squirt—let's hit the court and you can show me how much you've improved since last fall," Hazel called.

Ned stuck his head out the door.

"If you promise not to call me that, I *might* go one-on-one before we meet Frankie," he told her sternly. "But I'm in the middle of something right now."

The door slammed behind him.

Hazel realized her mouth was open and closed it. Last fall, Ned had pestered her constantly to shoot hoops. She knew how hard he'd been working on his shot during the school year; Hazel and Ned attended separate boarding schools but kept in touch by email. She'd assumed he would be eager to show off.

I bet this has something to do with my birthday next week, Hazel told herself as she headed back to her room.

Ned always gave her a present he'd made himself. This wasn't as feeble as it sounded, since Ned was so clever and pretty good with his hands. But his idea of what constituted a useful or fun gift didn't always match Hazel's—like the time he designed glow-in-the-dark remote-controlled spiders with realistic hairy legs. *Surrealistic* hairy legs, their dad had called them, after one of the spiders crawled into the shower with him.

11

Hazel flopped on the bed. Thinking about her father was starting to give her a headache. Her mind was going in circles like a cat chasing its tail; only she was chasing questions, the same ones over and over.

Where *was* he? What was he doing? Why had he left in such a hurry? Today was Wednesday. Had he even remembered that next Wednesday was her twelfth birthday? Would he make it back in time? Did he even care? What could be so important that he would take off without telling them?

This was nuts. She wasn't getting anywhere just lying here, waiting for Ned. By the time Ned was ready to go, they'd probably be too late to hit the court. She might as well go shoot some hoops on her own.

Although . . . technically she couldn't. That is, she couldn't leave Ned by himself. He was too young.

Great. She was stuck . . . trapped in an empty apartment badly in need of groceries, babysitting an antisocial genius who was probably building a bomb over the Internet. *Thanks, Dad.*

On the other hand . . . Hazel sat up. Maybe something good could come out of being alone and unobserved. Who was there to know, for example, if Hazel wandered down the hall to her father's study and took a look around?

I'd better act fast, before I lose my nerve.

Hazel could feel her pulse jumping as she tiptoed past Ned's door. As long as she could remember, she and Ned had never been allowed in their dad's study. They were never sure what he did there, but when it came to their father, they weren't sure about much. Hazel hadn't liked to admit it, but Ned was right—Dad was secretive. He had no family except them and never spoke of his childhood. He never spoke of their mother, either, claiming both subjects were too painful. All they knew was that Jane Frump had died when Hazel was not quite four and Ned was a baby.

Hazel had figured out a few things about her father over the years. The first was that he was pretty darn rich. Exactly how much money he had, Hazel wasn't sure, but he was wealthy enough not to have a job. The gallery Frankie was running was just one of Colin Frump's hobbies, like the building where they lived. Hazel knew from talking to the tenants that her father didn't charge enough rent to cover the costs of maintaining the building. Some of her neighbours didn't pay rent at all.

So, another thing Hazel had figured out was that her dad was not only rich, but he was generous. Yet, whenever she asked him about it, his nose wrinkled as if he'd smelled something icky, and he made a shooing gesture, as if Hazel were a fly buzzing around his ear. Then he would start asking about her marks in math class.

In the end, Hazel decided all she had really figured out was that her father was a mystery. Maybe all fathers were something of a mystery, but hers was more so. Over the years she had come up with so many questions she knew there was no point in asking—her father would never answer. There were big questions, obvious ones, like: Where did he come from? Where did he get all his money? Was Hazel at all like her mother? What was her mother like? Why wouldn't he ever talk about her? What were his parents like? Then there were the littler questions: Why didn't he really have any friends? Why did he always seem to be someplace else, even when Hazel was hugging him and telling him how happy she was to be home for the holidays? Why was that someplace else so far away and so . . . *sad*?

Years ago, Hazel and her father had climbed to the lookout at Pirate's Peak. She hadn't felt the least bit afraid as they peered over the edge, down to the valley far below. Not until her father had remarked: "You know, they say the fear is not that you will *fall*, but that you will *jump*." Ever since that moment, Hazel had been a little worried about her father. And very worried about heights.

Hazel stood before the door to her father's study. It might be locked, of course. She almost hoped it would be. Then she wouldn't have to screw up her courage to go inside.

But the brass handle turned easily and the heavy oak door swung open noiselessly.

This is hardly Bluebeard's chamber, Hazel thought. She was almost disappointed. Like the rest of the loft, her father had furnished the room sparingly, with stark, modern furniture and messy stacks of books. The only difference was that in the rest of the apartment just a few meticulously chosen paintings were hung with care.

"Here you can't see the paintings for all the art," Hazel said aloud.

There were hundreds of paintings, from oil canvases to watercolours. They covered the walls from floor to ceiling; there wasn't a blank patch of wall the size of Hazel's palm. Framed or unframed, they were leaning against bookshelves, heaped atop the sofa, and piled on chairs. In the centre of the room lay a stack of canvases, wrapped in brown paper, ready to be mailed.

"No wonder he doesn't want us in here," Hazel sniffed. "He could never complain about our rooms needing to be tidied once we saw this."

There had to be a desk hidden somewhere in the clutter. Hazel spied a long folding screen at the far end of the room. Maybe her father kept a work area behind it.

Carefully, she made her way past a precariously balanced canvas almost twice her height and narrowly avoided tripping over a group of marble statues concealed behind it. The area behind the screen was almost as cluttered, but here the mess consisted of notebooks, letters, and files piled on the floor and strewn across a broad antique desk. Here and there, jutting out like islands in the sea of paper, Hazel spied computer monitors, hard drives, two printers, and a telephone that looked very complicated.

"This is insane. It'll take me forever to find anything."

Hazel sat down gingerly. She noticed a small notepad to the left of the telephone. Her father was clearly in the habit of doodling while talking. She flipped through the three pages remaining on the pad. They were almost filled with scribbles—words and drawings.

"Time for a new pad, Dad," Hazel muttered. She'd take the sheets back to her room and try to decipher them at leisure. She could replace them later with no one the wiser.

Her father had left the computer up and running. It took only moments to locate his email account. There were two unread messages. The first was from someone named Oliver Frump. The subject heading read: Frump Family Reunion on Île du Loup?

Family reunion? But Colin Frump had no family. Hazel's finger hovered over the computer mouse, ready to click and open the message. Then her eye focused on the second unread message.

It was from someone named Inspector O'Toole.

Hazel froze.

The subject of this message read: Interpol investigation into Ned's website.

CHAPTER TWO

Hazel stared at the computer screen.

Interpol—that was some sort of international police thing, wasn't it? What did they investigate? Crime, obviously. Duh. But what sort of crime? Hazel felt stupid. Ned would know, of course. But she couldn't ask him.

Why would Interpol be investigating her little brother? What had Ned done?

She caught her breath. He wasn't *really* designing a bomb with that chemistry club, was he? Ned wasn't that clever, was he? She shook her head; wrong question.

Ned wasn't that *stupid*, was he?

Hazel had thought her brain was stuffed so full of worry and questions about her father that there was no room for anything else. But her head seemed to be expanding like a balloon, swelling with fresh questions every moment. Was this why her dad had left the country? Was he protecting Ned somehow?

But if Ned was in trouble, shouldn't Colin Frump be here?

Hazel's head felt dangerously close to popping. How could the police—the *international* police—be investigating Ned?

"He's just a little kid," Hazel thought aloud. Although

apparently he was a little kid who knew how to design a website. *She* didn't even know how to do that.

Maybe it wasn't a bomb. Maybe it was something to do with computer hacking, or designing viruses to mess up other people's computers. She'd read an article about that stuff for school. It seemed to be something smart kids—often boys—got into just because they could. Like a way of showing off.

Maybe that was all it was.

Except, hackers could go to jail. What if Ned had hacked into the computer system of a hospital and somebody had open-heart surgery instead of getting their tonsils taken out? What if he had hacked into a system that controlled traffic and gave everyone green lights so that they all drove into each other? What if he'd made the navy think a fishing boat was a nuclear submarine—and they blew it up?

This was crazy.

Hazel closed her eyes against the images that crowded her brain. Ned was a pest, but he was not . . . *bad*. He was not a criminal.

It had to be something else.

There was only way to find out. She had to open her father's emails.

Yet, as her fingers hovered over the keys, Hazel hesitated. What would her dad say when he found out she'd read his messages? Once she opened them, wouldn't he know someone had seen them?

Hazel scrunched up her face in concentration. She wished she'd paid more attention when Ned talked about computers. There was probably something she could do, some way to make the computer think she hadn't read the messages.

Ned would know. But she couldn't ask him, of course.

Hazel pulled at her thick, unruly hair. She would just have to open the messages and hope for the best. Maybe their father would understand. It's not like she had *wanted* to go snooping around—he'd left her no choice. If her dad had taken the time to talk to her before he left, if he had phoned from the airport, or emailed from his hotel . . .

Hazel slumped back in the chair. She could hear a faint tapping noise in the distance; Claire Holland, the artist in 3B, must be sculpting again.

Maybe it would be best to check her own computer one more time before she did anything rash. Maybe she'd find an email from Colin Frump explaining everything. Then she could ignore the messages, and no one would ever have to know she'd been in the study.

But even if her father came clean about this whole Interpol thing, there was still the question of that Oliver Frump guy and his family reunion. Finding long-lost family you never knew you had wasn't as important as figuring out why the cops were after your kid brother, but it was still worth looking into. Wasn't it?

Her fingers moved toward the keyboard.

The faint tapping noise became a loud thumping. That wasn't Claire Holland sculpting upstairs. That was someone banging on the apartment door.

"Hazel? Ned? It's me. Open up!"

Hazel jumped to her feet. What was Frankie doing back already? She glanced at her watch. How time flies when your world is falling apart. It was almost dinnertime. Frankie must have decided not to wait for them. She'd be wondering why the door was locked.

There was no time now to read the emails. Hazel would have to come back. She picked her way through the study as quickly as she could, without toppling anything over.

Ned was still in his room. Hazel could hear him tapping away at his keyboard as she ran to open the apartment door.

He really wouldn't notice if the place burned down around him, his sister reflected.

"Hey, Hazel—I hope you guys don't mind takeout." Frankie smiled and handed Hazel a shopping bag filled with cartons of Chinese food. "Should we eat here or over at my place?" Frankie enquired.

"Oh. Uh, let's eat here," Hazel answered. She was pleased to find her voice sounded calm.

"Where's Ned?" Frankie asked.

"He's in his room. I'll set the table if you can get him out," Hazel offered. "I've been trying—I think the hard drive ate him or something."

"So, you slept all morning and stayed inside all afternoon?" Frankie clucked. "What a shame—it's been so sunny and nice."

While Frankie went to rouse Ned, Hazel placed bamboo mats on the Lucite dining table and set chopsticks at each place. Normal, normal, normal, she repeated silently to herself. I must act *normal*.

As she poured glasses of ice water for everyone, Hazel resolved she would check her computer after dinner, just one last time. If she had no email from her dad, she'd find a way to sneak back into his office and read his. It was that simple.

Except, of course, it wasn't simple at all.

After dinner, Frankie insisted they all go for a stroll along the boardwalk, as the children had spent too much time "cooped up indoors." Ordinarily, Hazel loved to walk with Frankie; artists so often seemed to have a different way of looking at the world, and she could always count on Frankie to point out faces and patterns or shadows that she would never have noticed. But tonight, Hazel was so anxious to get back to her father's study, she found herself nodding without hearing anything Frankie said.

Hazel felt sure Ned and Frankie must suspect something

every time they looked at her, but no one said anything. Maybe she was a better actress than she realized. Maybe they figured she was just sad about Colin Frump leaving.

By the time they returned to the apartment it was late and darkness had settled over the city like a blanket. Frankie waited in the kitchen while the children gathered pyjamas, toothbrushes, and a change of clothes for morning. Hazel just had time to see that she still had no message from her father, before Ned was calling to her to hurry up so they could go across the hall to Frankie's place.

As the pair settled themselves on futons in Frankie's spacious guest room, Ned told Hazel that Frankie had made him promise not to even turn on his computer the next day. He and Hazel were to spend the morning shooting hoops in the park, and taking Frankie to lunch at Café Gentil.

Rats! thought Hazel.

Ned was quiet for a long time after Hazel turned out the light. When he finally spoke, it was in a whisper.

"Do you think maybe this time the dream was wrong?" he asked. "Because, nothing really terrible has happened. Yet."

Hazel was grateful for the darkness that hid her face. No, nothing terrible. Unless you counted that Interpol investigation and Dad's mysterious disappearance.

"That's what I've been telling you," she replied. "Frankie's here, I'm here. Everything's okay."

"Yeah." Ned sounded unconvinced. "But the dream's never been wrong before."

That was true. As Hazel searched for something reassuring to say, Ned asked the question he'd clearly been working up to, his voice tinged with dread.

"What if you have the dream again tonight?"

Hazel shivered. *Please, don't let me have the dream again tonight.*

"I won't," she said in the most confident tone she could muster.

It seemed to work because when Ned spoke again, he sounded almost normal.

"I'm sorry I kept you in all day." Ned's apology was muffled by his pillow. "I didn't really think about the fact that you couldn't go out if I didn't—not until Frankie pointed it out just now."

"That's okay," Hazel said. "So, uh, did you get a lot done?"

"What do you mean?"

"You know—with your chemistry club. Everything go okay?"

"I guess," Ned sounded suspicious. Hazel decided to change the subject.

"So, I've been meaning to ask you," she began. "This girl at school got into trouble for reading someone else's emails . . . and I was thinking. There was probably some way she could have disguised the fact that she'd read them, wasn't there?"

"It's wrong to read other people's emails," Ned said sleepily.

"Oh yeah, absolutely," Hazel agreed quickly. "But I just wondered why she didn't, you know, hide her tracks, or whatever. Because there's got to be something she could have done, right?"

Ned yawned.

"Well, I think most systems have a way you can mark the emails as "unread" if you look in the toolbar—you know, the thing across the top of the computer screen," he suggested. "But she could also have just deleted the emails after she read them, and then the person who sent them would have thought they got lost in cyberspace. Things disappear on the Internet all the time."

Hazel was thankful the room was so dark; she could feel her skin blush. Talk about stupid! Ned's solution was so simple it was ridiculous. What was her science teacher always saying? The easiest solution is often the right one? She didn't need any complicated computer wizardry: if she couldn't figure out how to mark the messages as unread, she'd just destroy the evidence.

Hazel thought about doing it right then. She could make some excuse to Frankie about needing a book or something from the apartment. It wouldn't take long to read those two messages (and any others that might have come in since). She didn't have to worry about memorizing them or anything, because it wasn't like she had to delete them right away. She could even print paper copies!

So long as she erased them before Colin Frump's return, no one would be the wiser.

Hazel stifled a yawn. She really, *really* wanted to find out more about Inspector O'Toole and Interpol . . . not to mention this Oliver Frump guy. But it had been kind of an exhausting day, and they must have walked for miles. Her legs felt like weights.

Ned was already asleep—she could tell by his breathing. Hazel wasn't surprised. Frankie's futons were awfully comfortable.

"I'll do it tomorrow," she told herself.

It was a decision she would soon regret.

· · · ·

Breakfast at Frankie's wasn't too horrible, since Hazel and Ned managed to convince her that cold cereal and fruit were just perfect, and no actual cooking was required. She made a great production of walking them to the park and actually watched them warm up for a few minutes before setting off for the gallery.

"She's serious about this fresh air thing," Ned observed, as he dribbled the ball up the empty court.

"You know, I really don't mind if you want to go back to the apartment," Hazel offered. "We can shoot a few hoops before we go, so we don't have to lie to Frankie."

"Nope," Ned replied. "I promised her I'd spend the day outdoors."

"Well, yeah, but . . . we could go home for a bit, and then come back and go one-on-one for an hour or so before we meet her for lunch," Hazel said.

"Why are you so eager to leave?" Ned demanded. He had stopped dribbling the ball and was staring at her. "I thought you'd be dying to show me you're still better than I am." Hazel could feel a flush creeping over her pale skin. She hoped Ned would think it was the heat.

"I'm . . . I'm not," she stammered. "Not eager to leave, I mean. In fact, I plan to kick your—I mean, I'm taking you to school, Squirt. Right now. Bring it on."

"Anyone named Hazel can't say 'bring it on,'" Ned said. "Face it. You're just not that cool."

Hazel grabbed the ball from his hands and launched a perfect mid-range jumpshot. The ball arced through the air and dropped through the hoop without so much as touching the netting.

"Nice," Ned said. "But you should also drop the 'taking you to school' thing. Makes you sound like you're trying too hard to be a 'baller.'"

"What is this? Your version of trash talk?" Hazel asked. "Do you really think you can throw me off my game?"

She launched another jumpshot but this one clanged off the rim.

"Looks like it," Ned observed.

That was enough to make Hazel set aside her worries about Inspector O'Toole and Colin Frump. For the next two hours they played Twenty-one, H-O-R-S-E, and competed against each other in countless drills they knew from school. It wasn't a fair contest. Hazel was tall and had played starting point guard on her school team ever since she began attending an all-girls boarding school three years ago. Ned was short and had only joined a team this past year, after he became a boarder at an all-boys school. Still, Hazel was quick to admit her brother had been working hard.

"You've really improved, Squirt. You've come a long way since the last time we played," she told him. They took a break in the shade of a leafy maple tree to swig Gatorade and catch their breath.

"Thanks," Ned said. "There's this kid at my school, William Cowan. He's been helping me with my layup. He's really, really good."

"Well, now you are too," Hazel said.

Ned wiped his hand with his mouth and peered at her, considering.

"Really," he said after a moment. "Don't you want to add anything?"

Hazel thought for a second.

"Okay. You still need to work on your crossover and your left-handed dribble," she ventured.

"No, I meant, like, a joke. Usually if you say something nice to me, you say something funny and kind of mean afterwards."

Hazel felt as if her face had just been slapped. "No I don't," she said. "Do I?"

"Not serious mean," Ned said. "Funny mean. It's like . . . it's sort of like a way of taking back the compliment."

Hazel's stomach lurched. Maybe it was too much sports drink. On the other hand, maybe it was guilt. Because now that he'd said it, she could see that she did do that, all the time. Not just to Ned, but to her friends and her teammates.

"I'm sorry, Ned," she said after a moment. "I didn't mean to hurt your feelings."

"You didn't," said Ned. "It's okay, no big deal."

He didn't look at Hazel as he spoke. He was too busy polishing his glasses with the edge of his T-shirt. Watching him, Hazel had the sensation of seeing him clearly for the first time. He was so much smaller than she, but he seemed . . . well, much older than she remembered. Boarding school must be agreeing with him.

"Anyway, you made me work hard enough that I wouldn't mind going home and grabbing a shower before we meet Frankie for lunch," Hazel suggested. "Do you think we have time?"

Ned looked at his watch.

"Nope," he said. "What is it with you and going home? We couldn't go even if there was time, anyway. I didn't bring my key."

"So? What's wrong with mine?"

"Hazel, you don't have your key! Didn't you notice Frankie borrowing your key to the apartment before she left?" Ned asked. "She took it from your knapsack. She said she might need to go back and pick up some papers from Dad's study."

"But Frankie has her own key to our place," Hazel said.

"She lost it," Ned said. He raised one eyebrow. "She told us last night when we were out on that walk, remember? She said she was sure she'd left it on her desk at the gallery yesterday, but when she went to leave, she couldn't find it anywhere."

"Oh. I guess I wasn't paying attention," Hazel confessed.

"No kidding," Ned said. "You were totally out of it last night."

"I didn't think you guys noticed," said Hazel. She stood up, stretching her right leg.

"I don't think *Frankie* noticed," Ned said. "She was too freaked out about losing the key, and trying to find some painting, and all those phone calls from some artist in New York that Dad was supposed to be meeting this week."

Hazel blinked. She really had been out of it last night. She had no memory of Frankie discussing any of this.

"You know, if you're done wiping the court with me, we should go to the gallery," Ned suggested. "Frankie could probably use our help."

Hazel nodded and stuffed the basketball and drinks into her bag.

The gallery was just two blocks away on a street that ran north from the lake. It was a street that served as an unofficial dividing line between the leafy residential neighbourhood to the east and the old warehouse district and dockyards to the west, which Colin Frump and a few other investors had turned into an artists' enclave and tourist attraction. The gallery was housed in an old chocolate factory. Colin Frump had chosen it for its soaring ceilings and giant windows, but Hazel swore it was the lingering smell of chocolate that encouraged buyers.

The gallery was known for featuring artists who were young or just starting out, selling "art for people who can't afford art" Frankie once said. So Ned and Hazel were taken aback to see a gleaming Ferrari convertible parked out front. Ned was so enthralled by the bright red car, he stopped dead in his tracks, a dazed expression on his face. Hazel didn't care much for cars, and was more interested in the fact that it was parked in front of a fire hydrant. She glared at the driver, who was still behind the wheel.

"Some people just think they can do whatever they please," Hazel hissed. But Ned didn't seem to hear her.

"What if there was a fire?" she continued. "He'd probably let the gallery burn down before he'd move out of the way. Is he napping, or what?"

She was tempted to approach the bored-looking blond man as he reclined against the leather headrest, his tweed cap pulled low over his forehead and his eyes shaded by dark glasses. But the local parking cop, Officer Cohen, beat her to it.

"Sir, you're blocking a fire hydrant. I'll have to ask you to move."

Without looking up, the driver slipped his hand into his shirt pocket and produced a fifty-dollar bill, which he dangled over the side of the car.

Big mistake. Hazel smiled to herself. Officer Cohen would never accept so much as a cup of coffee for free. Ferrari Guy had just guaranteed himself a ticket. It would be fun to watch, but they should be inside, helping Frankie.

"C'mon Ned," she urged, tugging at his sleeve.

"I'll be there in a second. Just want to get a better look at the car," Ned said slowly.

Hazel was sure he didn't even see the driver or Officer Cohen, just the sleek, expensive lines of the flame-red sports car.

"Whatever."

Hazel pushed open the glass door and noticed the bell that was supposed to tinkle every time the door opened or closed made no sound. She was about to call out to Frankie to ask if she'd realized it was broken, when she heard a low, angry voice—a man's voice—from the back of the gallery. Then a woman cried out in pain.

It was Frankie.

CHAPTER THREE

"I told you I have no idea what you're talking about," Frankie cried. "Please—you're hurting my arm—let go!"

Hazel stood, rooted to the spot.

She couldn't see who was hurting Frankie. Her view was blocked by a series of giant canvases staggered at intervals throughout the gallery. Was there more than one guy back there?

Hazel's mind was racing. If she couldn't see them, they couldn't see her. She drew a deep, steadying breath and called out to Frankie in as grown-up a voice as she could muster: "Ms. Yazer? Oh, Ms. Yazer! Is everything all right?"

Her voice trembled a little, but even to her own ears she sounded older. Hazel paused, but neither Frankie nor the man replied. So far, so good. At least she'd startled the man into silence. Now, if she could just make him leave.

"It's Susan Cummings, Ms. Yazer," she continued, using the name of a girl at school. "I just came by to pick up that painting and I . . . uh . . . I noticed a police officer outside. I hope that man in the red convertible isn't one of your clients, dear. I think he's getting a ticket."

She heard a muffled curse and the sound of heavy footsteps

on the creaking floor. Hazel just had time to duck behind a huge canvas covered in paint splotches. A heavy-set man with a large bulbous nose and bald head lumbered toward the door. Peeking around a corner of the painting, Hazel saw a jagged scar on the man's neck. An enormous diamond ring flashed from one of his fleshy fingers. He was quite possibly the ugliest man Hazel had ever seen.

"I'll be back. You'd better find that painting," he flung over his shoulder as he pushed open the door.

Hazel ran to find Frankie.

She was sitting on an antique chesterfield, rubbing her left arm. She looked shaken, but when Frankie saw Hazel, she tried to smile.

"Susan Cummings, I presume?" Frankie asked.

"It was the first name that popped into my head. Are you okay?" Hazel asked her. "Officer Cohen really is outside you know. I'll go and get her."

"No!" Frankie's voice was abrupt. But she seemed to realize it almost at once and covered her mouth with her hand. She shook her head apologetically.

"Hazel, I'm sorry. I didn't mean to snap. Thank you for . . . for getting rid of that man. It's just—I'd rather not get the police involved, honey. Can you understand?"

Hazel frowned. "No. I mean, why not? Does my dad know that guy?" she asked. "Is he some kind of client? Is he some kind of *friend*?"

"Oh, he's no friend of your father's," Frankie said emphatically. "I'm not even sure I would call him a client." She sighed and flexed her arm gingerly. "But I have seen him before. He was here a few days before your father left. And he's been phoning me. He says he left a painting with your dad . . . something old and valuable. He wants it back. I've been looking everywhere, but I can't find it."

"Maybe he made a mistake," suggested Hazel.

"No, no . . . I remember he did come in with a painting, and I'm pretty sure he didn't have one when he left. It wasn't very big, he carried it in a briefcase."

"What did the painting look like?" Hazel asked.

"Oh I never saw it," Frankie replied. "I only saw the package later, after your father had wrapped it in that brown paper he always uses."

"Well, anyway, he was threatening you, Frankie. And he talked about coming back. I think we should call the police."

"No! At least, not yet," Frankie insisted. "Something strange is going on, Hazel. I don't want to get your father into trouble. At least, no more trouble than he's in already."

Hazel's throat went dry.

"What makes you think my dad's in trouble?" she croaked.

"Frankie? Hazel? Where are you guys?" Ned's voice rang out from the front of the gallery.

"I have *got* to get that bell fixed," Frankie murmured.

"Back here," Hazel yelled. She turned to Frankie and whispered, "Don't say anything in front of Ned. I don't want to worry him."

Frankie looked surprised, but nodded.

"What a cool car," Ned said as he navigated his way through the canvases. "The guy driving it was a total jerk, though. He tried to bribe Officer Cohen, and then he tried to pretend it was all a mistake. Then, while she's writing him up for blocking this fire hydrant, this big ugly guy comes up and squeezes himself into the passenger seat. He must have been twice the size of Officer Cohen, but you could tell she made him nervous. I guess some people are just scared of cops."

"I guess," Hazel agreed. "So are they gone—Ferrari Guy and . . . Big Ugly Guy?"

Frankie gave a weak smile. "He isn't very attractive, is he?"

she observed. "His name is Richard C. Plevit. And he's very insistent about that middle initial."

"Well, they're gone anyway," Ned told them. "It was like they really didn't want to get another ticket. Ferrari Guy was so careful: signaling lane changes, driving half the speed limit. It was sort of funny, like watching a little old lady drive that sports car."

Hazel's stomach growled—time for lunch. They locked the gallery and headed to Café Gentil. Ned didn't seem to notice how quiet Hazel and Frankie were; he was too busy chattering about the Ferrari.

Café Gentil occupied most of the main floor of the building where Frankie and the Frumps lived. The Québecois pastry chef who ran it was a gruff man who loathed the tourists that thronged to his famous café, occasionally mocking them to their faces. But he had a longstanding friendship with Ned. Monsieur Gentil kept careful records of each day's baking, in an attempt to measure the effect of climate and weather conditions on the flakiness and flavour of his croissants. Ned had discovered this at the age of six and found it fascinating. They had been discussing temperature and humidity ever since.

As soon as they had ordered, and Ned had disappeared behind the counter to discuss the effect of a recent spike in air pollution, Hazel turned to Frankie.

"Why do you think my dad's in trouble?" she asked.

"Why didn't you want to talk in front of Ned?" Frankie countered.

"I didn't want to upset him," Hazel replied quickly. "He's a worrywart. You know."

Frankie agreed. "You're right. He's so clever, sometimes I forget he's just a little boy."

"So?"

"Oh. It's nothing I can put my finger on, honey. But your

father had been acting strangely for a while before you and Ned came home."

"Because of Big Ugly Guy?" Hazel asked.

"Who? Oh. Mr. Plevit—Richard C. Plevit," Frankie said. "He left so many messages, I'll never forget his name. . . . No, your dad was acting oddly before Mr. Plevit showed up. I think it was something to do with Ned."

Hazel swallowed.

"*Ned?*" her voice came out in a sort of squeak.

"Yes, that's why I wondered why you didn't want to talk in front of him. I wondered if your father had said anything to you."

"No. About what?" Hazel tried to keep the impatience out of her voice.

"Well, I don't know exactly. That's the trouble. It all started when Ned's art teacher telephoned. You know, Ned's never taken an interest in art, and the teacher knew how important that subject is to your dad. Well, I guess Ned had done a project on some obscure artist from the 1800s, and it was really fine work. Mr. McFarquhar was so impressed, he called your father to tell him about it."

Hazel stared at Frankie. An art project? Was she kidding?

"It was after that, anyway, that Colin started making a lot of phone calls overseas and spending a lot of time on the Internet. I don't know what it was all about, but I took a phone message the day before you kids came home, and it was from some Officer Somebody or Other!"

"*Bon! Vos croissants au jambon, salades, jus, café, eau!*" Monsieur Gentil had arrived with their food and drinks, Ned at his heels.

"Thank you, Monsieur Gentil," Hazel said, taking the glass of water and passing the coffee to Frankie.

"*Oui, merci, mon ami,*" Frankie said with a flawless accent.

Monsieur Gentil gave a pleased little bow and departed.

As they munched their sandwiches, Hazel studied Frankie. She looked worn out: there were shadows under her eyes and tiny lines creasing her forehead. She was obviously worried about Colin Frump and she'd probably been up all night painting. Hazel didn't like the thought of her heading back to the gallery alone. What if Big Ugly Guy . . . what had she called him? Richard C. Plevit! (And what was with the middle initial? He wasn't just a bully, he was a pretentious bully.) What if Richard C. Plevit came back?

"Frankie, you could check the gallery's voice mail from home, couldn't you?" Hazel asked.

"Sure, honey. But why?"

"Well, you've got a lot of painting still to do, and the gallery's probably going to be pretty empty this afternoon, anyway. Why don't you just leave it closed for the rest of the day and check the messages from home?"

Frankie tilted her head to one side. She looked at Ned for a moment, then turned back to Hazel.

"I think that's a good idea," she agreed. "What will you two do?"

"Oh, we'll hang out in our apartment for a bit, you know . . . read, email friends from school, that sort of thing," Hazel said airily.

"Okay, but you'll need your key back," said Frankie, fishing around in her leather satchel. "I borrowed it this morning, remember—in case I needed to get into your father's study."

"I can't believe you lost your key to our place," Hazel chided.

"Me either." Frankie shook her head. "Honestly, these last few days I feel like everything's been turned upside down. You know I always wear my own key around my neck so I don't lose it?"

Hazel nodded. Her father had presented Frankie with a silver chain after she'd lost her apartment key for the tenth time.

"Well, I should have put the key to your apartment on the same chain," Frankie said ruefully. "But I always kept it in a safe place, and I never lost it until just the other day."

"What kind of safe place?" Hazel asked.

"Oh, a little jar beside my desk at the gallery. I even stuck a label on it—Colin's Spare Key—so I wouldn't forget, or get it mixed up with the key I keep for Claire Holland, so I can feed her cat when she's away. But the other day when I went to check, it was gone. I can't imagine what I did with it."

"I'm sure it'll turn up," Ned said. He patted Frankie on the back, before heading to the men's room. Frankie watched him go, then turned to Hazel with a wan smile.

"I'm sure he's right. But between losing the key and losing track of that painting . . . I swear, when I walked into the gallery this morning, I felt like nothing was where I left it. Nothing seemed to be in the right place. . . . I'm probably just tired. Here comes Ned. Should we say *au revoir* to Monsieur Gentil?"

Hazel and Ned sent Frankie on ahead, while they stayed behind to collect salad, quiche, and pastries from Monsieur Gentil for dinner that night. While the food was being wrapped, Monsieur Gentil told Ned about a major storm that was headed their way, and the pair was soon embroiled in a discussion about the possible effect on tomorrow's baguettes. It took Hazel some time to pry Ned loose.

By the time they entered her apartment, they expected to see Frankie happily slapping oils on the canvas tacked to her wall. Instead the children found her sitting pensively in the armchair by the window, her knees drawn up to her chest.

Hazel felt her heart sink.

"Frankie? Is everything okay?" she asked.

Frankie sighed and unfolded herself from her chair.

"Well, there's this artist from the neighbourhood who's down in New York City, having his first big show, thanks to your father and his influence. But he left one of his best works behind. It's actually back at our gallery—I saw it today. He desperately wants it for the show. I offered to have it shipped immediately, but he's insisting someone take it to him in person. He's practically in hysterics. I know your father thinks very highly of him and wants this show to go well. I can't think what to do."

"Well, why don't we take it to him?" asked Ned. "New York flights leave the airport every half-hour and it's a short trip. We could be back before bedtime."

"Hey, I never thought of that," Frankie said, her face brightening. "Maybe we could even stay overnight. I can charge the trip to the gallery's account. I'm sure your father wouldn't mind, under the circumstances. I could take you guys to the zoo or the Museum of Modern Art!"

"Or maybe the American Museum of Natural History," offered Ned. "And there's an exhibit at the New York Public Library I'd like to check out. I guess for Hazel we could fit in a trip to the NBA store, or visit that basketball court she's always wanted to see—Rucker Park?"

"What do you say, Hazel?" asked Frankie. "Shall we all go?"

Hazel's heart leapt. New York would be a fantastic adventure and a great start to their summer holidays. Plus, they'd be far away from Richard C. Plevit and whatever trouble her father—or Ned—had stumbled into. Hazel was about to tell Frankie it was the best idea she'd heard in a long time, when she suddenly remembered something her father had said: their passports had expired.

Hazel felt a keen jab of disappointment. It was like waking up and thinking it was Saturday, only to realize a split second later that it was Monday. *And* you had a dentist appointment. *And* a history test you hadn't studied for.

"It would be great—if we only had passports," Hazel said

slowly. "Remember, Ned? Dad said getting them renewed was one of the chores we had to get done over the holidays."

The light in Frankie's eyes dimmed, and Ned made a sound like a balloon slowly deflating. Hazel gave herself a moment to silently mourn the lost opportunity to play pickup ball in a New York playground, then shook the image from her head.

"Look, we'll all get to New York someday, I'm sure. But in the meantime, Frankie, why don't you go? You've got a passport, right? And Ned's right, flights do leave every half-hour for New York City. It's 2:00 p.m. now. You can be there by dinner and back here by . . . well, maybe not bedtime, but before the airport closes, anyway. We'll be fine on our own until you get back. "

"Yeah, don't worry about us," Ned agreed, holding the quiche aloft. "We've even got dinner already organized."

"But what if I can't get back tonight?" Frankie asked. "The airports have been crazy lately with all the security alerts. And the weather forecast isn't great, either. What if my flight home is delayed? What if they close the airport?"

"What if this artist guy sues Dad for wrecking his big show and killing his career?" Ned replied.

After several more rounds of this kind of debate, Frankie finally gave in. Ned used her computer to book Frankie on a 4:30 p.m. flight to New York, while Hazel helped her locate her passport in the messy little room she called her home office. They both watched and waved from her living room window as the taxi pulled away.

"She *will* remember to stop by the gallery and actually pick up the painting, won't she?" Ned asked.

"Oh, sure. But will she pick up the *right* painting?"

They looked at each other and grinned.

"I know we said we'd sleep here, but we don't need to hang out here the whole time, especially with Frankie gone," Ned observed. "Why don't we go back to our place? I've got something I'd kind of like to finish before . . . well, before . . ."

" . . . before my birthday?" Hazel asked.

"I cannot answer that," Ned replied, raising one eyebrow, "on grounds I might incriminate myself."

Hazel couldn't help laughing at his expression, even as she wondered just what Ned had in store for her. But hanging out in their apartment was just what she wanted. With any luck, Ned would be so engrossed in his birthday project, she wouldn't see or hear from him for hours. Hours she could spend safely snooping. "Okay, let's go," she said.

Once inside their apartment, Ned headed straight for his room. "Let me know when you want to eat dinner," he flung over his shoulder.

"Perfect," Hazel told herself. "Alone at last."

As she walked down the hall toward Colin Frump's study, Hazel became aware of a curious feeling on the back of her neck. It was the uncomfortable feeling of being watched that you sometimes get, even when you know no one's there. As she turned the knob and pushed open the study door, she shivered slightly.

Don't be such a baby! Hazel thought. She set her shoulders and stepped inside. But what she saw froze her in her tracks. She couldn't breathe.

Colin Frump's study, which had been so messy and overflowing with art and books and papers just yesterday, was now as neat and empty as a classroom in August. The stacks and piles of paintings were gone. The statues she'd nearly tripped over had vanished.

Hazel's legs began to tremble so fiercely, she wasn't sure she could walk. Somehow she made it to the screen that divided her father's work space from his sitting area. His desk and chair were still there, and that was a good thing, because Hazel found she suddenly needed to sit down. Everything else had gone: the computer monitors, the hard drives, the printers, the files, and the masses and masses of papers.

It was as if they had never been there.

Hazel wasn't sure how long she sat there, dumbfounded, staring at the empty room. The only things left on her father's desk were a couple of empty trays labelled *Correspondence* and a small jar filled with paper clips.

Hazel's gaze focused on the jar. It reminded her of something. Something Frankie had said.

Her eyes widened: the key. Someone must have taken the key to their apartment from the jar on Frankie's desk in the gallery. Someone had used that key to break in here and steal . . . everything.

But why take *everything?* The art she could understand; it was valuable. But why take the papers and the computers?

Hazel wished now that she'd read those emails when she'd had the chance. She wondered what other clues to Colin Frump's disappearance had vanished along with them. She wondered whether someone was reading them right now.

Hazel stood up. What if that someone came back? What if it was Richard C. Plevit, or Ferrari Guy? In fact, it was probably more than one person—there would have been so much stuff to carry, heavy stuff—what if it was more than two people?

If they had a key, they could come back anytime. They could be coming up the stairs, riding the elevator right now. What if they were still in the apartment? Hazel hadn't checked any of the other rooms . . . she'd just come straight here. She flew down the hallway to Ned's room. As she neared his door, she could hear him tapping away at his keyboard. It was the greatest sound she'd ever heard. There was no time to waste in knocking; she burst through the door, calling his name.

"Hazel?" Ned pushed his chair back from the computer and

tried to block her view of the monitor with his body. "What are you doing? You'll wreck the surprise!"

"We have to get out of here *now!*" Hazel grabbed his hand and pulled him out of their apartment and across the hall to safety.

CHAPTER FOUR

Hazel was in the tower room again. She could feel the stone floor beneath her cheek. She could see the stars through the high, arched window. Her legs were numb and lifeless. She tried to move but couldn't. She was trapped, helpless.

Again? This was getting ridiculous.

Enough—enough of this stupid dream, Hazel told herself. I'm waking up—now!

"*Wait. Stay.*"

Whoa. This was new: a voice. A woman's voice. Nobody else had ever appeared in this dream before. Hazel was always alone.

"Who are you?" demanded Hazel.

Silence. Hazel twisted her neck, trying to see more of the tower. As far as she could tell, she was still alone. However, the room wasn't quite as empty as she'd always thought. She could see sheets or cloths draped over . . . over what? Furniture? She couldn't tell. Yet, the shapes were oddly familiar.

"Can you at least tell me why I'm here?" Hazel asked. "Why do I have to wait? Why do I need to stay?"

She didn't really expect an answer. So when the woman's voice came again, shock ran through Hazel's body.

"This is where you need to be."

The voice was firm, but gentle—not angry—so Hazel decided to try again.

"Okay . . . but why? Why here? Where am I? What is this place?"

There was a long pause. Now the voice was so quiet it was almost a whisper. It sounded like the wind sighing in the trees. It sounded sad.

"Home."

. . . .

A clap of thunder jolted Hazel awake. She wasn't in the tower—she was curled up in Frankie's armchair by the window. Rain was streaming down the glass outside, and the sky was as dark as night, but Hazel's sports watch showed it was Friday, 7:00 a.m.

Hazel yawned and stretched. She was tired, and her legs ached from being folded up in the chair. It had been a long night. Her first thought had been to call the police, but then she'd remembered that Frankie hadn't wanted them involved. If her father was in trouble, Hazel wouldn't make things worse for him. She'd decided to let Frankie decide what to do.

She'd also decided it would be better not to worry Ned unnecessarily. She didn't tell him about her previous snooping or the emails she'd found or the way Richard C. Plevit had threatened Frankie at the gallery. She told her brother only about the burglary, claiming she'd entered Colin Frump's study because the door was open, and found it ransacked. Then she had paced the floor of Frankie's apartment, anxious for her return.

And then, because this was the way everything seemed to be working now, Frankie had not returned.

It wasn't Frankie's fault, of course. In fact, when she phoned to say her fears of a storm had come true and she was stuck in New York, Frankie was so worried and guilt-stricken about having left them alone, that it was difficult to get a word in edgewise. Finally, Ned had put his hand over the receiver and whispered to Hazel: "We can't tell—she'll have a heart attack!" and Hazel had simply nodded. There was no point in making Frankie hysterical—not when she was so far away and powerless to help.

But after they hung up, Hazel had looked at Ned and felt the mantle of responsibility settle heavily around her shoulders. What had she gotten herself into? She'd succeeded, only too well, in keeping Ned from worrying; soon she was watching him snore contentedly, while she checked and re-checked the locks on Frankie's door. Hazel couldn't help feeling peeved. Perhaps she would wake her brother up and tell him about Plevit, or ask him about the emails. She'd see how easy he found sleep then. But no, that would be wrong.

Sleep was a long time coming to Hazel. Every muscle in her body tensed each time she heard a sound; she'd never realized how much noise the old pipes in the building made, or how eerie the wind could sound as it whistled through the streets below.

On the phone, Hazel had been impressed by her own ability to sound calm and confident as she reassured Frankie. That pride in her bravery and maturity had lingered for a while, even after Ned's infuriating snores filled the room. But it gradually ebbed away, to be replaced by uncertainty and, eventually, anger. Hazel realized part of her had hoped Frankie would just *know* that something was wrong, without being told. Why were grown-ups so quick to believe kids who said everything was okay? Why hadn't Frankie *guessed* Hazel was just being brave? Hazel banished that thought as unfair. None of this was Frankie's fault—she was trying so hard to help the Frumps, to keep the gallery and Colin's reputation intact. And, after all, it was Hazel and Ned who had insisted she go to New York in the first place.

No, it wasn't *Frankie* who had truly put them in this situation. It wasn't Frankie who had abandoned them. But Hazel refused to think about who had.

Now a bolt of lightning split the angry sky, lighting up the street below. Her ears ringing from the thunder that followed, Hazel peered down at a lone car splashing through a puddle that stretched from one curb to another, sending up great spurts of water from each of its wheels. If there had been any pedestrians around, they would have been drenched. But the sidewalks were deserted. Hazel and Ned were marooned. Alone.

"Looks like a good morning to stay indoors."

Ned had joined Hazel by the window. She nodded, trying to think of something comforting and grown-up to say to her little brother.

"I mean, so long as the bad guys don't come back," Ned said cheerfully.

Hazel looked at her brother. She raised her eyebrows. Both of them. "Who are you and what have you done with Ned?" she asked.

He grinned.

"Hazel, you have to admit this is way more interesting than most people's summer vacations," he said.

Hazel shook her head. Interesting, yes. But what was wrong with comfortable? What was wrong with safe? Clearly it was time Hazel and Ned had a little chat. She needed to know more about that art project Frankie had mentioned—and Ned's website. What exactly was he up to with his chemistry club? Could he already know that this Inspector O'Toole was investigating him?

This really was a ridiculous situation. It was all very well to be nearly twelve, practically a teenager, but disappearing dads and absentee babysitters and Interpol and burglars were more than she should be expected to handle.

Still, someone had to take charge.

"C'mon. Breakfast," Hazel said firmly. "We've got O.J. and slightly stale croissants and . . . there's gotta be some cereal somewhere."

"It does happen all the time," Ned continued, as Hazel rummaged through Frankie's kitchen. "Thieves break in, they steal stuff like televisions and CD players, and then they come back after you've replaced them, so they can steal the brand-new ones. It's very efficient."

Hazel gaped at her brother. How had she never noticed it before? Ned wasn't a genius. He was a *criminal* genius. He was probably working on a plan to control the weather. In fact, that storm that was raging outside . . . Hazel grabbed her head with both hands and held on tight. She took a deep breath.

"Okay that does make sense, sort of, but Ned, they stole art out of Dad's study," Hazel reasoned. "That's not something you can just replace, like a television or a CD player."

"You said they also took his computer," Ned pointed out. "They'd expect him to replace that. Anyway, maybe that was all they could carry the first time. Maybe now they'll come back for the television."

Hazel shook her head in disbelief.

"This is *soooo not* the way I planned to spend summer vacation," she muttered. Hazel shoved a bowl and several half-empty boxes of cereal in front of Ned and began tearing pieces off a croissant to quiet her growling stomach. Ned tilted his head to one side and gazed at her earnestly.

"Hazel, here's the thing I'm trying to say," he began. "The bad guys obviously got into our apartment using Frankie's spare key, which they stole from the jar on her desk in the gallery, right?"

"No kidding," Hazel said through a mouthful of croissant.

"My point is: these keys give you access to the elevator as well. So I don't think we're entirely . . . how shall I put this . . . *safe* staying here at Frankie's. I mean, unless you *want* to run into the burglars in the hall when they come back."

Hazel flashed a quick look at Ned, but he didn't seem frightened or even troubled by his own words. He seemed . . . happy.

"We could go find a locksmith and get the keys changed," Hazel suggested. "I mean, the locks and the keys."

"I think because the elevator's involved it's more complicated than that," Ned said thoughtfully. "I think maybe we need to find another place to stay . . . maybe we should ask Claire Holland if we could hang with her for now. And when Frankie gets back, the three of us should probably check into a hotel. Using aliases."

Hazel surveyed her brother through narrowed eyes. He really seemed to be enjoying himself.

"Room service, Hazel," Ned said dreamily. "Think of the room service!"

Hazel grinned. A hotel with Frankie did sound promising. But until Frankie returned, maybe Ned was right. Maybe they should find another adult. And stick close.

"Okay. Let's call Claire and see if we can stay with her," Hazel offered.

But there was no answer at the sculptor's apartment. Hazel left a message anyway, asking her to call them at Frankie's.

"What is it with the adults in this building?" Ned observed. "It's like they're disappearing, one by one."

Before Hazel could respond, the phone rang. For a second, she wondered whether it was Claire Holland, but despite bursts of static caused by the thunderstorm, the voice at the other end was unmistakably Frankie's.

". . . I just wanted to make sure you kids were okay after spending the night on your own," she was saying.

"We survived, Frankie," Hazel said. "Don't worry. When are you coming home?"

"The flights are all messed up, but I'm on the first one I could get," Frankie replied. Hazel could hear the apology in her voice.

"That's okay. So, will you be back by dinner or by bedtime?" Hazel asked.

"Err . . . bedtime," Frankie admitted reluctantly. "But you can reach me here at the hotel all day. In fact, why don't you check in with me every few hours, just so I know you're all right?"

After promising to call soon, Hazel hung up. Then, by tacit agreement, the pair headed downstairs to Monsieur Gentil's café. He was bustling behind the counter, struggling to keep up with the demands of the sodden tourists who filled the tables despite the weather. The sight of everyone going about their lives was relaxing, Hazel decided. In fact, just the sight of Monsieur Gentil was reassuring. Hazel gave a tiny, embarrassed laugh as she realized part of her had actually wondered if Monsieur Gentil might have disappeared as well.

Ned busied himself by clearing away the dishes left by the previous customer. He borrowed the waiter's rag to clean off the table. Then he turned to Hazel and fixed her with a very serious look.

"We need to talk," Ned announced. "I want to know whatever you know about where Dad is and what's going on."

Hazel's eyes widened then narrowed. "What makes you think I know anything?" she asked.

"You and Frankie were talking about something when we were in here yesterday and she seemed pretty upset. Plus, you've been climbing the walls since before the burglary," Ned answered. "I've been pretty patient, but time's up. Spill!"

Hazel reflected. Ned was ridiculously smart and she needed him on her side. And now that it was daytime and they were surrounded by people in Monsieur Gentil's café, she didn't feel quite so strongly about protecting her little brother.

"Deal," Hazel replied. "So long as you tell me about your website and your art project and whatever you've been cooking up with that chemistry club!"

Hazel sat back and crossed her arms in front of her chest, studying her brother's face. He didn't look startled or defensive or angry or fearful or any of the things she'd expected. He certainly didn't look guilty.

The only thing he did look was . . . confused.

"What the heck are you talking about? What website?"

"You know," Hazel stated. But even to her own ears, her voice sounded unsure.

Ned shook his head slightly. When he spoke again, he sounded like a parent trying to reason with a stubborn toddler.

"Hazel, I don't *have* a website; I've never had a website. If you want me to help you start one or something, I guess I could. But you know, I think right now we've got bigger things to worry about: Dad's disappeared, we've been burgled, and we pretty much seem to be on our own."

"Okay forget the website. What about the chemistry club?" Hazel demanded.

"Well, okay. Yeah I've been using the club to help me design your birthday present. But it's not quite finished yet. Anyway, it's Friday. Your birthday's not until next Wednesday. Don't you want to wait and see what it is then?"

Ned's voice still had that patient, condescending tone. It was starting to really bug Hazel. *She* wasn't the problem here.

"Look, Ned. I didn't want to tell you this before," Hazel drew a deep, steadying breath. "But . . . you know when I went into Dad's study yesterday? It wasn't the first time. I went in there on Wednesday, while you were working in your room. I wanted to try to find out why he took off like that."

Ned said nothing, but he raised one eyebrow. Hazel gritted her teeth.

"Yeah, I know, we're not supposed to go in there," she continued. "But it's a good thing I did, because now everything's gone. And the thing is, Ned, when I was in the first time, well . . . I think I found some clues!"

Ned leaned forward. He peered intently at Hazel. "I still can't figure out whether you're serious, or making all this up," he said slowly. "But go on. What kind of clues?"

"I am *not* making this up," Hazel replied. "Okay. For starters, I found some emails Dad hadn't opened yet, and one of them was from Interpol, from an Inspector O'Toole. And the heading on the message was something about his investigation into your website. So there!"

If she had been hoping to see the colour drain from Ned's face, Hazel would have been disappointed. Ned just looked baffled—interested, but baffled.

"Hazel, honest, I don't have a website. I don't know what the Interpol guy would be talking about."

At least the patronizing tone had disappeared from his voice. Hazel took another deep breath.

"Ned you're not . . . you're not building some sort of bomb or something with that chemistry club, are you?"

For the first time Hazel saw a flicker of something in her brother's eyes. Was it guilt?

"Not exactly," he said. But he looked down at the table.

"What, then?" Hazel whispered.

"I'll show you as soon as we're done here," Ned told her. "It'll mean going back into our apartment, though—just for a minute. And it'll wreck the birthday surprise."

Hazel nodded. She certainly didn't want to wait for her

birthday to find out what Ned had been up to. As for returning to their apartment, she wasn't looking forward to that, but at least it was daylight now.

Monsieur Gentil hadn't been surprised to see the children at 8:00 a.m., but then he knew all about Frankie's cooking. He didn't know, of course, that they had already eaten. However, excitement had sharpened their appetites, and there was something awfully comforting about chocolate-filled pastries. The café was so busy Monsieur Gentil had no time for talk of croissants and weather. That was fine with Ned. He just wanted Hazel to keep talking. When she told him about Richard C. Plevit and the missing painting, Ned almost choked on his *pain au chocolat.*

"I can't believe you guys didn't tell me about this," he said, his voice tight with anger.

"You're right," Hazel said. "I'm sorry."

Ned opened his mouth to speak then closed it, as if he didn't know what to say.

"There are just way too many secrets here," Hazel went on. "So from now on, I think we should promise to be straight with each other about everything."

Hazel had planned to talk to Monsieur Gentil before they left, to tell him about Frankie being delayed in New York. It was high time some responsible adult knew about their situation. But Monsieur Gentil was awfully busy, and she really wanted to see what her brother had been working on.

When the children reached the door to their apartment, they found it slightly ajar. Hazel hesitated, until Ned pointed out that they might have left it open themselves, in their haste to escape yesterday. He was probably right; she had no memory of stopping to close or lock the door behind them.

Now she gave the heavy door a gentle push and listened. And listened.

"Oh, come on," Ned said, pushing past her. "Let's get this over with."

Once inside Ned's room, Hazel closed the door behind her and leaned against it. She found herself studying his window, wondering whether they could escape that way if Richard C. Plevit suddenly reappeared. Ned, meanwhile, headed to his closet and pulled out a plain cardboard shoebox with the words *Caution! Do Not Open on Pain of Death* scrawled across its top.

"This is what I've been working on," he told her, yanking off the lid. "So, happy birthday."

Hazel took a step forward and peered inside the box. She looked at Ned.

"What is it?"

For answer, Ned switched on his computer and, with a few keystrokes, summoned up a website.

"This is what the chemistry club's been helping me build," he told Hazel. "We call it NIDS."

"Ned's Incredibly Disgusting Stinkbomb," Hazel read aloud. "Guaranteed to clear a classroom in six seconds flat and leave it uninhabitable for up to twenty-four hours."

She stared at her brother.

"Remember how you told me about the practical jokes some of the other girls in your dormitory were playing this year, and how everyone was always trying to find ways to get out of class?" Ned reminded her. "I thought a stinkbomb could come in handy for next year—like when you're trying to get out of a test or something. The only thing is, the stuff they sell in joke shops isn't very good. So I decided to make something myself. Well—with the club's help.

"It's really, really awful, Hazel. I mean, it's probably the best thing I've ever done. But I started working on this back when I was at school, and one went off accidentally in the lab. You wouldn't believe the smell. They had to close the room for two days! Luckily, I knew enough to get out of there fast. My skin didn't have time to really absorb the smell. I did have to burn my shirt, though. . . ."

Ned's voice trailed off. He was lost in the memory, eyes aglow with happiness.

Hazel didn't know what to say. She didn't know what to think.

"Wow," she said finally. "Uh . . . thanks. I'm sure it's what all the cool kids will be taking to school next year."

"It's completely harmless," Ned assured her. "I mean, it's not actually poisonous or anything. Of course, it can cause vomiting, itchy, painful eyes, skin rashes . . . but nothing *permanent*."

"Sometimes I'm really not sure we're even related," Hazel said, shaking her head. "Come on. Let's get out of here."

"Should I bring the bomb?" Ned asked eagerly. "I can finish it at Frankie's. You never know, it might come in handy—especially if the bad guys come back."

"Sure, whatever," said Hazel, rolling her eyes.

As they walked toward the door, Hazel recalled her dream from the night before. Maybe Ned's theory had finally been proved wrong. Instead of something bad happening, she'd found out something good: Ned wasn't building a bomb. Not a real one, anyway. A stinkbomb—even an Incredibly Disgusting one—hardly qualified.

"Hey, before we go, should we check to see whether Dad's sent you an email?" Ned asked.

Hazel didn't want to linger in their apartment any longer than they had to, but a message from their father was probably worth the risk. She nodded and headed for her room.

There were half a dozen emails from friends—mostly school-mates wanting to compare summer vacations—but nothing from their father.

"I can read those later," she told Ned. "Let's go."

"Wait. What's that?" Ned asked, pointing to a paper beside Hazel's computer. "A fax from Alysha?"

Alysha was one of Hazel's oldest friends. She had lived in the building with her parents until just last year, when her mother had accepted a position as head of the art department at a school in Paris. Alysha liked to fax Hazel funny pictures and articles torn from French magazines and newspapers.

But there was nothing funny about this one. Across the top of the clipping, Alysha had written: *Hazel! I found this newspaper in the street. I can't read Turkish but I think Frankie can. I hope this is all a big mistake. I tried phoning, but there was no answer. I hope you get this. Call me! Love, A.*

Hazel couldn't read the clipping either, of course. But her hands were shaking as she stared at the fax. Two grainy photographs accompanied the text. The smaller picture looked remarkably like Ferrari Guy, although she couldn't be absolutely sure.

But there was no mistaking the identity of the man in the larger photograph. That man—the one with the unshaven face and wild eyes, the one in handcuffs and a prisoner's uniform— that man was definitely their father.

CHAPTER FIVE

"Frankie, why would anyone put Dad in prison?" Hazel shouted into the phone. "Where is he? And why is Ferrari Guy in the story too? What does it say about him?"

Amazingly, Alysha was right about Frankie understanding Turkish. She had lived in Istanbul for a time when she was a student. But it was taking Frankie a long time to read the copy Hazel and Ned had just faxed to her hotel in New York. At least, it seemed to Hazel that it was taking a long time.

"I'm sorry, kids. My Turkish is a little rusty." Frankie's voice sounded rusty too, Hazel thought, like she was having a hard time getting the words out.

"It seems there's some sort of art scandal involving important galleries in Turkey and Cypress," Frankie continued. "And the article talks about arrests being made in connection with smuggling and . . . I guess that word means fraud or fake. There's a long list of names in this one section—I think they're talking about artists whose work was forged or something. I've really got to go find someone who can help me translate this more precisely."

"What does it say about Dad?" Ned asked her, his voice quiet.

He was standing in the doorway of Frankie's kitchen, listening on the extension.

"Not much, I'm afraid. They've arrested him for something to do with this art fraud or whatever, and they're searching for the man in the other photograph. They seem to think he's your father's partner or something."

"You mean, Ferrari Guy? The guy who drove off with Richard C. Plevit?" asked Hazel.

"Yes, I—at least, if you say so," Frankie answered. "Remember, I didn't see him yesterday. I only saw Mr. Plevit. But if this man in the picture is the one you saw *with* Mr. Plevit . . . well, then I'm really confused."

"Why?" asked Hazel. Her mouth was dry; her tongue seemed to be made of cotton balls.

"Well, the man you call Ferrari Guy is identified here as Clive Pritchard."

"So?" Ned asked.

"It's just that the paper says this Clive Pritchard is your father's partner—partner in crime, I guess—although I really need help with some of this vocabulary. But I've never seen him before."

"Well, then that's good, right? I mean, the paper's wrong— the Turkish police have made a mistake," Hazel replied.

"Yeah . . ." Frankie's voice trailed away uncertainly.

"What?" Ned demanded. "*What?*"

"It's probably nothing. But I recognize his name from some- where . . . Clive Pritchard, I mean. I think your father does know him . . . or maybe Colin *used* to know him a long time ago. But I have the impression your dad really doesn't like him. There's no way they'd be partners . . . or friends. More like enemies."

For a few moments Hazel and Ned were silent, staring at each other across the room. The only noise was the faint sound of paper rustling on the other end of the phone as Frankie continued to read.

"What are we going to do?" Hazel whispered. She was speaking to Ned, but it was Frankie who answered, and for once, she didn't seem flustered at all.

"Look, kids, I'm not going to come home," Frankie announced. "This will be one of the weirdest expenses I've ever billed your dad for, but I'm catching the next flight to Istanbul, as soon as the storm lets up. I've still got a few friends there, and your father's going to need a lawyer. But you can't stay there alone. Not with Richard C. Plevit hanging around. You'd better ask Claire Holland if you can stay with her for a few days. You can ignore the cat, Ned, right?"

Hazel looked at Ned. He raised one eyebrow. If they told Frankie about the break-in, she'd probably feel she had to come home. But now it seemed Colin Frump needed her help more than they did. *Somebody* had to go rescue him.

For a moment, Hazel considered telling Frankie she and Ned had to go to Istanbul, too. But they didn't even have passports.

"Sure Frankie, we'll be okay," Hazel said. Ned nodded silently. Hazel was on the verge of pointing out that Frankie couldn't hear a nod over the phone, when she realized her brother was trying to reassure *her*. She managed a weak grin in response.

"Frankie, make sure you get Dad a good lawyer," Ned advised. "Don't go for the cheapest help. Remember: Dad's *loaded*."

"All right," Frankie agreed. "Look, I promise I'll get to the bottom of this. Your father is a good man and whatever he's mixed up in, it's not his fault. We'll fix it, okay?"

We'll fix it? It sounded more like Frankie was going to fix it. Hazel loved her neighbour, but she wasn't all that sure Frankie was up to the task. She felt helpless and it was a feeling she disliked intensely. Hazel needed something to *do*.

"Okay, Frankie," Hazel agreed. "But look, isn't there anything that Ned and I can do in the meantime? We could go to the gallery and look for clues or something . . ."

"No! Stay away from the gallery," Frankie ordered. "I don't want you bumping into that Plevit man or this Pritchard guy, either. If you want to help . . . well, your father has an old friend at the museum: Ludwig Barta. He's the curator of the Mediterranean department. I know Colin went to see him before he left. Maybe it wouldn't hurt for you to go talk to him. He might even have some contacts in Turkey who could help me."

"Okay, we'll go right now," said Hazel. "We can get there before lunch."

"But promise me first that you'll go see Claire and let her know what's going on. You don't have to tell her everything. Just enough so that she understands you need a place to stay, okay?"

Hazel and Ned agreed, and Frankie promised to call again as soon as she could.

But there was still no answer at Claire Holland's apartment.

The children trooped downstairs to Café Gentil. It was eleven o'clock.

"Back again? I must try once more to have Frankie take the cooking classes," Monsieur Gentil sighed. "*Rien de compliqué, n'est-ce pas?* Just some simple omelettes—you know? Fresh ingredients, plain food."

"Actually, Frankie's not here right now," Ned informed him. "Do you know where Claire Holland is?"

"Ah, Claire. Now she is a much better cook," said Monsieur Gentil. "But she is away just now, at one of those—how do you say it—an artists' retreat, they call it, with the fresh air and butterflies. She is in the mountains. She took her cat."

Ned looked like he was about to explode. Hazel grabbed his arm and smiled at Monsieur Gentil.

"We have to go. But we'll be back for dinner. See you!"

Before Ned or the old man could speak, Hazel had bundled her brother out the door and into the streetcar that had just pulled up outside.

"What's the hurry?" Ned asked indignantly. "I was only going to point out that the adults in this building can't seem to stay put, that's all. Besides, I'm hungry."

"You're always hungry," Hazel answered. "And I didn't want you blabbing about everything to Monsieur Gentil."

"I. Never. Blab."

Hazel raised her eyebrows. A flush crept across Ned's cheeks.

"Anyway," Ned continued, "we can trust Monsieur Gentil."

"I'm beginning to think we can't trust anybody," said Hazel.

They glared at each other and didn't talk again until they were standing in front of the museum. The rain had stopped, but it had left a chill in the air and the sky was still dark, blanketed by ominous clouds. Staring up at the museum Hazel shivered. It was an imposing grey building built to impress passers-by in Edwardian times, and the years had done nothing to wear down its *hauteur*. Even the pigeons gathering on the carved, stone lintels and broad steps seemed to sniff as they stared at the two of them.

"I think if we go in the side door we can ask where the offices are," Hazel said.

But the receptionist there only stared at them coldly.

"The dinosaur exhibit is at the front of the building, just off the atrium," he informed them.

"We're not here for dinosaurs," Ned said hotly.

"I see. Well, lost children are supposed to report to the coat check desk," the receptionist replied.

"We're here to see Mr. Ludwig Barta please," Hazel said, elbowing Ned aside before he could speak again.

"Do you have an appointment?"

Hazel made her face a polite mask.

"Yes, of course," she replied.

"Really?" the receptionist looked disbelieving. "Mr. Barta is a busy man. He doesn't normally meet with . . . *children*."

Hazel stiffened. The receptionist was clearly one of those adults who didn't even pretend to like children.

"Actually, our father is the one with the appointment," Ned said. He spoke in a drawl Hazel had never heard him use. The word father became *faw-thuh*. It made him sound bored. "He wanted to discuss some big donation he's thinking of making. What was it Hazel, a new wing or something?"

Hazel swallowed. "I think it was more like a gallery. Something to do with Mediterranean studies, anyway."

She smiled at the man. There were daggers in her smile.

"We're supposed to meet our dad here, but I guess we're early. I hope he shows up soon. We're all having lunch at the Plaza."

"And what is your *faw-thuh's* name?" he mimicked, his tone brimming with disbelief.

"Colin Frump," said Ned, and jumped as a hand clapped him heartily on the shoulder.

"Colin Frump? Brilliant! I've been trying to reach him, but he's not answering his cell phone."

Hazel whipped around to see an elderly, bearded man in a leather jacket and jeans smiling down at her. A motorcycle helmet was tucked under one arm; the other arm was already steering Ned down the hall.

"Thanks, Willie," the man called over his shoulder. "When Mr. Frump gets here just send him on through."

"Right away, Mr. Barta."

The receptionist's tone was fawning. Mr. Barta was obviously an important person.

"I believe I heard you say something about lunch," Mr. Barta said hopefully, as they turned the corner and headed down a long, dimly lit hall lined with murky oil paintings. Mr. Barta strode purposefully toward a tall, carved wooden door at the far end of the hall. Ned had to trot to keep up.

"Did you say something about the Plaza?" Mr. Barta asked.

Hazel gulped.

"Yep—soon as our dad gets here," Ned said smoothly. "Have you known him long, Mr. Barta?"

"Why, yes," the elderly man replied, holding open the door with a courteous gesture. "And I've always wanted to meet you two. This way, my office is just up these stairs, down the hall, and around the corner."

Hazel marvelled at the silence as Mr. Barta led them down a hallway that was padded with Persian carpets and illuminated by tiny, recessed lights that twinkled like stars. As they rounded the corner, they entered a waiting area complete with elegant gilt chairs. Mr. Barta unlocked a door marked LUDWIG BARTA and ushered them inside.

It was one of the oddest offices Hazel had ever seen. The panelled room was filled with things that looked like they belonged in museum display cases. A sarcophagus leaned against a corner of the fireplace mantel, and a giant beetle in a glass jar was being used as a paperweight atop a stack of papers that teetered on the edge of the curator's desk.

"Now," Mr. Barta began, "Do we expect your father soon? I need to speak with him. Urgently.".

Hazel looked at Ned. He raised an eyebrow. Just then, a buzzing sound filled the room.

"Excuse me, I have to take this," Mr. Barta said, turning his back to the children as he opened his cell phone.

Ned stepped closer to Hazel.

"We never discussed what to say," he hissed. "What if he thinks we're nuts? What if he's not on Dad's side?"

"Don't panic," Hazel whispered. "He seems nice and Frankie

said he was Dad's old friend, remember? We'll just tell him . . . everything."

Mr. Barta turned back to face them.

"Oh, dear. Children, I have to leave you for a few moments. So sorry. Make yourselves comfortable, and if your father arrives before I get back, tell him I'll be with you presently."

With that, he was gone. Hazel let out a long breath.

"Saved by the cell," Ned observed. "Now, before he gets back, how exactly do you plan to explain everything that's going on and find out what he knows and get him to help Dad, when *we* don't even know what's going on or what kind of help Dad needs?"

"Calm down, Ned," Hazel said. "We trust Frankie, right? Well, Frankie obviously trusts Mr. Barta, or she wouldn't have sent us here. She said Dad visited him recently, so we'll just explain that our father's in trouble, and we need to know what they talked about and whether it had anything to do with this mess."

"Frankie trusts everyone," Ned pointed out. "Besides, didn't you say we shouldn't even trust Monsieur Gentil?"

"You're right," Hazel admitted. "But do you have a better idea? I mean, isn't this why we came here in the first place?"

Ned was silent for a few moments. Then he shrugged too.

"I guess so. Okay . . . tell him everything. I guess we have to trust someone sooner or later."

He threw himself down into a squashy armchair and stuck his legs out straight in front of him, studying his sneakers.

"Lunch at the Plaza, eh?" Ned queried, after a few minutes. He raised an eyebrow.

"A whole new wing? Wasn't that a bit over the top?" Hazel chided. But she thumped his shoulder affectionately, before throwing herself into the armchair next to Ned's. "Still, pretty quick thinking, Squirt."

"Yes it was," Ned agreed smugly. He added as an afterthought: "Of course, Dad probably *could* afford to pay for a whole new wing."

"Oh, I don't think he's all *that* rich," Hazel said, gazing at a stuffed eagle perched on the corner of a bookcase at the far end of the room. It appeared to have a stuffed mouse hanging out of its beak. This had to be the strangest office she'd ever been in.

"Trust me, he is," Ned replied. Something about his voice dragged Hazel's attention away from the bird.

"What do you know that I don't know?" she demanded.

Ned whipped off his glasses and began polishing them with theatrical energy.

"Ned!" Hazel's voice was stern.

"Hey, can I help it if I stumble across a few computerized bank statements when I'm minding my own business, working on my de-encrypting program?" he queried.

"You're kind of scary, you know that?" Hazel asked.

Ned grinned. "I'm going to the washroom. I saw a door marked MEN just outside in the waiting room."

"You can run but you can't hide," Hazel called as the door closed behind her brother. "This isn't over!"

Ned had been gone no more than a minute before Hazel heard the sound of voices raised in argument, coming from down the hall. She opened the door a crack. She couldn't see anyone yet, but the voices were getting nearer.

"I don't care if he's with somebody. I want to see him!"

That voice—Hazel knew that low, threatening voice.

"Please sir, I'm afraid if you don't come with me I will have to call security. Mr. Barta is expecting a very important donor any minute. He can't be disturbed."

The second voice sounded like the receptionist. But that first voice was definitely Richard C. Plevit. They were coming down the hall. As soon as they turned the corner, they'd see her.

Hazel bolted for the men's room. Ned was washing his hands at the sink. Apart from the two of them, the room was deserted.

"Hazel what are you doing in here! This is a *men's* room!" Ned hissed. "Get out before you get us into real trouble!"

"We're already in *real* trouble, Ned," Hazel countered. "Richard C. Plevit is coming down the hall. You know, Big Ugly Guy from the gallery?"

Ned joined Hazel at the door. They could hear the receptionist arguing with Plevit.

"Well, I'm not going anywhere; I'll wait until his meeting's done," Richard Plevit said. They could hear the antique chair creak as he sat down.

Hazel looked at Ned in horror. Richard C. Plevit was blocking their only way out.

"How long before the receptionist tells him a couple of kids are with Mr. Barta?" she whispered.

"How long before they realize no one's in there?" Ned asked.

"That would actually be okay. Then they'd leave," said Hazel. But that hope was dashed the next moment.

"Hey, buddy, where's the men's room?" Richard Plevit demanded.

Ned grabbed Hazel's arm. She glanced around the small bare room. Where could they hide? There were two sinks, two urinals (*ugh*, thought Hazel), and two stalls. Could she and Ned hide in one?

Hazel's mind was whirling. She really didn't want to be trapped in a men's room with Richard C. Plevit. What if he found them? Or what if he didn't but she had to listen to a lot of embarrassing noises? What if there were . . . smells?

The air was suddenly filled with a loud clanging. She looked at Ned. He had broken the glass fire alarm cover and pulled the lever. Without saying a word, her brother crossed the room and cranked open the casement window. Climbing up on the radiator, he was able to get his head and shoulders out the window. He turned and beckoned to Hazel.

"Come on," he mouthed.

They were on the second floor. Did Ned expect her to jump? Did he *want* her to break her leg? Her neck? They'd be better off taking their chances with Richard C. Plevit! Surely the man would leave now that the alarm had been sounded. Couldn't they just head for a fire escape and disappear into the crowd?

But the window overlooked Wodehouse Way, a meandering arboretum that led from the back of the museum to the university campus nearby. And as Ned was proudly gesturing, there was a stately, spreading maple tree positioned just outside the window.

If it hadn't been an emergency, Hazel would have refused. She hated heights. And although the tree's limbs were broad and inviting, they weren't quite close enough to reach. Besides, they were still slick from the rain. You had to jump—and grab—and she knew there was a distinct possibility that one of them might miss and tumble to the grass below. Still, somehow they each made it safely to the crotch of the tree. As they slowly lowered themselves from dripping branch to dripping branch, Hazel kept glancing back. It wasn't just because she hated to look down. She also wanted to make sure no one was watching—or even worse, following. But no face appeared at the window. The alarm was still clanging, and from her vantage point high in the tree, Hazel could see museum-goers starting to file out along the boulevard to the north of the park.

"Hurry up, Ned—there could be a lot of people in this park in another minute," she said.

Ned, who had already slipped twice and would have a few

bad scratches to show for it, just nodded. *He* had no fear of heights, Hazel reminded herself sourly.

They ran out of branches eventually and had to drop the final ten feet or so to the grass below. Ned got awkwardly to his feet, rubbing his leg.

"You know, I think this summer's turning out to be the greatest one ever!" said Ned, his eyes shining. "I've always wondered if you could get to one of those trees from the museum windows!"

"All I can say is, I'm glad Mr. Barta's office wasn't on the *third* floor," said Hazel, brushing grass off her T-shirt. She glanced upward. "Or the sixth."

"I may never get to pull a fire alarm again," Ned intoned solemnly. "But that has to go down as one of the most satisfying experiences known to mankind."

An older man occupying the bench beneath a nearby elm had stopped feeding the pigeons from his paper bag and was gazing at them with interest. Hazel waved to him as if dropping out of a tree was the most normal thing in the world; then she took Ned by the arm and walked him south, toward the university. The sky was clearing, and for now they were free of Richard C. Plevit.

"You did a great job on our escape," she told Ned.

"Yeah, but the mission was pretty much a bust," he pointed out. "We didn't get to ask Mr. Barta anything, and we almost got caught by that Plevit guy. It's like he's everywhere. Who knows where he'll turn up next?'

Hazel nodded.

"Maybe we should leave town or something," Ned said. "But where would we go? It's not like we have any relatives or family that we could stay with."

Hazel felt her jaw actually· drop. He was a genius. Ned was a genius. She, on the other hand, was a moron. How could she

have forgotten about that other email on her father's computer? What was the matter with her?

"Ned, you just said it. Family! That's what we need. That's
where we'll go."

"But we don't have any other family."

"Yes we do: Oliver Frump," Hazel told him. "He wanted a family reunion; he's going to get one. All we have to do is find him."

CHAPTER SIX

Ned, of course, had never heard of Oliver Frump. Hazel explained quickly about the other unread email she'd discovered on Colin Frump's computer. Ned was stunned; how could she have neglected to tell him about it?

Hazel apologized but tried to shift the conversation away from her forgetfulness. The truth was she had been preoccupied with the possibility Ned might be building a bomb. She could see now that her brother wasn't some evil genius, and the fact that she'd considered it, even briefly, wasn't exactly something she wanted to admit.

It was almost one-thirty and Hazel's stomach was rumbling. She tried to distract Ned with a picnic on the west lawn of the university campus, buying hot dogs and lemonade from a street vendor. Food usually worked wonders on Ned. Usually. Of course the weather wasn't exactly perfect for a picnic, not yet. And then there was the issue of Oliver Frump.

"So much for being straight with each other; so much for too many secrets," Ned scolded. "You're *sure* there's nothing else you should tell me? Like, maybe we won the lottery but you just forgot to mention it? Or maybe you got abducted by

Idiotrons from the planet Liargirl and they messed with your memory?"

"I swear there's nothing else," Hazel promised. "There were two messages—the one from Inspector O'Toole about your website, and this other one from the Oliver Frump guy, wanting to talk to Dad about a Frump family reunion."

"I still don't get that website thing," Ned said, swallowing the last of his hot dog. "Maybe that inspector has me mixed up with some other Ned Frump. Or maybe someone's stolen my identity and they're using my good name for evil. Identity theft is a big problem these days you know. Happens all the time."

Hazel relaxed. Ned may not have forgiven her for the oversight about Oliver Frump, but at least he was moving off the topic. They sipped their lemonade and gazed at the summer students going in and out of the elegant stone buildings.

"I wonder how this Oliver Frump guy tracked down Dad," he mused. "Do you think maybe he's a genealogist or something?"

Hazel hated it when her brother used words she didn't understand; she resolved not to ask what a genealogist was. It sounded like something to do with rocks but that made no sense. It was probably something to do with tracing your family tree.

"I dunno. Anyway, I don't have Oliver Frump's email address, so I'm not sure how we're going to find him," Hazel admitted.

They sat in silence for a few minutes. The air was warm and unpleasantly humid. Smog alerts had become commonplace in the past couple of years, and they made Hazel's head ache. Maybe if they *did* find Oliver Frump, he'd be living somewhere with cleaner air.

"What if we find him and he doesn't want us to come?" Ned asked. Now that the adrenaline of their escape had subsided Hazel thought his voice sounded tired, even a little worried. "Or what if he does invite us, but he lives in another country? We don't even have passports."

That reminded Hazel of something. She felt a tug at the corner of memory and tried to picture the email. There had been something, a French name . . . something about an island? But the more she reached for it, the more the memory wriggled away.

Hazel stood up, wadded her hot dog wrapper into a ball, and lobbed it into a nearby trash bin. She shared Ned's worries, but it was still worth a try.

"Let's just find him first," she said to her brother. "That's going to be the hard part."

But there she was completely wrong. Finding Oliver Frump proved surprisingly simple.

. . . .

Hazel and Ned weren't altogether comfortable about returning to the apartment building, but they agreed computers and telephones were needed to search for Oliver Frump. As Hazel turned the key in Frankie's door, she could hear the telephone ringing. She grabbed it before the answering machine could switch on.

"Hello?" Hazel said breathlessly into the phone.

"Oh, Hazel, you're there!" Frankie sounded harried. "My plane leaves at 2:40 p.m., so I just have a few moments before I have to board. I was trying you at Claire's, but there was no answer."

"Yeah. Um, Frankie, the thing is, I think Claire's out of town," Hazel said. "I don't think we're going to be able to stay with her."

"Oh. Ohhhhhh, that's right. She was going to the mountains on that silly retreat," Frankie recalled. "Maybe you could ask Monsieur Gentil—"

"No. Listen, Frankie. Ned and I think it might be a good idea for us to get out of town for a bit, or at least out of this building. We were trying to think of someone else we could stay with . . .

do you know . . . did my dad ever mention any relatives to you? Like maybe, somebody named Oliver Frump?"

Ned picked up the kitchen extension. There was a long silence on Frankie's end of the line. Finally, "Your father swore me to secrecy," Frankie began. "I mean, I really had to swear . . . I only found out by accident a few weeks ago."

"Found out *what?*" Hazel asked, trying to keep the impatience from her voice.

"Oh, Colin will kill me. I mean, I was only supposed to call his brother in case of emergency."

"Frankie—did you say *brother?*" Ned demanded.

"Do you have an actual number for Oliver?" Hazel asked.

"Oliver?" Frankie sounded confused. "I'm not sure that was his name . . . but, yes, Colin has a brother. And I'm definitely supposed to contact him only in an extreme emergency. . . ."

"Frankie! If this isn't an emergency, I don't know what is," Ned erupted. "We can't stay here anymore—our apartment's been burgled, and that Richard Plevit guy's following us all over the city!"

"What?" Frankie asked. "Oh, kids, they're calling my plane. I can't believe this! What do you mean burgled? When? No—wait! What did you say about Plevit?"

"Frankie, we're okay. Get on that plane and go help Dad," Hazel instructed her. "Just first, please, tell us how to find his brother."

"All I know is that he lives on an island. It's at the eastern end of Lake Ontario, at the mouth of the St. Lawrence River. Someplace called Land's End. His phone number is in my book, under *E.*"

"*E* for Frump?" asked Ned. "What kind of alphabetizing system do you use?"

"*E* for emergency," Frankie explained.

Ned was silent.

"I could hardly file him under *F* for Frump," she continued defensively. "Not when your father made such a big deal out of it being a secret."

"Okay, Frankie, I've found it," Hazel said. She had Frankie's address book. Under the *E* entries was written: Emergency Contact for Colin. There was a phone number and the words "Île du Loup" but no street address.

"Île du Loup," Hazel muttered to herself. That was it—that was what Oliver Frump had written: family reunion on Île du Loup.

"I've got to go, darlings," Frankie was saying hurriedly. "Promise you'll have Monsieur Gentil help you with all this—I don't know how long it will take you to reach your uncle, but in the meantime, Monsieur Gentil will make sure you are okay."

"Sure," Hazel agreed.

"Oh, and honey, it's Friday and I really don't know if I can get all this sorted out and have your father home by Wednesday, so you might as well take your birthday present to your uncle's place."

"Thanks, Frankie, but you can give it to me when you get back," Hazel offered.

"Actually, *I* haven't gotten you anything yet," Frankie said, sounding faintly embarrassed. "No, what I meant was that you should take your birthday present from Colin. He set it aside ages ago, for when you turned twelve. It's something you've wanted for a long time."

"But Frankie, we really were burgled," Hazel said sadly. "I know you won't believe this, but everything's gone from Dad's study, really. Everything."

"What? Oh. They're telling me I have to get on the plane now," Frankie said. "No, sweetie, the painting is in my office—my *home* office. Colin gave it to me for safekeeping just before he left. We were going to do this whole surprise party. . . . Anyway, it's in my closet, wrapped in that brown paper we use at the gallery. Take it with you. Goodbye."

After Frankie had hung up, Hazel and Ned argued briefly over which of them should be the one to make the call to Oliver Frump. A coin toss awarded the honour to Ned. He cleared his throat several times while listening to the phone ring on the other end.

"I don't think anyone's home," he whispered to Hazel, just as a recorded message began to play in his ear.

"You have reached the Frump family residence," a deep voice announced. "We can't get to the phone right now. Please leave your message and a number where you may be reached."

Ned cleared his throat again: "Hello. My name is Ned Frump and, uh, I'm looking for my uncle, Oliver Frump? A situation has arisen for my sister and me and . . . we urgently need to speak to you. In fact, we'd like to see you. To . . . visit your . . . to visit you. If that would be convenient. As soon as possible. Like, maybe today? Because, see, we need to leave town. I mean, we don't *need* to, but it would be . . . advisable. Under the circumstances."

Hazel made a face. She should have insisted on being the one to call. She knew it. At least Ned remembered to leave Frankie's phone number before hanging up.

"How was I?" Ned asked. "Did I sound strange? I was really nervous. Do you think he'll call back?"

"You were fine," Hazel lied. "I'm sure when he gets that message, he'll be curious to meet you."

She headed for the closet in Frankie's home office.

"I'm going to call back and leave my email address too," Ned called after her. "In case he doesn't get my message until late tonight or something. If he thinks it's too late to call, he could always email us."

"Why not leave another message saying he can call at any hour?" Hazel suggested as she rummaged among the boxes and bags piled haphazardly in Frankie's closet. "But if you want to leave the email address, I guess it can't hurt."

The package, when she found it, was tucked under a sheaf of old watercolours Frankie had stored on a high shelf. It was, as described, wrapped in brown paper. It was definitely her present. A yellow note stuck to the wrapping bore Colin Frump's handwriting: *For Hazel's 12th*.

Hazel lifted it down carefully and carried it out to the living room, where Ned was just replacing the telephone receiver.

"I left all our email addresses," he told her, "yours, mine, and Frankie's, just in case. I told him we'd probably be out this afternoon, but we'd check for messages at dinnertime. Want to go get a snack at Café Gentil?"

"Sure," Hazel agreed absently. She was staring at the package.

"Are you going to open that before we go see Monsieur Gentil?" Ned asked. "You might as well. Frankie already said it was a painting, so there's not much of a surprise left."

"Yeah," replied Hazel. "And she said it was something I'd always wanted. Which is weird, because I can't think of a painting I've always wanted. I mean, you know me; I'm not really into art. Not like Dad."

"That is sort of strange," agreed Ned.

Hazel ran her fingers down the sides of the package. An odd feeling of excitement was building inside her.

"There is one thing I used to ask Dad for, but he always said no," Hazel confessed. "A picture of Mum—you know, just a photograph. He said there weren't any. They burned up in a house fire. But Ned, what if there was a painting of Mum?"

"A house fire? He told *me* some cleaners he'd hired after a party threw them out by accident."

"That's silly; why would cleaners throw out photographs?" Hazel asked. "You must have gotten that wrong."

"Well he never said anything to me about a house fire," Ned averred. "And you'd think if there'd been a fire, other stuff would be missing."

"Well, I don't know—maybe there *was* a fire . . . just a little one, but he had cleaners come in afterwards and the photos got thrown out because they were damaged by water or smoke or something," Hazel said impatiently. "The important thing is—"

"Still, you wouldn't throw out all your photos after a fire, would you?" Ned continued doggedly. "It's not like they could be replaced. You'd keep them, just for sentimental purposes, because they were the only record of your children as babies or your wife, before she died. . . ."

"Well, maybe he threw them out because he still had this painting of Mum," Hazel said, "and now he's giving it to me!"

With a flourish, she ripped open the package and stared down at the small oil painting.

It was not a painting of their mother, or of anyone's mother. It was a dark landscape depicting a castle on the shores of a storm-tossed sea. The painting looked quite old; its surface was covered in tiny, hairline cracks, and something about it reminded Hazel of an exhibit her father had taken them to see.

As Hazel stared at the canvas, tears pricked at her eyes. She blinked them away, furious at herself. It was silly to feel disappointed. Colin Frump loved art so much, he probably thought she'd be thrilled to receive such a valuable painting. But why on earth had Frankie thought this was something she'd always wanted? She looked over at Ned to gauge his reaction. He was polishing his glasses.

"Well, it's certainly not what I expected," Hazel admitted.

Ned cleared his throat. "It's not what I expected, either," he replied. "Hazel, this is so weird. I care even less about art than you do, but I recognize this painting! I did a whole project on the artist who painted it!"

Hazel swallowed. Ned's art project. Frankie had said something about her father acting strangely after Ned's art teacher had contacted him about a project Ned had done for school. It hadn't made any sense at the time. It still didn't. Except—

"Ned, this painting. It's not very big. It would fit into a briefcase, wouldn't it? What if this is the one Richard C. Plevit wanted back from Frankie, from the gallery?"

"But why would Dad give it to you?" Ned asked. "For safekeeping?"

"I don't know. I don't think Dad would want to put me—well, either of us—in danger," Hazel said. "And even if he did want me to look after a painting for him, don't you think he'd just say so? I mean, he wouldn't try to pass off a stolen painting as a gift."

Hazel stared at the canvas and then at Ned, who was pacing back and forth, rubbing his glasses with the hem of his T-shirt.

"Okay, let's think about this. What do you remember about this painting? If it is the one from your project, I mean," Hazel demanded. "Who painted it? Is it valuable?"

Ned perched on the edge of the old valise that served as Frankie's coffee table. He concentrated fiercely.

"The painter's name was Paolo Cafazzo," Ned said. "He was some Romantic painter—as in Romanticism, with a capital *R*, this artistic period that lasted from about the late eighteenth century to the early nineteenth century. He basically became my whole project."

"Why did you pick him?" Hazel asked. "Did Dad suggest him?"

"No, I never talked to Dad about it," Ned said, frowning. "We were supposed to choose someone from the Romantic period. Most of the guys picked French painters, like Eugene Delacroix, or this Gericault guy. I wanted to do someone nobody else was doing, so I spent some time on the Internet and found these websites all about him."

"Websites?" Hazel asked. Her heart was pounding.

"Sure," Ned said. "He's got some bigtime fans, this Cafazzo guy. There are a couple of sites I found devoted just to him, and how he was like the greatest painter you've never heard of. And there were links to other sites, art history professors' sites, papers people had written about him."

"Show me," Hazel said. She could hardly breathe.

Ned shrugged and headed for Frankie's computer. Hazel stood behind him and watched as he entered his first website address. He made a *tsk* sound as the computer rejected his efforts, and tried again.

The room was silent but for the sound of Ned's furious typing. Again and again, he entered website names, only to be told the site could not be found. He swivelled the chair around to face Hazel.

"This is nuts!" Ned exploded. "I mean, I may not be remembering every site address exactly right, but some of those names I definitely know off by heart, and I know I'm entering them correctly. I don't understand how they could all just disappear!"

"What about books?" Hazel asked. "What books did you use?"

Ned looked a little embarrassed.

"Well, actually," he began, "I kind of did *all* my research over the Net."

"All of it?" Hazel repeated.

"Everything to do with Paolo Cafazzo, anyway," Ned said. "I mean, I used books to find out general stuff about the Romantic period, but I couldn't find anything about him in the books. It's like nobody knew about him until just recently. That's why I picked him—and I think that's why my art teacher liked the project so much. She said she'd never heard of him either, but when she checked out the sites I told her about, she was totally impressed."

Hazel looked at her brother. She felt as if she had been stuck, staring at a jigsaw puzzle for days, and all of a sudden she could see where the next pieces should go. There was so much more to figure out—so many giant gaps and so many little pieces that didn't seem to fit—but for the first time, Hazel believed they could solve it. They *would* solve it.

"Ned. I think I know what the inspector meant in his message to Dad," she said. "When he said 'Ned's website,' he didn't mean a site you *made*. He meant one you'd *discovered*—one about Paolo Cafazzo. It must be why Dad went to Turkey. It must have something to do with the whole art smuggling, art fraud thing in the newspaper."

Ned looked as if Hazel had hit him.

"Do you mean," and his voice came out in a squeak, "do you mean that it's *my* fault Dad's in trouble? It's my fault he's in jail?"

Hazel was about to say something reassuring (she just wasn't sure what) when Frankie's computer chirped. Both the children turned automatically to see who had sent the message. Hazel couldn't help herself. She gasped. It was from Oliver Frump.

With impatient fingers she reached over Ned's shoulder to click on the email. Together they read:

Dear Ned & Hazel,

> *Delighted to hear you can come for a visit. I have taken the liberty of booking two first-class, sleeper-car tickets on the overnight train to Frontenac. It departs Friday at 10:00 p.m.— you may collect your tickets 45 minutes before departure from the first-class lounge. You will arrive in Frontenac at 7 o'clock on Saturday morning. A car will collect you from the station and bring you across on the ferry. Don't worry about payment; I have taken care of everything.*

Please let me know by telephone or email if these arrangements are not suitable. Otherwise, I shall look forward to greeting you at Land's End tomorrow morning.

Yours truly,
Oliver Frump

CHAPTER SEVEN

Swinging her legs over the side of the bunk, Hazel contemplated the small closet where Monsieur Gentil had stowed their bags. They were travelling light: some clothing, Ned's stinkbomb, and, wrapped in tissue at the bottom of the battered suitcase Monsieur Gentil had insisted on lending her—the mysterious painting by Paolo Cafazzo.

Thinking of Monsieur Gentil, Hazel smiled. After they had filled him in on everything, the old man had insisted on accompanying them, first to the station to ensure they had no difficulty collecting their tickets, and then, right onto the train, just in case Richard C. Plevit or Clive Pritchard was lurking on the platform. The conductor would have refused Monsieur Gentil's request, Hazel was sure, had he not recognized the baker from his own visits to the renowned café.

"It's against the rules, but if they were *my* grandchildren travelling alone, I'd want to see them safely aboard as well," the conductor had said.

Hazel had been sure her brother would correct him. But Ned had simply taken the arm of his old friend and smiled his thanks to the conductor.

It hadn't been easy to fall asleep on the train, at least not at first. There was a great deal to talk about, and with Ned on the top bunk (Hazel was beginning to suspect his luck with coin tosses), and Hazel below, the two chatted until well past midnight. But the endless rounds of questions neither of them could answer proved exhausting. Eventually, Ned, and shortly afterwards, Hazel, succumbed to the combination of a long and tiring day and the soporific swaying of the train.

Now the pale light of the early-morning sun illuminated the sleeping compartment. Hazel wondered how Ned could still be asleep when there was so much to think about. Their father was still missing, locked in some prison in Istanbul, and the menacing Richard C. Plevit was still on the loose, not to mention his accomplice, Clive Pritchard. She and Ned were on their way to stay with an uncle they knew nothing about, save the fact that their father had kept his very existence a secret all their lives.

From the top bunk, Ned looked over at her.

"You awake, Hazel?"

"You can see that I'm sitting up. Why would you even bother asking that question?"

Ned rolled over and gazed out the window. Fields of corn and soybeans alternated with apple orchards and the occasional pasture dotted with grazing cows. In the distance he could glimpse the shimmering blue of the lake.

"Do you think he lives on a farm?" Ned asked, yawning again.

"Who? Uncle Oliver? Maybe. I was sort of picturing a small town, but I don't know anything more about Île du Loup than you do."

"I hope he's nice," Ned said. But he didn't sound worried, Hazel noted, and he wasn't polishing his glasses.

"Hey, Hazel! You didn't have that nightmare last night!" Ned said. "Do you think that's a sign?"

Hazel rolled her eyes.

"Don't be ridiculous," was all she said. But privately she couldn't help thinking maybe Ned was right. Maybe that was why she had woken up in such a good mood.

An early breakfast was being served in the dining car before they arrived at Frontenac. Over freshly squeezed orange juice and cold toast, the children rehashed their discussion of the night before. What would Land's End be like? Could they continue to search for clues to Colin Frump's disappearance and imprisonment? Would Oliver Frump be able to explain why his brother had given Hazel that painting? Would they ever have to see Richard C. Plevit or Clive Pritchard again? Monsieur Gentil had promised to check for telephone messages from Frankie and to call them that evening. Would he have any news by then?

After they had finished breakfast, Ned produced a pen and small pad of paper from the knapsack he carried with him.

"What's that for?" Hazel asked.

"We need to adopt a more rigorous approach to solving the problems that surround us," Ned said sternly. "We need a more scientific method. If only to make sure that *you* don't keep forgetting things. Valuable-information-type things, like emails from long-lost uncles, for example."

"Oh, really?" Hazel said, raising her eyebrows.

"Really!" Ned replied. "Don't you agree?"

Hazel stared at his bent head as her brother jotted down notes on the paper. It *was* a good idea, but that didn't mean she had to actually say so. Ned put the pen down with a flourish and pushed the paper toward her, raising one eyebrow.

"I hate it when you do that," Hazel said.

"I know," he said smugly. "So, have I left out anything?"

Hazel scanned the paper quickly. Ned's notes consisted of point form lists of names and events: *Richard C. Plevit; Clive Pritchard; Paolo Cafazzo; Inspector O'Toole; Colin Frump; art smuggling; fraud; Istanbul.*

"I was thinking," Ned continued, "that maybe I should add *Ludwig Barta*. I mean, he seemed nice, but it was kind of fishy, that Plevit guy showing up at his office. What if Barta left the room just so he could call Plevit, and tip him off that we were there?"

Hazel resisted the temptation to roll her eyes again.

"I don't think Mr. Barta had time to tip anyone off about anything," she said carefully. "But Dad did meet him just before he disappeared, so maybe he's involved somehow. . . . Sure, put Barta's name down."

"Okay," Ned agreed, taking up the pen again, "and I think I'll add *disappearing websites* to the list, too."

"Also—what was the style? *Romanticism*," Hazel urged, warming to the task. "Can you remember anything else from the Internet that might be helpful?"

"Like what?" Ned asked, pen poised above the paper.

Hazel shrugged. What *did* she mean?

"Like . . . other names, I guess," she said finally. "Art experts you quoted in your project."

Ned nodded. "Maybe we can track them down some other way, even if the websites aren't working."

He thought for a moment then added: *Professor Levi Triccar; Dr. Chip Vilecart;* and *Critic Reva L., Ph.D.*

"Those are some weird names," Hazel observed. "What's with this Reva L. person? Doesn't she have a last name?"

Ned shook his head. "Nope. But it may be sort of a Net name. Reva L. turned up in a lot of places. I think she must be one of those Internet junkies, you know, with her own sites and chat rooms and probably more than one blog."

Hazel nodded. She didn't spend anywhere near as much time on the Internet as Ned did, but she knew some kids—and a few grown-ups—who seemed to live online.

"Well, that's all *I* can remember," Ned said, pushing the paper away with a sigh. "Are you sure there's nothing else *you* can remember?"

"I never saw the websites," Hazel replied.

"No, I mean stuff from when you went snooping in Dad's study, before everything got stolen," Ned answered.

Hazel shook her head.

"There were just a lot of paintings and papers that I didn't get a chance to look at," she answered, "and then when I came back, they were gone. Oh! Wait!"

Ned peered owlishly at her. "What—another email you forgot to mention?" he asked.

"No. Paper!" Hazel responded. "I remember now—I tore some pages off a notepad Dad kept beside his phone—they were all covered in doodles and scribbles."

"Well? What did they say?" Ned demanded.

"I never looked at them again," Hazel confessed. "I was in such a hurry. I figured I'd do it later, but there's just been so much going on. . . ."

There was a grinding noise from the other side of the table. Ned appeared to be gnashing his teeth.

"Where. Are. The. Papers. Now?" he asked.

Hazel could not remember doing anything with the scraps. Were they in her room? Did she have them at Frankie's? Where had she put those pieces of paper?

"Okay," Ned gave a theatrical, long-suffering sigh. "Think about it. You're in Dad's office. You see this notepad. You tear off some pages and you put them . . . where?"

Hazel closed her eyes.

"In my pocket," she said. "My jeans pocket."

"What jeans?"

"These ones," Hazel replied. She dug into her pocket and pulled out several crumpled scraps of paper.

"Whoa!" Ned exclaimed. "Good thing you don't do laundry that often."

Hazel was too excited to think of a withering reply. She smoothed the papers out on the table so they could both examine them.

The bad news was that Colin Frump's writing was almost illegible. The good news was that some of the scribbles looked remarkably like names Ned had just written down.

"Hey! Does that say Levi Triccar?" Ned asked.

Hazel nodded. "And I think that must be Critic Reva L.," she added. "I'm not sure about this bit at the bottom of the page . . . does that say 'Call S?'"

They had agreed one of the scribbles resembled the name Clive Pritchard and another seemed to spell Richard C. Plevit but were puzzling over the others when they were interrupted.

"Are you two finished?" The waiter was hovering at Hazel's elbow. "I don't mean to rush you, only we'll be arriving at Frontenac soon."

The train was indeed slowing down. Hazel darted a quick look out the window. The farmers' fields had given way to rambling, grey limestone houses and gardens overflowing with roses and hollyhocks. It was charming, in a peaceful, sleepy way, she thought. It seemed . . . safe.

"Thank you," Hazel said, grabbing Ned's arm and pulling him to his feet.

The Frontenac train station was worlds removed from the one Monsieur Gentil had escorted them through the night before. There, Hazel had felt as if she was in a sort of giant cathedral, one that demanded passengers stop to admire its vaulted ceilings, soaring windows, and ornately carved stone walls. Here, the train simply halted outdoors beside a small platform and a tiny brick building decorated with Victorian "gingerbread" trim.

Hazel had been nervous about finding the car their uncle had mentioned, but Ned spotted their driver almost immediately. She was tall, with tanned, freckled skin and long brown hair pulled back into a pony tail. She wore jeans and a cotton shirt, and held a hand-lettered sign that read FRUMPS. When Ned waved, she waved back immediately and began walking toward them.

"Hello, I'm Charlotte," she called. "Olly sent me to pick you up."

"Hello," Hazel said politely. "I'm Hazel, and this is my brother, Ned."

"Is that all you have? Just the one suitcase and your backpacks?" Charlotte enquired. "Goodness, I know Oliver's hoping you'll stay for more than a couple of days."

Hazel shot a glance at Ned. Charlotte spoke as if she knew their uncle well. She must be more than a hired driver—perhaps a friend?"

"I think if our uncle wants us to stay longer, we probably could," Ned answered.

"Your *uncle?* Oh, I'm sure *he'd* go along with that," Charlotte said, hoisting the suitcase into the back of an old and somewhat dented blue pickup truck.

Hazel hesitated. Why had Charlotte said 'your uncle' like that? Something seemed . . . not quite right. But before she could put her finger on it, Ned had pushed past her and scrambled into the cab of the truck. Charlotte was still holding the door open, her eyes fixed on Hazel with a look Hazel couldn't decipher. Were those *tears* in the woman's eyes? Just what, exactly, was going on here?

"Climb on up Hazel," Charlotte was saying. "I'm afraid my van isn't working, so I had to bring the truck. It'll get us to Land's End just as safely. But it's not quite as comfortable. We'll have to get our air conditioning the old-fashioned way." She pointed to the truck's open windows.

Hazel took a deep breath and managed a thin smile in response, as she climbed in beside Ned.

The drive to the ferry took no more than five minutes. As she steered the truck through the winding streets of Frontenac, Charlotte told them a little about Île du Loup.

"It's not a very big island and it's made up mostly of farms. The ferry will take us to O'Connor's Corners, but that's nothing more than a marina, a church, and a gas station. The only real shopping is in Ville St-Pierre, on the opposite side of the island—right near Land's End, in fact. But it's geared more to the American tourists who come across the border by boat. You know: cafés, antique shops, galleries, that sort of thing. Locals generally take the ferry across to Frontenac for their shopping. . . . And here we are at the docks."

They had arrived just in time to see the island passengers disembarking. As they waited in line to drive onto the boat, Hazel wondered again who Charlotte was. She was pondering how to broach the subject when Ned broke in.

"So how do you know our Uncle Oliver?" he asked.

Charlotte wrinkled her nose. The ferryman waved the car ahead of them onto the boat. She glanced at Ned and shook her head. Shifting the truck into gear, Charlotte followed the ferryman's directions. When she had steered the truck into place, she switched off the ignition and paused, her hand still resting on the keys.

"How long have I known . . . *who?*" she asked.

"Uncle Oliver," Ned repeated.

"You mean, Uncle *Seamus*," Charlotte corrected.

"No, he means our Uncle Oliver," Hazel said. She could feel a knot forming in her stomach. "Oliver Frump. Our father, Colin Frump, is his brother. You're supposed to be taking us to Oliver." Despite her best efforts, Hazel's voice wobbled slightly.

"It's okay," Charlotte said soothingly. "I *am* taking you to Oliver."

"Then who's Seamus?" asked Ned.

Charlotte paused.

"You know what? I think I'll let Oliver explain that," she said. "Now, if you'll excuse me, I have to go see a man about a horse."

"I beg your pardon?" Hazel asked.

"Did I mention I'm a vet? That fine gentleman over there could use a gentle reminder about paying my last bill," Charlotte explained. "Why don't you two stretch your legs, enjoy the fresh air—just meet me back here before we dock."

With that, she was gone. Hazel and Ned looked at each other. Ned shrugged.

"Let's go see what there is to see," he suggested without enthusiasm. They clambered out of the truck and made for one of the narrow metal staircases that led to the decks where passengers, soaked in spray, leaned over the rails and chatted as they surveyed the circling gulls and the few sailboats hardy enough to brave the choppy waters.

But as they reached the deck, a scuffle broke out below them. Turning, Hazel and Ned saw two fair-haired boys, roughly Hazel's age, trying to break free from one of the ferrymen. The man had one of the boys by the ear and the other by the neck of his T-shirt. A taller boy with dark curly hair was hanging back, watching the scene with narrowed eyes. The girls at Hazel's school wouldn't have given the fair-haired boys a second look, but the other one? They wouldn't have taken their eyes off him, Hazel thought.

"You think soaping the windows of people's cars is funny?" bellowed the ferryman. "Let's just see how funny you think it is to clean it off then!"

"It wasn't us," whined the larger of the blond kids. He had

stopped trying to get away; he pouted and his shoulders slumped in defeat.

"No? Then what're you doin' with this, mister?" the ferryman demanded, thrusting a bar of soap under the boy's chin.

Hazel could see that two of the cars parked below had something rude written on their rear windows.

"He was trying to wash my mouth out with soap," giggled the smaller boy. The heavyset boy scowled at him before turning to the dark-haired boy.

"C'mon, Hank, tell him it wasn't us," he whined.

Hank. Now there's an old-fashioned, country sort of name, Hazel thought. Someone named Hank just had to be a baseball player, she decided, not a hockey player, and definitely not a basketball player.

Hazel hadn't realized she was staring at the boy until Hank looked straight at her. Their eyes locked for a moment. Then Hazel looked away.

"You're on your own, Billy," Hank said in a careless tone. "I was watching a bird. I don't know what you two were up to."

Hazel steered Ned toward the far side of the boat. When she glanced casually back, Hank was gone.

"What do you think Charlotte meant about Uncle Seamus?" Ned asked. "Do you think there's a whole bunch of uncles we don't know about?"

"At this point, nothing would surprise me," Hazel replied. "Maybe there're aunts, too."

"And cousins."

"Well, we'll find out for ourselves soon enough—there's the dock, over there."

As they started to make their way back to Charlotte's truck, Hazel scanned the crowd for the boy called Hank. She caught sight of him over by a gleaming black pickup truck parked at the front of the ferry, the two other boys beside him. The ferryman was there too, arguing with the driver of the truck—a slim man in jeans and a T-shirt, with blond hair peeking out below his cap. A pair of sunglasses shielded his eyes.

"I wonder if that's their dad," Hazel murmured.

As she strained to get a better look at the man, he turned. Hazel caught a glimpse of his face. She let out a squeak and pinched Ned, hard.

"Ow!" Her brother yelped. "What's the matter with you?"

A middle-aged woman glanced up from her newspaper, curious, but Hazel ignored her. Putting a finger to her lips, she grabbed Ned's arm and pulled him behind a gaggle of chattering teenagers. Her heart was beating wildly.

"You're freaking me out," whispered Ned, but his voice was calm.

"Did you see? Did you see the man with those boys—that Hank guy and the other two?" hissed Hazel, peering around the corner.

"What man?" demanded Ned.

"There, with the sunglasses—getting into the pickup truck." Hazel pointed. "It's, you know, Ferrari Guy—whatsisname—the one the newspaper said was Dad's partner. It's Clive Pritchard!"

The black pickup was the first vehicle to drive off the ferry. The children drew back slightly as it passed. The three boys were sitting in the cab; the back of the truck was covered with a tarpaulin that had come untied at one corner. Hazel glimpsed a stack of packages wrapped in brown paper.

They were slim and flat—like paintings ready for shipping.

"Hey, Frumps!" It was Charlotte, beckoning them to the blue truck.

"We'll talk about it later, right?" Hazel muttered. Ned nodded.

"We're coming!" the children chorused.

The drive to Land's End took about half an hour and passed

by nearly a hundred farms. All three occupants of the blue pickup seemed pre-occupied with their own thoughts. No one spoke until they crested a long hill that opened up a postcard vista of the lake, with dozens of sailboats and a couple of larger vessels that looked like passenger ferries.

"What are those?" Hazel asked, pointing.

"This is where Lake Ontario meets the St. Lawrence River," Charlotte explained. "Those are tour boats that take Canadian and American tourists to the area called the Thousand Islands. They circle around Île du Loup on their way out, because we're so 'picturesque.'"

As they drove on down into Ville St-Pierre, Hazel could see it was bigger than O'Connor's Corners, where the ferry had docked. But it was still, as Ned put it, "no thriving metropolis." Hazel noticed a greengrocer's, a general store, a butcher's shop, a repair shop, a half-dozen antique shops, and a café with a sign that read ART, TEAS, BOOKS AND ANTIQUES. There was no sign of Clive Pritchard.

Just beyond the village, Charlotte stopped the truck. They were at the entrance to a long, winding driveway flanked by spreading maple trees. On one side of the driveway sprawled an old apple orchard, on the other, a rolling expanse of lawn. But it was the house that amazed both of them. Except it wasn't a house at all.

It was bigger than the biggest mansion Hazel had ever seen—more the size of a large school—and built of rough-hewn stone, overgrown in places by ivy. The grey walls were punctuated at odd intervals by tall, arched windows, and Hazel counted three round towers. Two had conical slate roofs, but one was open at the top, perhaps to serve as a lookout over the lake. The walls of that tower alternated between high and low sections. There was a word for that, Hazel knew, but she couldn't remember it.

"Battlements!" Ned breathed. "An actual castle with actual battlements."

Hazel wondered what sort of battle the castle's owners might have waged. It looked awfully familiar. Could she somehow have seen it before? She glanced at Ned; his mouth had fallen open. She turned to look at Charlotte.

"It sure is something," Charlotte agreed, putting the truck in gear again and heading slowly up the drive. "People around here call it The Folly. Your family always calls it Land's End, though. This road is Land's End Lane. I think your cousins consider the word *folly* a bit hard-hearted.

"Still, it was a crazy project. It was built 130 years ago by a French immigrant for his Irish wife. It's meant to combine elements of a castle near her home in the south of Ireland with one near his home in the north of France. It makes for an unusual collaboration of architectural styles I suppose you'd say. . . . He died before he could finish it."

"I feel like I've seen this place before," Ned said, in a strangled voice. Hazel was about to ask him where, when it hit her: this was the castle from the painting. This was Paolo Cafazzo's castle!

CHAPTER EIGHT

Hazel stared. This castle had to be the one from the painting! Except . . . something wasn't quite right. Maybe it was the angle, the view from the truck. As she puzzled over it, the pickup reached the top of a small rise, giving Hazel her first glimpse of the lake beyond the castle. She caught her breath. A fat stone tower was clearly visible some distance behind and to the left of Land's End. There was something about that tower. Hazel couldn't take her eyes off it. It drove all thoughts of Paolo Cafazzo's painting from her mind. She *knew* that tower.

"What's that place?" she asked. "I can't see it very well from here, but it looks too far away to be part of this Folly or Land's End place."

Charlotte nodded. "That's a Martello Tower," she said. "It's on a little island just behind Land's End. There are a few such towers around Frontenac, left over from the days when they were needed to help guard the town and the port. Some have been turned into museums, but not that one. It's sort of . . . abandoned, I guess. A few of the villagers say it's haunted."

Hazel shivered. Charlotte looked at her in some amusement.

"You don't believe in ghosts, do you?" Charlotte asked.

Before Hazel could answer, a loud beeping noise pierced the air. Charlotte braked, reached into her purse, and pulled out a pager.

"Oh, heck—Carol Jupiter's horse is in trouble again! I've got to dash. Do you kids mind if I drop you here? You can tell Oliver I said hi, and that I'll come by later to discuss . . . er, your visit with your uncle."

"Sure," Hazel said faintly. "No problem."

As the blue pickup sped down the road, Ned gripped Hazel's arm so tightly she winced.

"Hazel, do you realize where we are? Ned asked. "This is the castle. *The* castle—the one in Paolo Cafazzo's painting!"

Hazel nodded. But she was still thinking about the tower. It wasn't in the painting. So why did it seem so familiar? She felt almost as if it was calling to her.

Ned was still talking.

" . . . and, of course, this has to mean Uncle Oliver's loaded too, just like Dad." He frowned. "Or maybe he isn't, Hazel. I mean, maybe Dad inherited all his money. All the Frump money, I mean. Maybe Dad got all the money and Uncle Oliver got the castle. I think if it was me, I'd rather have the castle."

Ned was still pondering the pros and cons of fortresses versus fortunes when they reached the end of the long driveway and stood, hesitating, in the shadow of the castle. They were wondering whether they ought to climb the stone steps to the great wooden door, or if there might be a less forbidding entrance somewhere, when a small boy skidded around the corner and stopped in front of them.

"You made it! You made it!"

Hazel caught her breath. The boy had ruler-straight dark brown hair and glasses. He was almost the same height and weight as Ned, perhaps an inch shorter. The resemblance was uncanny.

"You must be Ned," the boy said, holding out his hand.

"Yeah," Ned confirmed, shaking hands a bit stiffly.

"And you must be Hazel." The boy turned to smile up at her before pumping her arm energetically.

She nodded and returned the smile, wondering when he would introduce himself.

"I'm . . . I'm pleased to meet you," the boy said after a slight pause. "Welcome to Land's End or, as they say in the village, The Folly."

"Thanks. Who the heck are you?" Ned asked bluntly. "And where's our Uncle Oliver?"

"I'm . . . I'm your cousin, of course," the boy stammered. "Come on up—we should let Deirdre know you're here."

With that, the boy turned and led the way up the short flight of broad stone steps to the verandah. The castle was girded round by a narrow stone terrace. It was covered by a flat roof, which created a covered porch below and an open terrace above. This lower level felt far too grand to be called a porch, but that was clearly how Uncle Oliver treated it. Books and games were scattered about on wicker chairs and a bin was jammed full of tennis rackets and baseball bats. There was even a porch swing.

"Wait! Who's Deirdre?" Ned demanded. But the boy had run ahead and either couldn't hear him or wouldn't hear him.

"Deirdre—our visitors are here!" the boy yelled.

A wooden screen door at the far end of the porch opened and a sandy-haired girl in shorts and a faded T-shirt stepped out. In her arms she cradled a copper bowl filled with peas still in their pods. She was the same height as Hazel but appeared to be older, although that might have been due to the intimidating scowl on her face.

"Oliver, what are you talking about?" the girl asked. "You're supposed to be helping me shell the peas! What do you mean, visitors?"

But when she saw Hazel and Ned she stopped dead in her tracks.

"Oh. I . . . omigosh . . ." her voice trailed off as she stared at the children. She wasn't frowning now; she looked as if she'd seen a ghost. The bowl slipped out of her hands and clattered to the floor below, pods scattering across the flagstones.

"Oh my. Oh my goodness. You're . . . you're Hazel and N-Ned," she stammered.

Hazel looked at Ned. He raised an eyebrow.

"Yes, I'm Hazel, and this is my brother, Ned," Hazel began slowly, her voice conveying a patience she didn't feel at all. "But we're a little confused. We came to visit our Uncle Oliver."

The girl turned to the younger boy, who was now perched on the porch swing, grinning nervously.

"Oliver! What have you done?"

"Wait a minute. *You're* Uncle Oliver?" Ned demanded, pointing an accusing finger at the boy.

"What's going on?" Hazel appealed to the older girl.

"That's what I'd like to know," she said, turning to the boy. "But it looks like my brother's the only one who can answer that. Well, Oliver?"

"They called—I mean . . . he called . . . Ned." Oliver replied. "I think he must have been looking for Dad, but somehow he had my name, instead. He said they wanted to come and visit. So I said sure. Don't be mad, Deirdre. It's what we've always wanted."

"I did call," Ned agreed. "And I did ask for Oliver. I thought that was our uncle's name."

"Nope. Our dad's name is Seamus; *I'm* Oliver," the boy explained. "But when I got your message, I figured you'd probably only come if you thought it was Dad inviting you. You might not have come if you'd known it was just me."

No wonder Charlotte had decided to make Oliver explain.

She'd probably guessed that he was behind the confusion. But why hadn't Frankie set them straight? Hazel thought back to their hurried phone conversation. Frankie had said their father had a brother, but she had never actually called him Oliver. In fact, hadn't she said Oliver didn't sound right?

"I thought . . . I mean, I found an email to my Dad from an Oliver Frump, about a family reunion," Hazel said slowly, thinking aloud. "And then we found out that there was a brother. I mean, an uncle. So I guess we just assumed—I assumed—that the uncle was named Oliver. We didn't know there were any other relatives. . . ."

"A classic case of two plus two equalling five," Ned observed, shaking his head.

"Wait a second. You emailed Uncle Colin?" Deirdre's hands were on her hips. She glared at Oliver. "Oh, you are so busted, mister. Wait until Dad finds out."

Deirdre turned back toward Hazel. Her blue eyes no longer blazed with indignation. Now they were just bewildered.

"But how did you get here?" the girl asked, looking from Hazel to Ned and back again. "I mean, Oliver's right. We've all wanted you to come for ages, but now you suddenly show up. It's like magic."

"There's nothing very magical about booking train tickets online and hiring Charlotte to pick them up at the train station and bring 'em over on the ferry," Oliver said airily.

"*You* did all that?" asked Ned in tones of begrudging admiration.

"I hope you used some kind of magic to pay for everything," Deirdre said. She was looking at Oliver with one eyebrow raised. "Considering the last time Dad found out you'd used his credit card to buy something over the Internet, he flipped out."

"Look, if there's a problem, we can pay you back," Hazel said. An uncomfortable feeling was growing in the pit of her stomach. She felt as if she had arrived at a party only to find her invitation had been issued by mistake.

"Gosh no, I'm sorry. There's no problem," Deirdre hastened to reassure her. "I'm really glad you guys came. *Everybody's* going to be glad."

"Everybody?" asked Hazel. "Who is everybody?"

Deirdre slipped an arm around Hazel's shoulders and guided her to a wicker loveseat, motioning to Ned to follow. Sweeping a pile of jigsaw pieces out of the way, she plunked herself down on the footstool facing them.

"Okay, here's the thing," Deirdre said, taking a deep breath. "My name's Deirdre, and I'm your cousin. I'm fourteen. You also have a cousin named Oliver—this scheming little imp over here. He's eight. Then there are our older brothers, Matthew and Mark. They're seventeen. They're twins and they're adopted. That doesn't make them any less your cousins, of course. I only mention it because, well, they're black. I mean black is what they say. Their dad was from Montreal and their mum was from Trinidad, but their biological parents died a long time ago."

"But there is an Uncle too, right? Uncle Seamus? You're not *all* orphans," Hazel interrupted. It might just be nerves, but the older girl seemed awfully chatty.

Deirdre blinked.

"Oh, no! I mean yes. I mean no, we're not orphans, and, yes, there is an uncle." Deirdre shook her head like a swimmer trying to empty water from her ears. "Our father—your father's brother—is Seamus: Seamus Frump. You don't have an Uncle Oliver, just a cousin who likes to pretend and thinks he's clever. Understand?"

Hazel nodded.

"So I guess you don't remember . . . I mean, I guess you two don't really know anything about us, eh?" Deirdre asked softly.

Hazel shook her head. Her brain was spinning: how could their father have hidden all these relatives from them? Why would he keep them a secret?

"Nope. We've never heard of any of you," Ned said. "You didn't mention an aunt. Is there one?"

Deirdre flicked a glance at Oliver and cleared her throat.

"No," she said reluctantly. "Our mother died when I was six years old."

"Oh. Sorry," Ned said. "Our mother's dead too. She died when I was a baby."

"I know," Deirdre murmured.

For a few moments nobody spoke. Hazel felt suddenly very tired. She was vividly aware of how soft the cushion on the loveseat felt and how a nearby trellis, overgrown with climbing roses of a pale yellow, was filling the air with a heavy perfume. She could hear bees humming in the vines and the singing of a cicada. She heard Ned's stomach growl. It must be almost lunchtime.

"So, where *is* Uncle Seamus?" Ned asked. "Does he even know we're coming?"

The boy Oliver shook his head. Deirdre grimaced.

"Well, that should be the first topic for discussion once the twins get back from sailing," she said. "Dad's away, and he's actually not due back for days, maybe even weeks. I'm sure once he hears about you two, he's going to want to come home as soon as possible, so we'll have to decide when to break the news."

"Where is he?" Hazel asked.

"He's in Ottawa, trying a case before the Supreme Court," Deirdre informed them. Hazel thought she detected a note of pride in her cousin's voice.

"He's a lawyer?" Hazel asked.

"A really good one," Deirdre answered. The pride was undisguised now.

"Well, that could come in handy," Ned muttered. Hazel jammed an elbow in his ribs.

"I beg your pardon?" Deirdre asked.

"Uh, got any candy?" Ned asked, rubbing his hand over his stomach and, more surreptitiously, his side. "I'm starved."

"Oh goodness, where are our manners?" Deirdre chided Oliver. "Take your cousin inside and find him a snack! Or better yet, why don't you boys get started on lunch? Hazel and I will come and help in a few minutes."

Deirdre was a little bossy as well as a little chatty, Hazel reflected. But as long as the bossiness was directed at someone other than her, she wouldn't protest. Hazel nodded to Ned.

"We'll be right behind you," she told him. "Don't do anything I wouldn't do."

She hoped Ned would take the hint and keep quiet about Colin Frump's imprisonment. Uncle Seamus might be just the person they needed right now, but until they found out more about why he and their dad were estranged, Hazel didn't know if they could trust him. Ned nodded and slid off the loveseat.

"After lunch, want to see my room?" Oliver asked. "I have the coolest chemistry set you've ever seen."

"Oh, I really doubt that," Ned replied. "But sure, I'll check it out."

After the screen door had slammed behind the boys, Hazel turned to Deirdre. It was time to gather information.

"So . . . it can't have been easy growing up as the only girl in a house with three brothers," Hazel remarked. "It's too bad we didn't have each other to talk to, all these years."

"Uh-huh. Want to go for a walk along the beach, or take a tour of the castle?" Deirdre asked brightly.

For someone who so clearly loved to talk, Deirdre wasn't exactly grasping the chance to dish the family gossip, Hazel observed. Well, she wasn't about to give up. A tour of the family home should provide lots of opportunities for questions.

"Sure. I'm dying to see the rest of the castle," Hazel said, smiling back at the older girl. "Let's go!"

Stepping over the scattered peas, Deirdre opened the screen door and led Hazel through the largest kitchen she had ever seen. Monsieur Gentil would flip if he saw it, Hazel knew. The room was so long and wide that there was space for tables, bookcases, and armchairs, as well as fitted cupboards and counters. The flagstone floor was worn smooth in front of the old-fashioned iron stove. Next to the stove stood an enormous fireplace, with a hearth opening so tall that Oliver was demonstrating to Ned how he could walk right into the chimney. Hazel fell in love with the place instantly and would have been happy to spend the rest of their visit in the strange yet welcoming room. But Deirdre was already ushering her into the hall.

Hazel's plan to interrogate her cousin would have to wait. She couldn't help it; the castle commanded her full attention. The ceilings were so high, she was pretty sure you could attach NBA regulation-height hoops to most of the stone or wood-panelled walls, and still have loads of room to spare. There was a full suit of armour standing at attention in one passageway and Hazel desperately wanted to sneak a peek behind its visor, but Deirdre was setting a brisk pace. There were so many rooms and hallways, it was impossible to fix them all in her memory. There was an actual ballroom in the main part of the building, and in one of the towers Hazel was thrilled to see a two-storey library. It was a completely round room, lined from floor to ceiling with books. A narrow circular staircase led to an equally narrow balcony that encircled the room. Hazel itched to climb the stairs and examine the upper tiers of books, but Deirdre was already pulling her into another corridor.

Hazel had lost count of living rooms, parlours, games rooms, and bedrooms by the time Deirdre led her through a rounded oak door into a courtyard.

"Cloisters!" exclaimed Hazel. "I thought that was something you only found in churches or monasteries?"

"Land's End has almost everything you can imagine," laughed Deirdre. "Except a swimming pool; with the lake right outside you don't really need one. You haven't seen the best thing yet. Come on!"

She pulled Hazel through another door. This one led directly to a small, circular stone staircase, which Deirdre climbed, two steps at a time. When they reached the top, Deirdre was out of breath and needed Hazel's help to push open the trapdoor.

"Wow," breathed Hazel, as the girls scrambled out into the afternoon sunshine. They were standing atop the open tower with the battlements. Hazel's stomach was turning flip-flops and her head felt light and woozy; she really did not like heights. She stayed a few paces behind her cousin, as Deirdre moved closer to the crenellated wall that encircled the platform. Up here the breeze was stronger, more like wind, and the girls' hair was blown about their faces. But when Hazel pulled her hair back and gazed at the glittering lake, she had to admit the view was spectacular. Terrifying, but spectacular.

"This tower is actually taller than the others," Deirdre pointed out. "The northwest tower is where the boys' rooms are, and the southwest tower is where my room is, and Dad's room, and a guest room—you can have that one tonight, if you like. Anyway, we don't really know why this tower doesn't have a roof like the others, but if you ask me, it does have the best view. I'm kind of glad they never finished the fourth tower; it makes this one more special, even though it does ruin the symmetry.

"From here you can see that the castle is built on a sort of peninsula. Beyond the orchard and the hill, there's an even better beach, with sand dunes and the whitest, softest sand. And way, way beyond *that*, there's a really interesting old lighthouse. It hasn't been used to warn ships in almost a century, but it's still standing. We'll take you there for a picnic or a midnight bonfire some night. Oh—and we have the greatest tree fort you've ever seen. It's really, really old, and it's incredibly big and stretches from tree to tree to tree!"

Deirdre's eyes were shining.

"Please," Hazel said, putting her hand on Deirdre's arm. "I don't mean to be rude. It's great that you and Oliver are being so friendly and everything, but . . . don't you see how strange this is for me? You and Oliver act like you know all about me and Ned, and you're talking about picnics and bonfires and stuff. But we just met you! We didn't know you even existed until a few minutes ago!"

Deirdre looked uncomfortably at Hazel.

"I know. It's got to be weird for you guys. But I'm not the right person to explain it all."

"Just tell me why my dad never told us about your dad. Did they have a big fight or something?" asked Hazel.

Deirdre winced.

"You see . . . it's a whole, big, complicated thing and I'd just mess it up," Deirdre said helplessly. "I mean, I'd leave out stuff or I'd get it wrong. And it's so important that you hear the whole story—but you should hear it from the right person."

Deirdre paused. She seemed to be choosing her words carefully.

"*Our* father never kept you two a secret," she said finally. "So, yeah, we know your names, and how old you are, and there are a few old photographs around. And, well, you saw how much Ned and Oliver look alike. As soon as I saw you, I knew who you were."

She paused again. When she resumed, her voice sounded strained.

"But you have to believe me when I say that I can't explain why your dad never told you about us, or why we've never met. You just have to wait for Dad."

"But . . . does our father know you guys live in a castle?" Hazel asked. "Because I just can't believe he would've kept this place a secret from us."

"Does he know?" Deirdre echoed. "Well, yeah—he was born here. They both were, our dads I mean. They're twins. I guess I didn't mention that. Identical twins, not fraternal, like Matt and Mark, but not, like, freaky identical. I think if they were standing together, you could tell them apart. But if you only had one in front of you, it might take you a minute to figure out which one he was."

Hazel's mind was spinning. Her father had an identical twin? How could she not know something like that? How could he not have told her? And how could he not have told her he'd grown up in a castle?

Hazel raised her eyebrows. This family, she decided, was insane. When she grew up, if she had kids, she'd tell them every-thing—*everything*—even stuff they didn't want to hear.

Deirdre was studying her with a worried look.

"Oh, Hazel, don't let it drive you nuts. Please? We're so happy to have you guys here. We've wanted to see you for ages, and we've been pestering Dad and everything.

"I'd never let on to Oliver, but if you ask me, he's done everyone a big fat favour. My dad and your dad will definitely agree. You'll see. In the meantime, we should take advantage of our fathers not being here and just . . . have a blast. You know?"

Hazel sighed. Okay. If Deirdre wouldn't confide in her, she wouldn't confide in Deirdre—at least not yet. Maybe one of the other cousins would be willing to talk. In the meantime, she might as well steer Deirdre toward happier subjects.

"So . . . Matthew and Mark aren't identical twins?" she asked.

Deirdre's face relaxed.

"No, no. Matt and Mark don't look alike at all. And they *hate* being compared to each other, so of course Oliver and I do that all the time. But if you ask me, I'd say they get along really well. With each other, I mean. They're typical older brothers to me and Oliver—you know, always putting us down. They never, ever take me seriously. They're starting university this fall, but they'll be going to different schools. I'll miss them like crazy, but don't ever tell them that. They each have an ego bigger than this whole island already."

Hazel had stopped listening. Looking past Deirdre, beyond the parapet, she gazed out toward the island with the Martello tower. Deirdre hadn't mentioned that tower when she was pointing out the scenery. Why not?

"Does somebody own that island?" Hazel asked, gesturing toward it.

"Hmm? Oh, we do, but I haven't been there in years," Deirdre said carelessly. She didn't even glance in the direction of the island—too busy examining her nails, Hazel noticed.

"I'd like to go see it sometime," Hazel said, more to herself than Deirdre. But the effect on her cousin was electric.

"Oh no, no, no," Deirdre said, shaking her head. Her voice sounded a little shaky too, Hazel thought. "That tower's falling apart and the island is pretty small, and, well, it's not like there's anything to *do* there."

Deirdre took Hazel's arm as if to steer her away from the sight of the tower. Was it Hazel's imagination, or had Deirdre turned a little pale? And she was . . . babbling.

"I mean, gosh, the current's much too strong to swim over

there, and even if you took a boat, well, pretty much the whole place is covered in poison ivy. Some kids even say the tower's haunted. Of course that's silly, but still, I mean, why take chances—right, Hazel? Hazel?"

Hazel was staring at the tower with narrowed eyes. There was a man leaning out of one of the tower windows. He was too far away to get a good look, but she had the grim feeling that his bulky frame and bald head were horribly familiar. Her heart slammed against her ribs.

"Do you see that man?" Hazel asked.

Deirdre turned to look.

"Where?"

"Just there, in the window!" Hazel almost growled with frustration. But the man had drawn his head back inside the tower.

"No one's there," Deirdre announced. "Anyway, Mark and Matt must be home by now. Aren't you just dying to meet them?"

Hazel nodded, although for now she didn't care the slightest bit about meeting her cousins. She just wanted to warn Ned that Clive Pritchard wasn't the only man they had to worry about on Île du Loup.

Richard C. Plevit was here too.

CHAPTER NINE

"Hey, Hazel—come and meet Matt and Mark! Oliver calls 'em the M&Ms; you know, like the candy!"

Ned was sitting beside Oliver on the porch swing. For one disconcerting second, Hazel wasn't sure which boy was which, but it passed so quickly she wondered if she'd imagined it.

Ned seemed different somehow. Had she ever seen her brother look so completely relaxed at home?

He's really hit it off with Oliver, she thought to herself, as the younger boy whispered something in Ned's ear that set the pair of them giggling like crazy. Mark and Matthew were leaning against the stone balustrade, surveying the younger boys with amused expressions.

This was all very cozy, but Hazel needed to get Ned to herself, to tell him about seeing Richard C. Plevit in the tower. Unless she wanted to share the news with everyone . . . but they'd probably think she was nuts. Or making it up.

"Hi, Hazel. I'm Matthew, but everyone calls me Matt," said the shorter of the twins. "Nobody ever calls me an M&M," he added emphatically. (That set off a fresh round of giggles from the direction of the porch swing.)

They were definitely not identical; Hazel wouldn't even have known the teenagers were twins if Deirdre hadn't told her. Matt had a stockier build, lighter skin, and close-cropped hair. He wore a sober expression that seemed to suit his plain denim jeans and white tennis shirt. Mark's skin was very dark and he was at least six inches taller but looked as if he weighed considerably less than his twin. He wore his hair in cornrows and had a pair of tinted glasses perched at the end of his nose. His Hawaiian shirt was unbuttoned, revealing a tattered T-shirt that read: Dandelions Don't Cause Cancer—Lawn Chemicals Do.

"Hi," Hazel began, but she was interrupted by Mark, who crossed the porch in three swift strides, lifted her off her feet in a giant bear hug, and twirled her around before setting her gently down again.

"Hey, little cousin—long time no see!" he roared.

"Ahem!" Matt cleared his throat.

"Yeah, whatever . . . I meant, great to see you," Mark said breezily. "Ned was just telling us you guys might stay for a while. That's terrific; best news we've had in a long time."

Hazel stared at her cousin. Mark might be skinny, but he sure was strong. Hazel was tall for her age, and thanks to all those hours on the basketball court, she had muscles too. She was *solid*. People didn't just go around picking her up like she was a little kid or a doll or something. What did he think she was—six?

"We are *all* very happy to see you," Matt said, more formally. "We were just talking about the fact that we should tell your uncle Seamus about you two . . . he'll be very happy too, of course. But maybe we'll just wait until he calls."

"He's supposed to check in tomorrow, right?" Deirdre asked.

Matt nodded.

"The thing is, this case he's trying is a little tricky and we don't want to do anything that would throw him off," Matt continued. "I mean, we don't want to disturb him."

"Sure," Hazel agreed. That would give her a little more time to talk things over with Ned and decide how much to tell Uncle Seamus and the cousins.

"Oh—there's the phone," Deirdre said. "Oliver, you get it!"

She really is bossy, Hazel thought. Deirdre was standing much closer to the screen door than her little brother. But Oliver leapt up obediently and headed into the kitchen. He was back in a few moments, holding a portable phone.

"There's some guy with a really thick French accent asking for 'Azel or Ned," Oliver announced.

"Oh, that's Monsieur Gentil, our neighbour. We left him your phone number. He probably just wants to make sure we got here okay," Hazel explained. "Ned, we should talk to him."

Almost imperceptibly, Hazel jerked her head toward the kitchen door. This was her chance to get Ned away from the others.

"So give her the phone, Squirt," Deirdre ordered Oliver.

Hazel blinked: Squirt was what she sometimes called Ned. This was weird.

"Actually, do you mind if we take it inside?" Ned asked.

"Go ahead," Matt replied. "We'll be out here."

Their conversation with Monsieur Gentil did not last long; he was still in the midst of a late lunch rush of tourists from a nearby exhibition. Ned and Hazel assured the old man they were safe. He told them that a locksmith friend had already changed the locks on the door leading from the staircase to the floor where the Frumps and Frankie lived, as well as the locks on the doors to their apartments. Ned was about to ask about the elevator, when Monsieur Gentil gave a quiet little cough.

"I worked a little sabotage on the elevator, myself," Monsieur Gentil said. "I will apologize to your father on his return, but in the meantime, I promise you, no one will be using it. Everyone must take the stairs. It is good for their health, *non?*"

The entrance to the staircase was right beside Monsieur Gentil's café, Hazel realized. This way, the old man could easily keep track of who was coming and going from the apartments . . . so long as he wasn't distracted by his baking.

"Thanks, Monsieur Gentil," Ned told him. "We'll be in touch."

After they had hung up, Hazel told Ned she didn't think there would have been any more disturbances at the apartment building anyway.

"Well, Ferrari Guy—I mean, Clive Pritchard—is here on the island," Ned agreed. "But don't forget about Richard C. Plevit—the one who hurt Frankie."

Ned's eyes widened as Hazel described seeing Plevit lean out of the tower.

"Do you think they're following us?" Ned asked, removing his glasses. "Should we tell the others?"

From outside the children heard laughter and the murmured conversation of their cousins. Hazel watched Ned for a moment. His glasses were off, but he wasn't actually polishing them. Did he feel it too, she wondered? Did he feel safe?

"I don't think they're following us," Hazel mused aloud. "Frankie said she thought Dad knew Clive Pritchard from a long time ago. I wonder if it could have been from here, from Île du Loup. Deirdre says Dad was born here, and grew up here."

"Man—how could he grow up in a castle and not tell us?" asked Ned in disgust. "That's cold."

"Oh, that's not all," Hazel said. "Get this. Apparently he and Uncle Seamus are identical twins."

Ned grimaced.

"I've changed my mind," he announced. "Dad's not secretive; he's nuts. How could he have an identical twin *and not tell us?*"

"I'm right there with you," Hazel agreed. "But in the meantime, we still have to deal with Clive Pritchard and Richard C. Plevit being on the island. It's strange, but when I think about it now, I don't actually feel afraid . . . even though I probably should. Isn't that weird?"

Ned nodded. "It *is* weird, but I kind of feel the same way," he replied. "I feel a bit nervous and sort of excited, I suppose. But not scared. Maybe it's just because we're better off now."

"What do you mean?" asked Hazel.

"Well . . . we're not alone anymore," Ned pointed out, "and Matt and Mark are *almost* like grown-ups, and staying in a castle just has to be better than hiding out at Frankie's and waiting for the burglars to come back. I sort of wish there was a moat, though."

Hazel grinned.

"I think we should tell them everything—they might be able to help," Ned said in a serious voice. "I think there are way too many secrets in this family."

"You're not worried they'll think we're crazy?" Hazel asked.

Deep down, she knew Ned was right—they had to come clean. Still, she'd feel better about it if she knew why Colin and Seamus were estranged.

"What about the note Dad made?" Ned reminded her. "He wrote 'call *S*.' He might have meant 'call Seamus.' Maybe he was going to tell Uncle Seamus everything. Or maybe he already *did* tell him."

"Huh. Well, maybe you're right. Okay, we'll tell the cousins everything we know," Hazel said. "But let's do it tomorrow, okay? Let's just give ourselves what's left of this day to get to know them and let them get to know us. Hey, weren't you guys supposed to be making lunch? I'm starved."

Oliver wasn't quite so firmly under Deirdre's thumb as Hazel had thought. It turned out that as soon as the girls had embarked on their tour, the boys had grabbed a handful of cookies and headed straight for Oliver's room—a place, Ned assured Hazel, that boasted something closer to a chemistry *lab* than a simple chemistry set. Oliver was going to help Ned refine the NIDS.

"We might have to change the name to NOIDS—for Ned & Oliver's Incredibly Disgusting Stinkbomb," Ned said happily.

"Stinkbomb?" Mark poked his head through the screen door. "Oh, man—are you another chemistry freak like young Olly? One was bad enough!"

"Oliver makes stuff too?" Hazel asked.

"Don't get me started," Mark said darkly. "Listen, you guys, we were all just talking about taking a picnic to the beach. It's too late for lunch and too early for dinner, so we thought we'd just throw a whole bunch of food in a basket and spend the rest of the day eating and swimming and eating and swimming and maybe eating again. What do you say?"

Hazel and Ned needed no persuading. Oliver promised to find Ned a spare swimsuit in the jumble of his room, and the two boys set off together, whispering non-stop. Deirdre smiled at Hazel and gestured for her to follow.

"I'm sure I've got something you can borrow, if you didn't pack a swimsuit," the older girl promised. "And I'll show you the tower room where you'll be sleeping while you're here."

"Hey, be quick, you two! None of that girly stuff. No giggling and trying stuff on and looking in mirrors," Mark called after them, as they hurried up the stone staircase. "Time's a-wastin'! Surf's up!"

With Mark's words ringing in her ears, Hazel was determined to be the first one changed. She barely glanced at the perfectly round room that would be hers later that night, taking only seconds to pull on the swimsuit Deirdre had thrust in her hands and stuff her unruly hair into a ponytail. But the castle's layout was confusing, and by the time Hazel had found the kitchen again, the twins had finished assembling an impressive array of sandwiches, fruit, and drinks for the picnic.

Assuming that they were just headed to the pebbly shore a few metres away, Ned was mystified by the elaborate preparations.

"No, we're going to the real beach—the sand dunes," Oliver explained finally. "They're the best ones on the whole island. Come on, follow me!"

Hazel and Ned practically lived at the beach in the city. But the sand there was coarse and, as often as not, littered with candy wrappers, pieces of glass, and bits of plastic. The beach at Land's End had the softest, whitest sand Hazel had ever seen. The dunes—undulating waves of sand crested with tall grasses—appeared with startling suddenness just beyond the edge of the old orchard. One minute Hazel was walking under tree boughs laden with small unripe fruit; the next, she was sliding down a steep grassy slope and gaping at the broad crescent of sand that stretched before her, and the sparkling water beyond.

The rest of the afternoon passed so peacefully, Hazel felt as if they had entered another world. She swam for a while, but the water still had that early-summer chill and the lure of the sun and the sand proved stronger. Lazing on her borrowed beach towel, Hazel talked with Mark and Deirdre about harmless topics like boarding school, basketball, and Mark's difficulty in deciding whether to be a lawyer like Uncle Seamus or a great chef.

After hours of watching Ned and Oliver construct the most impossibly elaborate sand fortress, Hazel had almost succeeded in forgetting the events that had brought them here. At least until Matt emerged from a lengthy swim to take a seat on a nearby towel and ask: "So, what made you guys decide to come visit us, anyway?" He was sitting with the sun behind him; to look at him, Hazel had to squint and shield her eyes with her hand. She fumbled for words.

"Uh . . . well, our Dad had to go out of town, and then the woman who was staying with us, she had to leave too—unexpectedly," Hazel said. She could feel her skin flushing and hoped Matt would think it was the sun. "So we decided it would be . . . more fun to come visit than to . . . you know, stay in the city by ourselves."

"The babysitter left too?" Deirdre asked in a shocked tone. "If you ask me, that's just terrible! She shouldn't have left you kids alone."

Hazel could feel the beginnings of anger stirring inside her; who said anything about a *babysitter*? And who was Deirdre to call *her* a kid when there were only two years between them?

"Actually, DearyMe, in this province Hazel's old enough that she doesn't need a babysitter," Mark pointed out, "legally speaking, I mean."

"Still, if the woman was being paid," Deirdre began to argue.

"I didn't say she was *hired* to look after us," Hazel said frostily. "She's a friend of the family. And she had a good reason for going! It was a family emergency!"

"Oh," replied Deirdre. She smiled at Hazel. It was an apologetic smile, Hazel realized.

"I'm really sorry—Dad's always telling me to stop and think before I speak," Deirdre admitted. "I didn't mean any disrespect to your friend."

"It's okay." Hazel's voice was somewhat muffled. She had rolled over onto her stomach and put her head down on her towel. She meant it. She wasn't upset, not really. But she needed to end this conversation before she divulged more than she wanted.

Matt looked at his watch.

"It's getting late," he announced. "Why don't we pack up, go back home, and throw some clothes on. We can take a walk into the village for some ice cream or something."

Everyone agreed. They gathered the picnic things and towels and headed back to the castle. As they climbed the steps to the porch, they could hear the telephone ringing in the kitchen. This time, Deirdre was the one to grab it.

"Hello? Oh, Mr. Gentil? No, I'm Hazel and Ned's cousin. But they're right here. I'll get them for you."

Hazel caught her breath. Why was Monsieur Gentil calling back so soon? Had something happened? She stretched out a trembling hand for the phone, but Ned beat her to it.

"Hello? It's me, Ned," he said. "What's up?"

Hazel watched as her brother listened for a few minutes.

"Oh. Well, no, it wasn't," he said finally. "You can tell her if she calls again. Okay, well, thanks. We'll talk to you soon," Ned said. "Bye."

"Everything okay?" asked Deirdre, eyes bright with curiosity.

"Sure, fine," Ned replied. But he looked at Hazel as if he wanted to say more and couldn't.

"Well, let's everybody meet back here in ten, okay?" Matt asked. "Come on, Deirdre, you already showed Hazel and Ned their rooms. They can find their own way."

Alone at last in the kitchen, Ned gazed worriedly at Hazel.

"Well, what?" she demanded. "What did Monsieur Gentil want?"

"He just wanted to tell us that Frankie called and she made it to Istanbul," Ned began. "She hasn't seen Dad yet, but she wanted to know how we were. So Monsieur Gentil told her we'd made it safely here and he'd talked to us. She wanted to know if you'd looked at the painting yet. . . ."

"Why?" Hazel asked. "Did she say something about Paolo Cafazzo?"

Ned shook his head.

"No, but it sounds like maybe you were right before, Hazel," he replied. "Frankie told Monsieur Gentil she hoped it wasn't too big a shock for you, finally having a portrait of our mother."

"Our *mother?*" Hazel repeated. "But . . . that means . . ."

"I know," Ned nodded. "You've definitely got the wrong painting."

"They must have gotten switched somehow—in the gallery or something," Hazel mutttered. "But if I've got the wrong painting, then so does Dad."

"I wonder if that's why he's in jail?" Ned asked.

CHAPTER TEN

The cousins were determined to show Hazel and Ned Ville St-Pierre. Her mind still reeling from Monsieur Gentil's phone call, Hazel went along, but she could scarcely take in the scattering of quaint shops or the brightly painted boats in the harbour.

They had just sat down on the steps of the empty bandshell to eat ice-cream cones, when Charlotte pulled up in her truck.

"Hi, Frumps," she called. "Getting to know each other? Listen, I'm sorry to bother you, but I need a hand. A couple of horses up at the Deacons' farm were hurt when a stray dog got into their paddock. It doesn't sound too serious, but I could use some hands to help corral them and calm them down so I can inspect the damage. Any volunteers?"

Matt, Mark, and Deirdre were already tossing their cones into the garbage bin.

"What about you guys?" Mark flung back over his shoulder as he climbed into the front seat. "Hazel? Oliver? Ned?"

"No, thanks," Oliver answered. "I got my foot trampled last time I helped—remember?"

Ned looked at Hazel; she shook her head. Last year, she had been thrown by a cranky mare during riding lessons at boarding school and had landed in a pile of manure. Hazel wasn't crazy about horses.

"No, thanks," Ned replied. "If you've got enough to manage without us, I think we'll just walk home."

With Mark's long, skinny arm waving out the rear window of the cab, the truck disappeared down the darkening street.

"So, Oliver, your foot got trampled by a horse?" Ned asked as they began retracing their steps toward home.

"What?" said Oliver. "Oh, that. No, it wasn't the horse. We were helping Charlotte with a sick foal, and Mark tripped over a barn cat. He landed on my big toe. Mark, I mean, not the cat. It really hurt."

The route back to Land's End Lane took them past a basketball court. Dusk had fallen while they were finishing their ice cream, and it was getting hard to see. But as they approached the court, Hazel could hear voices. Something about them sounded vaguely familiar. She could make out a low, whining voice, a higher-pitched giggle, and a quiet, bored tone.

As the three Frump children drew alongside the court, the ball players turned to stare at them. Hazel recognized the two fair-haired boys, who had soaped cars on the ferry, and the dark-haired one named Hank.

Beside her, she could hear Ned suck in his breath, while Oliver made a tiny, uncomfortable sound. They'd recognized the boys, too. Hazel wished the boys weren't within earshot, so she could ask Oliver who they were and whether they meant trouble. She wondered what their connection was to Clive Pritchard.

But the three boys had stopped talking now and were simply watching the Frumps. She nodded curtly toward them, then turned to Oliver and said: "We should be getting home. Let's go."

Oliver looked relieved, but they had only taken a few steps

when the younger, giggly boy called out, "Hey, Frump! Hey, Chump! Olly Chump! Where are you going?"

Oliver looked at Hazel. He whispered so that only she and Ned could hear: "It's okay, that's just what he calls me to hurt my feelings. We should just ignore it. That's what my teacher always said. Ignore it, and he'll get bored and go away."

"Hey, Chump! Who're your friends?" It was the older, whiny boy, trying to sound threatening. In the dark, deserted park it should have worked. But oddly, when Hazel glanced at him, she couldn't help remembering how this boy had cowered before the ferryman.

"You know, maybe ignoring these guys worked out well for your teacher, but it doesn't look like it's working out so well for you," Ned muttered. He had taken off his glasses and was polishing them with his shirt, but to Hazel's eyes, her brother looked more angry than worried.

"It's okay, really. Let's just go." Oliver tugged at Hazel's sleeve and turned to go.

Thwack! A basketball, thrown hard, landed squarely between Oliver's shoulder blades, sending him sprawling onto the ground. As Hazel and Ned helped him to his feet, Oliver gulped and managed to keep from crying.

"I'm okay," Oliver said shakily. "Let's just get out of here."

Hazel's stomach twisted. This was sick. There was no bullying allowed at her boarding school. There was meanness; she didn't think you could ever get rid of that. But until now, Hazel had never realized how lucky she was not to have encountered a bully. She picked up the basketball and turned around to face the boys.

"That was clever," she said flatly, her voice so calm that Ned, who could tell how angry she truly was, peered curiously at her.

"Not to mention brave, whipping a ball at somebody's back . . . somebody littler than you."

She made no move to return the ball. Instead, Hazel began bouncing it up and down on the path beside her; a slow, steady dribble she maintained without ever glancing down at the ball, not even when she switched from one hand to the other. She kept her gaze steady on the three boys. Waiting.

The one called Hank, who had looked so bored on the ferry, didn't look bored now. He'd been staring at Hazel. Now he turned and cuffed the younger, giggly boy on the head.

"What did you do that for?" Hank asked. "Apologize to . . . Oliver."

"No way," the unrepentant reply came, as the younger boy rubbed his head. "What's your problem, Hank?"

"*My* problem?" repeated Hank in disbelief. "I don't have a problem. But I'm starting to think maybe you do."

"You *guyyyyyys*, make her give me my ball back," whined the older boy.

Hazel laughed. She was dribbling the ball faster now, passing it behind her back and between her legs, still never taking her eyes off them.

"Make me," she taunted. "Make me. You want the ball back, how about you *play* me?"

"Play you?" repeated the older boy stupidly. "You mean, for the ball? You mean the winner keeps *my* ball?"

"Yeah, Einstein," answered Hazel.

"But . . . but that's not fair. It's *my* ball," the boy asserted.

Hank looked like he was trying not to smile. "Look, this is dumb. Say you're sorry, Kenny, and maybe she'll give you back Billy's ball."

"Or maybe you guys don't know how to play?" Hazel continued. "Maybe you just stand around *holding* the ball 'cause you think it makes you look cool."

Hazel was spinning the ball now, while balancing it atop one finger. She and Alysha had spent months practising that particular trick last year. Billy—that appeared to be the name of the whiny older boy—let his jaw hang slack. Spinning a ball impressed onlookers, Hazel knew. That was the only reason she and Alysha had practised. It really didn't mean anything as far as playing went, though.

"Hey, Ned, maybe that boy didn't mean to hit Oliver in the back," Hazel suggested conversationally. "Maybe that was his idea of a pass."

"This is crazy," said Hank, shaking his head.

"Um, Hazel?" whispered Oliver timidly. "You could just give them their ball back. I'm okay, really."

Hazel turned and smiled reassuringly at Oliver, then shook her head. Even Kenny was wide-eyed as she rolled the ball across her shoulders and down her arm, catching it in her right hand. She strolled toward the asphalt court, dribbling the ball.

"Hey there . . . Kenny, is that your name?" she said politely. "My cousin Oliver says he's been told to ignore you. But I think we're all done ignoring you. I think it's time to pay attention, what do you say? Let's all pay really close attention to how well Kenny can play ball."

"You're weird," scowled Kenny.

"You have no idea," sighed Ned. He had followed Hazel onto the court.

"Three on three," Hazel announced briskly. "You three: Kenny, Hank, and Billy? Are those your names? It's you three against Oliver, me, and my brother. First team to twenty points wins."

"Uh, Hazel, I don't really play basketball that much." Oliver sounded embarrassed.

"You'll be fine," Hazel assured him quietly. "You're a Frump, aren't you? Just keep moving. I'll get you the ball and when I tell you to pass, you pass. If I tell you to shoot, you shoot."

It was the shortest game Hazel had ever played. Hank turned out to be the best player of the three, but that wasn't saying much. Besides, when Oliver dropped the ball and Hank scooped it up to score on an easy layup, Hazel could tell his heart wasn't in it. Kenny and Billy wanted to win, but it was plain to everyone, or should have been, that this simply wasn't going to happen.

None of the three boys seemed to have a clue about how to play defence, and Hazel drained jumpshot after jumpshot without so much as a hand in her face. After she had run up eleven points, including a shot from the far end of the court, Hazel figured it was time to set up her teammates. She knew Ned liked to shoot from the corner. Stripping the ball from Kenny's hands, she fed it to her brother. Ned drained two baskets in a row from the corner, with Hazel grabbing the rebound and passing the ball back to him before Billy had taken a single step.

Oliver's contributions consisted mostly of jumping up and down excitedly and clapping every time Hazel scored, but she was determined to make her little cousin part of the victory. After another easy basket, Hazel called a time out. Walking over to Oliver, she whispered: "When you hear me count three, I want you to throw the ball up at the basket, hard as you can."

Her startled cousin gaped at her.

"I can't . . . I can't shoot," he croaked in an agonized whisper.

"Trust me," Hazel flung over her shoulder as she walked away. "Okay, game on!" she hollered to the waiting boys.

Oliver stood his ground at the foul line. Glancing nervously at the approaching Kenny, he bounced the ball once, twice . . .

Hazel broke into a run; as she neared the basket, she yelled, "Onetwothree!"

She turned her head in time to see Oliver hurl the ball skyward just as Kenny and Billy converged on him. If she had the timing right—Hazel leaped, twisted, and caught the ball in mid-air and lofted it into the basket, before landing.

"Hey, Billy! I thought you were guarding her," Kenny called. "Nice job!"

"It's not my fault," Billy said in an aggrieved tone. "I thought you were supposed to be guarding her."

"Oh . . . you're playing zone defence?" enquired Ned politely.

Hank laughed. "Nice alley-oop," he told Hazel.

Kenny scowled. He didn't like losing. Hazel didn't care for it either, of course, but she could tell Kenny really, *really* didn't like losing. Now, doesn't that just figure, she told herself, as she drove past Hank to the basket. On top of everything else, he's a sore loser.

Crunch! Hazel's ribs were squeezed as Billy and Kenny slammed into her from opposite sides. She fell to the ground, Billy landing heavily on top of her. Above their heads, the basketball she'd just tossed up rolled twice around the rim before dropping through the hoop and into Hank's waiting hands. He glanced back at Hazel in time to see Kenny, who'd kept his balance, grind his foot into Hazel's wrist as she struggled to get to her feet.

"Hey!" cried Hank, as Hazel gasped in pain.

Without stopping to acknowledge what he'd done, Kenny darted forward, grabbing the ball from Hank's hands, to shoot from just below the basket. The ball bounced off the backboard and Kenny caught it again, taking another shot. He didn't seem to notice that all the other players had stopped, or that Hazel and Billy were still on the ground.

"I scored! Did you see that?" Kenny crowed as, on his third try, the ball rolled through the hoop.

"Yeah, that was great, Pritchard," said Hank sarcastically. He helped Hazel to stand up. She just stared at Hank. *What* had he called Kenny?

"Are you okay?" Hank asked her seriously. "We should probably take you to a doctor."

No one made a move to help Billy. He flapped one arm feebly to draw attention and began to moan piteously.

"Ow, ow, somebody help me up! I think my leg is busted. I think I broke my ribs."

Oliver and Ned each raised a single eyebrow; then Oliver extended a hand to the older boy, who staggered upright. Ignoring his friend, Hank asked Hazel again whether she was all right. She nodded. Actually, her wrist was probably sprained, and the truth was it hurt like heck. But Hazel wasn't going to give these boys the satisfaction of knowing that.

"Hey, where's your defence now?" taunted Kenny, who had managed to sink another basket, this time on his fourth try. The ball rolled toward Ned, who picked it up soberly.

"The game's over, Pritchard. They won," said Hank irritably. "Stop being such a jerk."

"They didn't win," contradicted Kenny indignantly. "They got nineteen points. She said first team to get twenty! That means they still need one more basket!"

"Don't be stupid," Hank yelled.

Pritchard. He really *had* said Pritchard. Kenny Pritchard. For a moment Hazel couldn't move. Then she shook her head. It was a coincidence, it just *had* to be.

But if it wasn't, well, it was too late now.

Hazel didn't even look at Kenny. She lifted her head and stared at the basket. Wordlessly, she held out her good arm toward Ned. He tossed the ball gently to her.

"Now *you're* being ridiculous," muttered Hank, gazing at her in disbelief.

Hazel hoisted the ball to her shoulder. It was no longer dusk; night had fallen and the net was barely visible. She narrowed her eyes. Then she lofted the ball, using only one arm, high into the air.

Six pairs of eyes followed its graceful arc until silently, neatly, the ball dropped precisely through the hoop and came to rest on the asphalt below.

There was a moment of silence. Then several voices spoke at once.

"I can't believe you," Hank said flatly.

"My leg hurts," whimpered Billy.

"What happens to the ball?" demanded Kenny.

Hazel looked wearily at Oliver. She raised her eyebrows. She really, *really* wished she could raise just one.

"Keep it," Oliver instructed Billy.

"Yeah, you guys could use the practice," Ned added matter-of-factly.

Hazel turned and silently led the way out of the park.

"Wait up," Hank cried.

But the Frumps kept walking. Hazel gazed at the lighted homes, wondering if one of them was Kenny Pritchard's. He probably was related to Clive, but how? Was Clive his father? Did he know, or care, just how messed up Kenny was? Kenny could have broken her wrist, and she was pretty sure he wouldn't have cared.

In silence, they walked past the closed shops toward Land's End Lane. As they passed a dimly lit shop selling art and antiques, Ned stopped abruptly. He stared at a small oil painting at the back of the window.

"What now?" Hazel asked.

"Hazel, does that painting remind you of anything?" Ned asked, his voice barely concealing his excitement.

Hazel sighed. Her wrist really was quite sore and she was tired. She just wanted to get home . . . or at least, back to Land's End. She peered through the glass.

The painting did look familiar. It was in the same dark, Romantic style as the Paolo Cafazzo painting of the castle she'd carefully hidden in her room earlier that day. The setting for this painting was also a storm at night, and in the foreground the painter had placed a violent shipwreck; in the background there was an island with a ruined old tower, crumbling into the sea.

"Hey, that reminds me of our tower," Oliver said matter-of-factly. "What do you think, Ned?"

A shiver ran down Hazel's spine. It *did* look like the Martello tower where she had spotted Richard C. Plevit that morning.

"Yeah, kinda," Ned replied, his voice deliberately casual. "It also reminds *me* a lot of this painting I saw once on the Internet."

He turned to look meaningfully at Hazel, as if to make sure she understood him: another work by the supposedly obscure Paolo Cafazzo. She nodded once, not wishing to attract Oliver's attention. But he seemed to have something else on his mind.

"Hey, Hazel," Oliver said, scuffing the ground with the toe of his sneaker. "I'm really sorry about tonight—about getting your hand hurt and all."

Hazel shook her head at him and smiled.

"Don't be silly. You weren't the one who stomped on my wrist," she said firmly. "Besides, I'm the oldest and I was the one who wouldn't walk away. But you know what? I'm not sorry, not at all."

Oliver smiled back at her, relief showing in his eyes.

"We should probably get going," said Ned, reluctantly pulling his eyes away from the shop window. "Maybe tomorrow we could come back and take a closer look, when this place is open."

"You never can tell with some of these shops," Oliver said as they trudged down the road. "That one's really just for tourists. Nobody around here much likes the guy who owns it."

"Why?" asked Ned.

"Well, you know that boy Kenny—the one who hurt Hazel?" Oliver asked. "It's his uncle Clive who owns it. Nobody around here likes Clive. He hasn't really lived on the island for years, but he comes back now and then to visit Kenny's parents."

Okay, maybe *now* I'm a little bit sorry, Hazel thought to

herself. Ned appeared to trip over nothing, stumbling, but not quite falling. Oliver put out a hand to steady him.

"You okay?" Oliver asked.

"It's too soon to tell," Ned muttered. "But I bet it won't take long to find out."

Before Oliver could respond, they heard pounding footsteps behind them. Squinting into the darkness, Ned made out the figure.

"Hey, Hazel! I think it's that Hank guy," he said quietly.

Hazel sighed. The tree-lined driveway to their uncle's home was just ahead. Light was spilling out of some of the gothic windows on the lower floors. The others must be back already.

"I'll deal with him. You guys go on up and let them know we're okay," she told Ned and Oliver. "They're probably wondering where we are. I'll be right behind you."

"Are you sure?" asked Ned skeptically.

"If I'm not up there in five minutes, send out the M&Ms and they can challenge this guy to a duel," joked Hazel.

"Okay, I'm timing you on my watch," said Oliver earnestly, and the two boys darted toward the driveway.

"I was kidding," Hazel called after them. "You know that, right?"

"Hi," said Hank breathlessly. Hazel turned to face him.

"Hi," she said evenly.

"So . . . uh, your name's Hazel," Hank said awkwardly.

"Yes," Hazel said shortly.

"That's an interesting name," replied Hank.

"I guess."

"Well, so . . . Hazel?"

"Yup, that's still me."

"I'm really sorry about what happened."

"Oh," Hazel replied. "Well, good. You should be." She waited. Her wrist was starting to throb.

"Anyway, well, I'm sorry."

"You said that already," Hazel pointed out, more sharply than she'd intended, but really, her wrist was starting to hurt quite a bit.

"Yeah."

"So, okay, it was, er, interesting to chat with you, Hank," Hazel said, turning on her heel. "It's kind of late, so if you don't have any more friends who want to beat me up, I guess I'll be going."

"Wait! I, I wanted to tell you I think you're a really good basketball player," Hank blurted.

"Thanks," Hazel said flatly. "I know I'm good."

She glanced back at the dark-haired boy. His hands were jammed in the back pockets of his jeans, and he was dragging the toe of his right sneaker back and forth through the gravel and studying the effect. But she could tell he was waiting for her to speak again.

"Okay, look. You could be good too," Hazel sighed. "But only if you stop hanging around with jerks like that and spend a little time practising and playing real games with real players. Anyway, whatever: it's none of my business. Good night."

She turned and began to walk up the drive.

"So will you play with me?" called Hank. Hazel stopped again and looked back, eyebrows raised.

"That sounded better in my head," Hank said. He grinned at her. "I meant . . . will you play basketball with me?"

"Maybe," Hazel answered, as she headed up the driveway.

"At least think about it?" Hank called after her.

"Don't you have a home to go to?" Hazel hollered over her shoulder. But Hank clearly wasn't ready to leave.

"So will you? Think about it?"

Hazel was halfway to the castle now. She took a deep breath.

"Okay, I'll *think* about it."

"What?"

Hazel took a deeper breath and turned to yell into the darkness.

"I'll *think* about it. Now, go away! Go home!"

It was just like that time a stray dog had followed her home. She bet if she was back down there at the bottom of the driveway, she'd see that same look in Hank's eyes, the same dopey, hopeful look that dog had given her.

Except, Hank's eyes were prettier.

"Oh. Okay! Good," Hank called back.

Hazel didn't answer. She was on the veranda now.

"So . . . I'll see you." Hank's voice was so faint now she could hardly hear him. "Later, I mean . . . bye!"

Hazel let the screen door swing shut behind her. *Boys.* Like she wasn't in enough trouble already.

CHAPTER ELEVEN

Hazel could feel the dusty stone floor beneath her cheek. She could see the night sky through the tall, arched window. Her legs felt like lead; they refused to move.

She couldn't be back here, not again. She had to get out of this place.

She tried to move her arms. A stab of pain shot through her hand.

"I don't understand: why am I here?" Hazel pleaded.

There was no answer.

The stars through the window cast a cold, bright light over the tower room. Hazel could tell now that many of the shapes covered by white sheets were artists' easels.

The brightest beam of moonlight fell across the easel directly in front of her, causing its canvas shroud to appear to glow. Suddenly, Hazel knew what she had to do. She had to remove the canvas. She must reveal what was hidden underneath.

Hazel struggled to get up. She had to see, to find out—everyone was counting on her. But there was so little time. And she couldn't move.

"I'll never do it," Hazel sobbed. "It's too hard. It's not fair. I can't, I can't."

Yes you can. You will.

The woman sounded so sure, so calm, that for a moment, Hazel believed her. But then came a new voice—cold and hard.

"No you won't," laughed Clive Pritchard.

• • • •

Hazel awoke as suddenly as if she had been thrown from a horse and feeling as bruised and sore as if that was, indeed, the case. She was drenched in sweat and the sound of her breathing filled the small circular room. With wide, staring eyes she scanned her surroundings. She was in the guest room above Deirdre's room, in one of the towers at Land's End. She was *not* trapped. She could move her arms and legs, although her wrist, where Kenny Pritchard had tromped on it the night before, was swollen and aching. Early morning light was filling the perfectly round room.

She was alone.

The sun was just rising, and the sky was dark and streaked with pink and grey clouds. Hazel knew she wouldn't be able to return to sleep; the dream had been too disturbing. Besides, the pain in her wrist wouldn't let her. Opening the tall curved window beside her bed, Hazel felt a gust of cooling wind on her face. The trees in the orchard were rustling, and the lake beyond looked black, swollen, and menacing.

If sleep wasn't possible, breakfast was, Hazel decided. She checked first, to make sure the Paolo Cafazzo painting was still where she'd hidden it yesterday. She'd wrapped it in a sweatshirt and tucked it in a secret compartment under the window seat that Deirdre had shown her.

Hazel made her way carefully down the stairs and into the

deserted kitchen. It didn't surprise her that the others had slept in. They had all stayed up late last night, rehashing the game and hearing about the injured horses. The cousins were clearly intrigued that Hank had followed Hazel back to Land's End, but for the most part they restricted themselves to theatrical coughs or meaningful silences. Only Matt had ventured a comment and Hazel wasn't entirely sure what he meant by the cryptic: "Hank's all right. I'm just glad it's not his brother who's sniffing around."

Thinking about it now, Hazel could feel her cheeks flush. She scooped a handful of ice cubes from the freezer, wrapped them awkwardly in a dish towel, and held it over her wrist. It took time to fill a tray with cereal and orange juice using only her right hand, but once she had the tray carefully braced between her hip and her arm, Hazel was able to unlatch the screen door and manoeuvre her way onto the porch.

"Good morning," Mark said cheerfully. He was stretched out on a wicker sofa that was not quite long enough to accommodate him, his feet dangling off the end.

Hazel jumped and almost dropped the tray.

"I didn't know anybody else was up," she said.

"Just us," Mark answered. "I think it's going to storm. I heard a noise a while back, so I got up to check it out. It was just the shed door blowing open. But I latched it last night, so that means we're talking about a pretty strong wind. Rain can't be far behind. I thought I'd just lie here and watch the storm build. Don't you love storms?"

"I guess," Hazel answered dubiously.

She lifted the bowl of cereal from the tray and winced, realizing it would hurt too much to try to hold it in her left hand, while eating with her right. Mark sized up the situation instantly. Unfolding himself from the sofa, he pulled a chair over to the table and pushed Hazel down into it. Then he gently lifted her left arm, supporting the bruised wrist with one hand. Despite his care, Hazel flinched.

"I think Kenny Pritchard did more damage than you thought," her cousin remarked.

Hazel reached for the ice and covered her wrist with it.

"I've been injured before. It hurts, but it's just a sprain," she assured him.

"Can you move your fingers?" Mark asked.

Hazel waggled them obligingly.

"Hmmm. I think that means it can't be broken, but Matt's the one who wants to be a doctor. Or a vet. Anyway, drink your juice," he said. "I'll be right back."

Hazel expected the screen door to close behind him, but the breeze caught it and pinned it open against the outside wall. She could hear the wind gathering force; tree boughs were creaking, leaves were fluttering. Out on the lawn, a flower pot toppled over.

"Wow, the rain can't be far off now," Mark said, returning. He had to raise his voice to be heard over the din. "I called Charlotte; she's having car trouble, so I'm going to go pick her up in a few minutes. You wanna wait out here, or inside where it's quieter?"

"Why are you getting Charlotte?"

"Well, she lent the truck to a friend and her van is in the shop."

"I get the car trouble thing, but I meant, why is she coming over?" Hazel asked.

"Well, Doc McCormack is on vacation and somebody should look at your wrist," Mark explained. "Charlotte said it doesn't sound like it's broken, but she wants to check it out anyway."

Hazel nodded. There was a flash of lightning, followed almost instantly by a deafening clap of thunder. Mark and Hazel both jumped.

"Look, I'd better get Charly before the storm really hits," Mark said. "You go inside soon, okay?"

Hazel nodded. But she stayed on the porch, watching, as Mark dashed to the truck. The pickup hadn't been gone more than a minute before the rain started. It was heavier than any rain she had ever seen. In a few minutes she could no longer make out the lake, or the orchard, beyond the first row of trees. She stood up and took a step toward the door; the roof above the porch began to clatter, as if a giant was tossing marbles down on it.

"Whoa! That's serious hail!"

Matt was standing just inside the kitchen, his face pressed against the screen. Hazel turned to see small white pellets hitting the lawn. The willow trees that marked the way to the pebbly beach bent beneath the force of the wind. Hazel wondered if they would break. The sound of the hail on the roof was so loud she didn't notice Matt had joined her on the porch until he was shouting in her ear: "The wind's coming from two directions!"

She looked back at him blankly. *Who cares where the wind is coming from?* But Matt yanked her into the kitchen, pulling the door closed behind them. Inside it was quieter, although Hazel could hear voices and footsteps on the stairs. It sounded like someone running.

"Listen, City Slicker, when you have hail and wind coming from two directions, you sometimes get tornados," Matt explained, grabbing a flashlight from the cupboard and draping Hazel's dressing gown over her shoulders.

"Wow," Hazel breathed, glancing back toward the door. "So, do we go to the cellar?"

Matt nodded his answer just as Oliver and Ned barrelled around the corner. Both boys were slightly out of breath and, behind their glasses, their eyes were wide with excitement.

Ned had borrowed Oliver's clothes, and as Hazel looked at them, clad in matching sweatpants and T-shirts emblazoned with the stencilled image of Albert Einstein, she reflected again that the pair could be brothers, they looked so much alike.

A yawning Deirdre was bringing up the rear, still dressed in the faded tank top and gym shorts she had slept in—and from the pillow marks that still creased the skin on her cheek, that sleep must have ended just moments ago, Hazel judged.

"We found Deirdre, but we couldn't find Mark," Oliver said, his voice squeaking with excitement.

"Oh no. You wouldn't. He went to get Charlotte," Hazel explained. She held out her wrist. "He thought she should make sure Kenny didn't break anything."

Matt opened a door and all five of them piled down a steep staircase into the cellar below. It wasn't at all what Hazel had expected.

"This is very cool," observed Ned, looking around. "Not your ordinary, everyday dungeon!"

The castle had been built in the late 1800s, Hazel knew, but the cellar looked as if it might be even older. The walls were made of stone, and the timbers above their heads had been hewn from giant trees. The air was cool, much cooler than upstairs, and somebody had seen fit to stock the cellar with brass lamps and old arm chairs, faded cushions, a sofa, and some trunks and packing cases.

"We used to play down here when we were little," Deirdre explained. "We'd build forts and clubhouses and make a lot of noise. I bet inside that case there's still . . . aha!"

From the largest trunk, Matt pulled a stack of comic books and held them aloft.

"Behold our reading entertainment while we wait for the all-clear," Oliver told Ned. The two boys dived into the pile.

"Meanwhile, how long ago did Mark leave to get Charlotte?"

Matt asked Hazel. He had lowered his voice so the boys couldn't hear, and Hazel could tell he was worried. She thought hard.

"I sort of lost track of time, watching the storm," she confessed. "But I know it had just started to rain when the truck left the driveway."

Matthew's face relaxed and he let out his breath.

"That's all right then," he said. "Charlotte's only a couple of miles away. He'll have had enough time to make it to her place and take shelter in her cellar."

Hazel was relieved. She was really starting to like these cousins and wouldn't have wanted Mark to be caught out in the storm because of her.

Now that they were no longer worried about Mark, Deirdre and Matt proposed giving Hazel a tour of the cellars. Deirdre kept chattering about how there hadn't been a tornado in the area for ages, so Hazel knew she was a bit nervous. But if Matt was trying to provide a distraction, it worked. He led the way through a warren of rooms, some empty and cavernous, some cozy and furnished. Deirdre pointed out the wine cellar, stacked with racks and racks of dusty bottles, and a room filled entirely with miniature trains and endless looping tracks.

Once Matt had demonstrated just how the electric trains worked, the older Frumps all agreed it was time to see whether the storm was still raging. But Ned and Oliver were still engrossed in the early adventures of Superman and had no interest in going back upstairs. After admonishing them to stay where they were, Matt, Deirdre, and Hazel headed up to the kitchen.

"It sounds like the storm's passed," Matt observed, as they crossed the floor. Opening the screen door, he let out a low whistle.

"It did a lot of damage in such a short time," Hazel said.

"Let's go up the lookout tower and get a better view," Deirdre suggested. "Maybe it really was a tornado."

The tower's worn flagstones were slick with rain, and Hazel felt even less safe than she had during her previous visit to the lookout. Still, it did provide a dramatic view of the damage the storm had caused. Several of the old apple trees had lost limbs, and one of the old willows lay completely uprooted by the shore of the lake. Some of the storm's effects made little sense. The wind had picked up two large garden urns and set them down, unharmed and right end up, about twenty metres away from their original position on the lawn. But it had also flattened the garden shed Mark had latched before leaving.

The storm had caused the temperature to drop considerably, and Hazel could understand why Deirdre shivered as they peered down from the lookout tower. She hoped the older girl would suggest they descend the stairs and return to the warmth of the rooms below. But a moment later, when a shudder ran through Hazel's own body, it had nothing to do with the cold.

"Looks like we have a visitor," Deirdre observed, following Hazel's gaze.

A black pickup had pulled up in front of Land's End, and a slender man in jeans and a cap emerged.

Hazel opened her mouth to speak, but no words came out. A feeling of dread was welling up from the pit of her stomach.

"He's going to the front door, but the boys won't hear. They'll still be in the basement," said Deirdre, chagrined.

The man, having had no answer at the front door, was walking around the side of the castle, as if looking for another way in. A gust of wind blew his cap into the air. He caught it quickly, but not before the three of them had seen his face.

"Isn't that Kenny Pritchard's uncle?" asked Matt, just as Deirdre yelled, "Yoohoo! Mr. Pritchard!"

As Clive Pritchard glanced around, Hazel found the use of her voice.

"No! Get back, get down," she hissed, stumbling toward the trapdoor. In her haste she staggered against Matt, and the two fell heavily to the floor. As Deirdre bent to help them up, Hazel pulled the girl down on top of them.

"What's with you?" Deirdre asked.

Matt looked at Hazel. He had raised one eyebrow, but she was too worried to resent it now.

"Well, it's a heck of a coincidence, Kenny's uncle turning up here the day after that kid tangles with Hazel and the squirts," he said. "Clive's got a reputation around here, and it's not great. If half the stories are true, he has a mean temper. So, I know why I don't feel like inviting him in . . . but what's your story?"

"Well, I don't want to be, you know, melodramatic or anything," Hazel said with an unconvincing laugh.

"If you ask me, I think you're there already," Deirdre said, rubbing her arm.

"Well . . . we saw Clive Pritchard in the city, before we left," Hazel began. "He and this friend of his were arguing with my neighbour. And then Ned and I saw him on the ferry, and then I think I saw his friend after we arrived. Remember, Deirdre, the man in the Martello tower?"

Deirdre shook her head, then stopped abruptly.

"Oh, yeah. Hazel said she saw a man, but when I looked, I didn't see anyone," she told Matt.

"Anyway, the thing is, he's part of the reason we left the city," Hazel admitted. "Our apartment was burgled, and we think he had something to with it. There's more stuff that has to do with my dad, and Ned and I were going to tell you guys all about it today. Just trust me: I don't think we want to let him in."

Matt was already moving toward the trapdoor.

"Where are you going?" asked Hazel.

"This isn't the city, Hazel," Matt replied. "We don't lock our doors around here. Not in the daytime."

"Oh, no," Hazel cried. "The boys are downstairs—alone!"

But Matt had already vanished down the circular staircase.

CHAPTER TWELVE

Hazel flung herself down the stairs after her cousin. She could hear Deirdre following close behind. The circular staircase that led down from the tower was completely enclosed, but at each floor there was a door leading to a passageway beyond. When Hazel reached the first door it was ajar, and she could see Matt in the hall. He was standing beside a small wooden table, holding an old-fashioned telephone receiver in his hand. He turned to face Hazel as she entered, a breathless Deirdre at her heels.

"I thought I should call someone—Charlotte maybe," Matt muttered. He sounded as if he was talking to himself.

"Matt—what's going on? What's wrong?" Deirdre asked.

"The phone line's dead."

Hazel stared at Matt.

"What about a cell phone?" Hazel asked.

Matt shook his head. "They don't work at Land's End. Something about the hill nearby. It cuts out the signal."

Hazel bit her lip. They were completely cut off from the village, or from any outside help. As she watched Deirdre fumble with the phone, Hazel's mind began to race. Why was the phone dead? Was it the storm? Or had someone cut the line?

"I think we should go find the boys," Deirdre said, setting down the phone. "I still think you guys are crazy, and I'm sure Mr. Pritchard doesn't mean any harm, but . . . well, we might as well all stick together."

"What if he's already in the house?" Hazel asked. "Can we get to the boys without running into him?"

Matt nodded. His eyes reflected Hazel's concern. "And I'd like to get there *before* he finds them," he added. "C'mon, you two—the secret staircase!"

"There's a secret staircase?" Hazel demanded. But Matt and Deirdre were already pelting down the corridor.

Later, when Hazel tried to reconstruct their flight in her mind, she found she could recall nothing but a blur of hallways and rooms, some of which she knew Deirdre had shown her before, but others she could swear she'd never entered. There were occasional pauses, when Matt would stop dead in his tracks, put his fingers to his lips, and listen. They would hear footsteps, and then Matt would change direction, leading the girls away from the sound, down new corridors and through different rooms, but somehow always working their way toward the secret staircase.

The footsteps had to belong to Clive Pritchard, Hazel figured. Deirdre suggested he was just there to offer help after the storm. But if that was the case, Hazel would have expected him to call their names. At the very least, he should have been calling: "Hello? Anybody home?" the way people always did in movies when they entered eerily deserted houses. Instead, it seemed the man was making as little noise as possible.

They had arrived in what appeared to be a music room; a baby grand piano stood in one corner, an old harp next to it. But there was no time to look around because Matt was tapping one of the wooden wall panels and it was sliding back, opening onto a dank, dusty set of steps.

"Come on," Deirdre said impatiently, as she pushed Hazel in front of her. Matt had already headed down the stairs without looking back to see whether they were following.

"I can't see," Hazel whispered.

"Me either, but our eyes will adjust," Deirdre observed. "If you let me squeeze past, I'll go first, and you can hold onto me as we go."

It was a tight fit, but they managed it somehow. Hazel shuffled down the dark steps, her right hand clamped firmly on Deirdre's shoulder, her injured left tentatively brushing against the wall, ready to pull away the instant something creepy or crawly approached. It seemed to take forever before they came to the bottom. Matt was waiting, in what appeared to be a small box room. At least, in the gloom Hazel thought she could make out large, crate-like objects here and there.

"I can hear Ned and Oliver," Hazel whispered excitedly.

"Yes, and I *don't* hear that Pritchard guy," Matt said. "I'll grab the boys. You girls wait here. And keep quiet!"

As they waited for him to return, Deirdre passed the time wondering aloud whether Clive Pritchard would suddenly jump out of the shadows behind her, or whether he was lying in wait in the next room, ready to pounce on Matt and the boys. Hazel passed the time wondering to herself whether that feeling of crawling skin was nerves, dust, or a tarantula that had decided to explore the back of her neck. As their eyes adjusted, Deirdre pointed out a cigarette butt on the floor near their feet, and then a lighter on a nearby steamer trunk.

"I guess someone's been experimenting with smoking!" she sniffed. "Wait until I tell Dad."

"Who knows how long it's been there?" Hazel whispered dubiously. "Maybe it was Uncle Seamus who was doing the experimenting."

"Hey. What's up?"

It was Ned's voice, and he was shining a bright light in their eyes.

"Quit that!" Deirdre scolded, her voice a little too loud. She was nervous, too, Hazel decided. Ned pointed the flashlight at their feet.

"I thought I told you to be quiet," Matt said from the darkness, as he reclaimed the flashlight from Ned.

"What's going on?" piped up Oliver. "If this some sort of kooky game, can we play it later? 'Cause Ned and me were having a perfectly good time on our own."

"Ned and I," corrected Deirdre automatically.

"No. Me. You weren't playing. You guys took off ages ago," Oliver argued.

"Enough," Matt groaned. "Listen!"

Everyone looked at Matt expectantly.

"Well?" Deirdre asked. "We're listening. What?"

"No, listen," Matt said, through gritted teeth. "Do you hear anything? Or anyone?"

It was so still, all Hazel could hear was Oliver's slightly adenoidal breathing. Then—

"Footsteps," said Ned, who had excellent hearing. "Is Mark back with Charlotte?"

The footsteps were getting closer and louder.

"That's too heavy to be Mark or Charlotte," Deirdre whispered.

"Besides, they'd be calling out to us," Matt muttered. "Maybe we do need to get out of here. Follow me."

He led them deeper into the box room. The beam of the flashlight illuminated the stacks of packing crates and revealed the existence of a low door behind the staircase. Matt opened it and gestured to the others to follow.

"I'll go first with the light, then Oliver and Ned," he said in a whisper so quiet it was barely audible. "Then Hazel, then

Deirdre—and Deirdre, you have to close the door behind us. Okay? Everybody keep close together."

Nobody said a word until they were all inside the passage-way with the door closed behind them. The younger boys looked scared but excited, and Hazel tried not to think about how much darker and dirtier and insect-friendly this passage looked than anywhere else she'd ventured that day. She had the oddest sensation that there was something familiar about this place. A shiver ran through her body.

"Kind of cold in here, isn't it?" Deirdre whispered, giving her arm a sympathetic squeeze. "Makes you wish we'd had time to get dressed; these pajamas aren't very warm."

"Um, can I ask a question?" It was Ned, sounding determined to remain calm.

"Shoot," Matt answered tersely, as he began gingerly leading the way down the corridor.

"Who are we running from?"

Hazel put her hand on her brother's arm.

"It's Pritchard," she whispered.

"Kenny?" squeaked Oliver, sounding alarmed.

"His uncle," said Matt.

"Can I ask another question?"

"You just did," Matt pointed out. Then he sighed. "Sorry, Ned, I didn't mean to be snotty. Go ahead, ask your question."

"Where are we running *to?*"

There was silence for a moment. Hazel began to wonder if Matt knew the answer.

"Of course we're not actually *running,*" Deirdre observed, "although we may want to pick up the pace soon. This place is sort of creepy."

Matt ignored his sister; when he spoke it was to answer Ned.

"Dad always said there were secret passages leading out of

the castle," he told Ned. "He showed me the entrance to this one once and promised me we'd explore it some day. The guy who built this place supposedly thought secret passages would make it more romantic. But there were rumours about smugglers using them too."

"Dad never told *me* any of this," said Deirdre, wounded.

"Well, he didn't want any of us getting lost down here," Matt said. "He wasn't sure how structurally sound it was. He was worried there might be cave-ins."

"Hey, now. *There's* a happy thought," said Hazel. She was trying to sound casual, but there was a slight tremble to her voice. She couldn't shake the feeling that she had been here before. But that was impossible. Wasn't it? She felt Ned pat her arm.

"Well, I'm sure we don't have to go very far into this passage," Matt said. "I just want to make sure we're not being followed."

They shuffled along in silence for a few more minutes before anyone spoke again.

"Did you hear that?" Ned said suddenly.

"What?" Matt asked sharply.

"I heard a door opening," Ned replied. "Do you think maybe *now* would be a good time to pick up the pace?"

"Run!" hissed Matt, following his own order instantly.

It was amazing how quickly and quietly they were all able to move, despite the narrowness of the passage and the roughness of the ground. Ned stumbled once, but Hazel grabbed her brother before he could fall. Without thinking, she used her injured hand, forgetting about Kenny Pritchard's violence until the pain sliced through her wrist. She bit back tears; Ned paused, realizing something was wrong.

"I'm okay." Hazel gave Ned's shoulder a gentle shove with her good arm. "Let's just keep going."

A few seconds later, all slightly out of breath, they found themselves at a place where the passage widened into what was almost a small room. Here, the tunnel branched off in several directions, and Matt appeared to be trying to decide which passage to take. Hazel was sure they should go right. It was like the day in science class when they'd held the magnet in one hand and the paper clip in the other. She could feel a pull. She opened her mouth to say "Shouldn't we turn right?" but she was distracted by faint sounds from behind them in the passageway.

"Left," Matt whispered, and they all obeyed.

Presently, Hazel realized the tunnel was growing lighter, and she could see her brother and Oliver much more distinctly.

"We're coming to the end," Matt announced with satisfaction. "There's an opening just ahead."

A minute later they were stumbling, bent almost double, out of the low mouth of a cave. Blinking in the light, Hazel saw that they had arrived at a beach. But it wasn't the pebbly beach nearest the house, and it wasn't Sandy Bay, the lovely, white sand beach where they had picnicked and swum what seemed like a lifetime ago.

"Where the heck are we?" Ned asked. He'd taken off his spectacles and was busily polishing them. But a quick glance told Hazel he wasn't worried—just covered in dirt and dust from the passageway.

"This is the cove just beyond Sandy Bay," Deirdre said in wonder. "I never knew there was a cave here."

They stood for a few minutes staring at each other. Nobody seemed quite sure what to do next. Matt spoke first.

"I'll sneak back into the tunnel a ways and see if Clive is still following," he said slowly. "You guys wait here. If you hear me give the signal, start running."

"What's the signal?" asked Ned.

"How about I just holler 'Look out!' or 'He's coming!'?" Matt flung wearily over his shoulder as he re-entered the cave.

Hazel plunked herself down on the shale beach and rested her head on her knees. *At least it isn't raining*, she thought as she gazed at the clearing sky. The lake even looked calmer; the water lapped the rocks along the shore with a soothing rhythm.

Hazel closed her eyes. She didn't think she'd have the energy to run if Clive Pritchard himself walked out of the cave.

"Pritchard must have turned the other way at that fork in the passage," Matt announced. Hazel started as her cousin emerged from the cave once more. "Either that or he went back to the house. There's no sign of him, anyway."

"So what do we do now?" asked Oliver.

"Mark and Charlotte are bound to show up soon; we'll rest for a bit, then walk back to the house."

They sat in silence for a few minutes, listening to the gulls keening overhead. The sun was struggling through the clouds now, and the warmth felt good on Hazel's skin. She examined her cousin. His face was grimy and set in lines of worry.

"Thanks for getting us out of there," Hazel told Matt.

Her cousin shrugged. "I just wish I knew where that guy went," he said. "Not to mention what he wanted."

Hazel looked at her feet. She hated the thought that she and Ned might somehow have brought danger to Land's End.

"Is anybody else hungry?" asked Ned conversationally. And suddenly five stomachs were acutely aware of the passage of time.

"Yeah. Well, if everybody's had a chance to catch their breath, I say we head back home," Matt said.

By tacit agreement, they headed back along the rocky shoreline instead of re-entering the tunnel. At Sandy Bay, the children could see more of the damage the storm had wrought. The white dunes were littered with driftwood and bits of plastic and other debris that had washed ashore.

"Ah, behold the flotsam and jetsam," pronounced Oliver solemnly.

"Well, flotsam anyway," Ned said. "I think jetsam means something else."

"If you ask me, it's just one big clean-up job," sighed Deirdre.

As the bedraggled troupe made its way out of the orchard, clambering through wet grass and over fallen tree limbs, they heard Mark and Charlotte calling their names.

"Over here!" called Deirdre, and in minutes they were all together at the side lawn.

"We were getting worried about you," Charlotte said, relief evident in her voice. "It took us forever to get here. There was so much debris blocking the roads."

"We tried to phone, but all the lines were down after the storm," Mark said.

So Clive Pritchard hadn't cut the phone lines to the castle. Hazel felt a little foolish and wondered if the others did, too. But then she thought about the newspaper clipping with the picture of her father in handcuffs and the photo of his "partner" Clive Pritchard. The foolish feeling evaporated.

"We tried to phone you guys too," Matt said. "We wanted to make sure you were okay."

"Well, we spent some time in Charly's cellar and let me tell you, that's not a place you want to linger," Mark drawled. "I vote we take up a collection and buy this nice woman a chair for her basement . . . maybe a light bulb, too. Anyway, we survived. Where were you guys, though?"

"And why are you all still in your pajamas?" Charlotte asked, cocking her head to one side.

"It's a long story," Matt sighed. "We'll tell you over lunch."

CHAPTER THIRTEEN

"First things first," Charlotte said as they gathered in the kitchen. "I need to take a look at Hazel's wrist."

After a few minutes of careful prodding, Charlotte pronounced herself satisfied that the wrist was not broken.

"But I do think it's a nasty sprain," Charlotte frowned. "So just to be safe, we'll go into Frontenac to have it looked at by a doctor."

"Right *now?*" Hazel groaned. She was really starting to feel quite tired. Not to mention hungry. A bath or shower also might be nice; in that tunnel, who knew what sort of insect might have decided to hitch a ride in her hair? Her unruly mop was so thick she'd never notice a bug until the thing crawled across her face!

Charlotte laughed. "Actually, no," she answered. "Right *now* I'm putting your arm in a sling to support your wrist. Right *now* I'm giving you these pills to help with the pain and swelling—and they're regular people pills, nothing for dogs or sheep or anything like that, so you needn't give me that look. And right *now* we're all going to get something to eat. Then one of you is going to please make me some coffee while somebody—anybody—fills me in on what's been going on here."

The cousins were obviously used to Charlotte ordering them about. Within a few minutes Hazel's arm was resting in a sling, Matt had set the table, bacon was frying on the stove, seven glasses had been filled with orange juice, coffee was percolating, and fruit, bread, and cheese had been slapped on plates. And Ned and Oliver were explaining how Hazel had come by her injury in the first place.

"Oliver, I am so sorry that nobody realized this child was bullying you," Charlotte said, when the full story of the basketball game had been recounted. "But why on earth didn't you tell any of us?"

Oliver squirmed at the question.

"It's embarrassing," he finally managed to squeak.

"Plus, his teacher said if he ignored it, Kenny would leave him alone," Ned remarked.

"I always said that teacher was a fool," Mark said flatly. "That's the same teacher that let Hank's older brother get away with all kinds of stuff a few years ago."

Matt put his hand on Oliver's shoulder: "Hey, Squirt, bullying is never the fault of the person being bullied."

"Right," agreed Charlotte. "Also, it's not something that's easy to fix on your own. We'll get this sorted out together, all right?"

Oliver was studying his shoes, but he nodded silently.

Matt gave the girls a meaningful look and pushed his chair back from the table. Squaring his broad shoulders and leaning forward slightly in his chair, he took a deep breath and began. "Hey, uh, Charly? Kenny's bullying isn't the only Pritchard problem we may have to deal with." Just then the telephone rang. Deirdre sprang to answer it.

"Hello?" she said quickly. "Oh, hello, Dad."

The room became suddenly very still.

"No, we're fine," Deirdre said reassuringly into the phone. "Well, yes, some trees. And the shed was, like, pulverized! The phones were down for a while so—yes, we went to the cellar. Of course we went, and if you ask me—"

They were silent as Deirdre listened.

"Wow, really? They're sure it was a tornado? That close, eh? Boy, and here I was just telling Hazel that we haven't had one in these parts since . . . uh . . . since . . ." Deirdre's voice trailed away as she realized what she had just said.

"Hmm? Oh, yeah . . . Hazel *and* Ned. Uh-huh. Well, not long, of course. I mean, they really *just* got here. Practically. So, Dad, you know what? Charlotte's also here, and if you ask me, she probably should talk to you right now," she said brightly. Without waiting for an answer, she held out the phone to Charlotte.

Charlotte looked around the room.

"Let me guess. You didn't call him to say Hazel and Ned were here." Nobody answered. Hazel looked at her plate.

Charlotte took the phone.

"Seamus, hi. Everybody is fine, and the place is still standing," she said smoothly. "But we've been having a bit of trouble with the phones."

She paused to listen.

"Why don't we talk first, and then I'll put them on," she replied. Cupping her hand over the phone, Charlotte made a shooing motion toward the door.

"Out," she urged them softly. "All of you. But don't go far—especially you, Matt. You'll have to talk to him in a few minutes."

All of them bolted for the porch. Charlotte closed the screen door and then the heavy wooden door as well. Now nothing of the phone conversation could be overheard. Hazel surveyed the grounds. The sun was shining cheerfully now, making the rain-soaked lawn sparkle. Except for the pulverized garden shed and the relocated urns, you wouldn't know there had been such a savage storm that morning, Hazel thought. Everything seemed . . . normal. Why, then, did she feel so worried? An involuntary shiver ran through her body.

"Are you cold?" asked Deirdre, concerned. "Is your wrist hurting?"

"No, I'm okay, although I would like to get out of these pyjamas. It's just . . ." Hazel tried not to sound too worried. "Do you think your dad will be mad?"

"At you guys?" asked Mark. "No. No way. But he might not be thrilled with us."

"I guess we should have called him right away, as soon as you arrived," said Matt heavily.

"Maybe the storm was a blessing in disguise," suggested Deirdre. "Dad sounded pretty worried at first. He heard on the news a tornado really did touch down near here—just on the American side of the border. So he's got to be relieved we're okay. Maybe that will take the edge off things."

"Oh, yeah. He'll be in a fine mood," agreed Matt with a touch of sarcasm. "Until he hears about Hazel's wrist and our wild goose chase through the secret tunnel."

"What wild goose chase?" Mark demanded.

"But the sprain isn't serious, and anyway, that's not your fault," protested Hazel at the same time.

"And Charlotte's positive it's not broken," added Deirdre helpfully.

"Oh, well then, that makes everything okay," replied Matt morosely.

"Hey! Helloooo!" Mark waved his long, skinny arms in Deirdre's face. "Will one of you tell me what's going on? What secret tunnel?"

Before anyone could answer, the door opened and Charlotte reappeared.

"Seamus had to ring off—he's heading into an important

meeting. But he's going to phone back in an hour, and he wants to talk to Hazel and Ned when he does."

"Great," said Mark. "In the meantime, somebody can start explaining about the wild goose—"

But he didn't get a chance to finish his sentence. At the word *goose*, Charlotte jumped and looked at her watch. For the first time that day her face wore a genuinely panicked look.

"Goose! Oh my goodness—kids, I'm sorry, but I have to fly. I promised Janet Cram I'd have a look at her sick goose—that prize-winning one that she's always fussing over. This time I think it actually might be serious—and what with Hazel's wrist and the storm and everything, I forgot all about it. I'm going to need to borrow the truck, I'm afraid. Mark, can I have the keys, please?"

Then she was gone.

"It's a funny thing about grown-ups," Ned remarked to no one in particular. "They really don't seem to hang around much."

Mark slid to a kneeling position and clasped his hands together as if in prayer.

"If somebody doesn't *please* tell me right this second *what* wild goose chase and *what* secret tunnel, I will expire. I will pass away. I will become deceased. I will . . ."

"You will get a clout on the head, if you keep that up," growled Matt.

"We'll tell you all about it, Mark. Of course we will," Deirdre said soothingly. "If you ask me—"

"Yeah, I *do* ask you. I *have* asked you, I *am* asking you!"

"It's just a figure of speech!" Deirdre huffed.

"But you do say it pretty often," Oliver piped up.

"It's called a verbal tic," Matt concurred. "And it is sort of annoying, Deirdre."

"*If* you ask *us*," Oliver said.

Before the conversation could deteriorate further, Matt launched into a description of their flight from Clive Pritchard.

Then it was up to Hazel to explain just why she had insisted they avoid the man.

Hazel took one look at Ned and knew that he agreed it was time to confess everything. But it took a long time to tell *everything* from Colin Frump's disappearance, right up to their discovery, the night before, of another Paolo Cafazzo painting in Clive Pritchard's shop. So much had happened in such a short time, Hazel found she kept forgetting details, prompting Ned to interrupt.

When she had finished, Hazel sat back, exhausted, and waited. But no one spoke. Hazel's eyes met Ned's. Were their cousins regretting their presence at Land's End? Now that the truth was out, would they ask Hazel and Ned to leave?

"So, your friend Frankie is over there right now, trying to help your father," Mark said finally.

Hazel and Ned nodded.

"But she's an artist, not a lawyer or a detective or anything," said Deirdre dubiously.

"No, but she speaks some Turkish, and she mentioned she had some friends there who might be able to help," Hazel replied.

"Hmm . . . that's great, of course," Mark said. "But I'd say we'd better bring Dad into the picture. He really is a very good lawyer, Hazel, and I'm sure he'll want to help."

"But I thought he and Dad had some kind of fight or something," Ned piped up. "None of you guys will talk about it, but it must have been serious for them to keep us apart all our lives. Is Uncle Seamus really going to want to help?"

Matt, Mark, and Deirdre each made as if to speak, then appeared to change their minds. Scanning the table, Hazel noticed Oliver looked just as confused as she and Ned did. Whatever was going on between Seamus and Colin Frump, Oliver was in the dark, she decided.

It was Mark who broke the silence.

"Of course, Dad's going to want to help," he said firmly. But to Hazel it sounded as if he was trying to convince himself as much as her. "And when Charlotte gets back, we'd better tell her, too."

"So what's the deal with Charlotte?" Ned asked, looking at no one in particular. "She's a veterinarian, a sort of island taxi driver, and what else? Uncle Seamus's girlfriend?"

"No! She's our cousin, silly," Deirdre said. To Hazel's annoyance the girl was looking at Ned with one eyebrow raised. Could *everyone* in this family raise one eyebrow, except Hazel?

"I mean our second cousin, technically, of course," Deirdre added.

"*Of course*," Ned responded, sarcasm oozing from his voice. "How were *we* supposed to know she was your cousin?"

"She's your cousin, too," Oliver interjected.

"Really? You mean she's a Frump?" Ned asked.

Mark appeared to choke on air and began coughing theatrically. Deirdre thumped him on the back absently, her eyes fixed on Matt.

"Oh . . . you know how confusing family trees are," Matt said after a minute. "Anyway . . . we're all related somehow . . . even if we can't remember all the details right now, and Charlotte and Dad have always been good friends. Hey, speaking of Dad, why don't we all go and get some real clothes on before he calls back?"

With her injured wrist, it took Hazel took a little longer to change. By the time she returned to the kitchen, everyone else had reassembled, and Matt was on the phone with Uncle Seamus. Matt handed the phone to her and nodded to Ned to pick up the extension. Then their cousins left the room. Hazel took the phone with some trepidation, but Mark had been right after all—their uncle did want to help. He listened without interrupting, as Hazel and Ned recounted their tale for the second time that day. When it was his turn to speak,

Uncle Seamus's voice was warm and friendly and, most of all, reassuring. It sounded a good deal like their father's voice, only slower and more ponderous. *That might be a lawyer thing,* Hazel reflected, remembering what Deirdre had said about Uncle Seamus advising her to think before speaking.

" . . . the most important thing is that you are both safe and at Land's End," Uncle Seamus said. "I'm very much looking forward to seeing the two of you, and if it wasn't for the situation with your father, I would leave this court tomorrow and head straight for the island."

"But I thought the case you were working on was really big," said Ned.

"Big? Oh no," Uncle Seamus said, with a low chuckle. "But it does hinge on a very interesting point of law. Still, the fun part is mostly over now, and I can leave the rest to my associates."

Fun? Hazel had never thought of law as fun. She had never pictured lawyers even *thinking* about fun. But Uncle Seamus was still talking.

" . . . so I thought I would head to Istanbul on the first available flight," their uncle was saying. "I just have to consult a few colleagues and make some calls first. You don't happen to know where your friend . . . where Frankie was planning to stay in Istanbul, do you?"

"No," Hazel replied. "But you might check with Monsieur Gentil, our neighbour back home. She may have called and told him."

"An excellent suggestion," Uncle Seamus said. Ned gave him the phone number, and Uncle Seamus read it back correctly. There was a pause.

"Now, children," Uncle Seamus said slowly, "I know you must have a great many questions. But I must ask you to be patient a while longer. I cannot explain things over the telephone, and I think we may all agree that my priority must be to secure your father's release from prison and his safe return home."

"I know," Hazel said. "But—"

"I will endeavour to return to Land's End as quickly as I can," Uncle Seamus broke in. "I promise that when I get home I will answer every question you wish to ask. I will tell your father this when I see him. There are to be *no more secrets* in this family. Do you understand?"

"Yes," Hazel answered and somehow, without meaning to, she added, "sir."

"Okay," agreed Ned.

"Good. Now please give my love to your cousin Deirdre and your cousin Oliver," Uncle Seamus said. "You may tell them that the radio is reporting serious damage from a tornado that touched down not far from Land's End, on the American side of the border. Dozens of buildings were flattened. Oliver will find that fascinating and the thought of such a near miss may distract my daughter from feeling left out. I simply do not have the time to speak to everyone just now."

Hazel smiled. Uncle Seamus was pretty sharp, she decided.

"I will be in touch," Uncle Seamus concluded. "And as soon as it can possibly be arranged, I shall return, with your father. I am a very good lawyer and a very persuasive man, rest assured."

Ned was smiling now, too.

"In the meantime, try to stay out of trouble. Stay clear of Clive Pritchard and any of his associates, including that nephew, Kenny," Uncle Seamus ordered. "And if you think of anything else I should know, the children have my cell phone number."

After Hazel and Ned hung up, they went looking for their cousins. They could hear someone playing jazz on a piano; following the sounds, they wound up in a games room down the hall. Mark was lying on a long, tufted leather chesterfield. With eyes screwed shut, he was throwing darts at a board hanging on the wall opposite. Deirdre and Oliver were stretched out on the floor, engrossed in a game of Chinese checkers. The pianist was Matt. Hazel was taken aback. She hadn't pictured him as a pianist or a jazz lover. But all four ceased what they were doing as soon as Hazel and Ned entered.

"So, is Dad on his way to Istanbul?" Deirdre asked.

"Yup," answered Ned. "And he wasn't cross with us for showing up here."

"I told you so," Oliver said.

"Well, he *does* want to have a word with you about using his credit card," Matt informed his brother, who turned slightly pale. "But he said it could wait until he got home."

"So anyway, we were thinking," Mark said, "at least, we were *hoping*, that maybe we could help you figure out what's going on with the Pritchards and the painting and everything. Sound like a plan to you?"

"Sounds like a great plan," Hazel replied. "Where should we start?"

"I think we should start with the painting your father gave you," Deirdre said.

"I think we should start with the websites," Oliver argued.

"Let's put everything together in one place," Matt said. "Like when you study for a test. Hazel, we'll need the painting and whatever notes you and Ned put together. Bring that newspaper clipping too. Even though none of us can speak the language, maybe there'll be something useful in the photographs. Mark, we'll use your room. You've got the best computer."

"Aye, aye sir," Mark said in a mocking tone. But Hazel could see the excitement she felt reflected in his eyes. All the cousins were caught up in it—maybe they would finally figure out what had happened to Colin Frump!

But a half-hour later, after they had each examined the painting carefully, turning it over and over, all anyone could agree upon was that the castle did look very much like the

Land's End folly the cousins called home. The newspaper clipping also proved useless, since they already knew what Clive Pritchard looked like, and, as Matt had admitted, none of them could read Turkish. Ned searched again for the websites that had extolled the virtues of the little-known Romantic artist, Paolo Cafazzo, but again came up empty-handed.

Things didn't start looking up until Ned produced the list he'd begun on the train, with names he'd remembered from the missing websites, and Hazel found the page she'd torn from the notepad on Colin Frump's desk.

As six pairs of eyes scrutinized the scraps of paper, Deirdre let out a yelp.

"Oh! They're anagrams!" she said. As everyone turned to stare at her, the girl began to blush. "Well, okay, I'm sure you all knew that. Just like me to state the obvious . . ."

"What are you talking about?" Ned demanded.

"Well . . . you mean, you didn't know?" Deirdre asked hesitantly, looking around the room.

"I know an anagram is when you transpose letters to form new words," Matt began.

"Transpose means you move the letters around and make new words," Ned said helpfully to Hazel.

"I got it," she muttered. Turning to Deirdre she asked, "Okay, so where are the anagrams?"

"Don't you see it?" Deirdre asked incredulously. "Wow, I guess it's just like one of those puzzle things, you know, those inkblots, where you have to stare at something a long time and then it just turns into something else. If you ask me . . ."

"We. Did. Ask. You." Mark spoke through clenched teeth. "So tell us already!"

"Well, some of these names are anagrams," Deirdre answered. "Who are these people, anyway?"

"Well, Critic Reva L., Ph.D., was all over the Net, talking

about the painter Paolo Cafazzo," Ned explained. "And so was Dr. Chip Vilecart. I found links to academic papers by Professor Levi Triccar on Romanticism and Cafazzo."

"Okay," Deirdre said. "A professor, a doctor, and a Ph.D. That's all sort of the same thing, right?"

Now it was Matt's turn to glare at his sister. "A Ph.D. is a short form for someone who has their doctorate in something, and most professors do, yeah," he answered. "So if you had a history professor, for example, at a university, then I guess he could sign his name Professor William James or Dr. William James or just William James, Ph.D. But I think I speak for everyone when I say: So what?"

"Well, it's simple," Deirdre answered. "Take away the word *professor* and substitute *Ph.D.* What do you get?"

She grabbed a blank sheet of paper from Mark's desk. In big block letters she wrote:

CRITIC REVAL. PH.D.

And below it:

LEVI TRICCAR PH.D.

And finally:

DR. CHIP VILECART

"Don't you see? Each name uses the same fourteen letters, just in different arrangements."

"So . . . so what? It's a coincidence? Or do you think they're not real people—just made up names?" Hazel mused aloud.

"Or they're all the same person, just playing a weird joke," Matt suggested.

"Could that mean all those websites and all that stuff about Paolo Cafazzo was written by *one* guy?" Ned asked. "That's sort of nuts."

"You know, these are all pretty weird names," Mark commented. "I mean, if you were setting out to make anagrams, I bet there'd be easier combinations of letters to use."

"Ned's right, this *is* nuts. I mean, what sort of person would do this?" asked Matt.

"That's easy," Deirdre said. The smile on her face suggested she was enjoying their confusion, Hazel thought.

"Again, I speak for everyone when I say: Huh?" repeated Matt.

"You *know* who did this?" Ned asked.

For answer, Deirdre took the paper again, and beneath the first three names, she added two more. When she turned the paper around so the others could see, Hazel read aloud:

RICHARD C. PLEVIT and
CLIVE PRITCHARD

"It's the same fourteen letters every time," Deirdre announced.

Hazel felt a sudden chill, as if someone in the room had just switched on an air conditioner. This was deeply weird. Disturbing. Unsettling.

"But, what exactly does this mean?" Hazel asked, looking at each of her cousins in turn.

Matt gave her a troubled look and Mark shook his head, but neither said a word. Deirdre frowned. Oliver raised one eyebrow. The silence stretched until it became uncomfortably long. Finally, Ned removed his glasses and began polishing them with the corner of his T-shirt. He cleared his throat before he spoke.

"It can only mean one thing. We're dealing with a madman."

CHAPTER FOURTEEN

Ned was sure the anagrams proved that a criminally insane mastermind was behind everything from the disappearing websites to Colin Frump's imprisonment. But the more the six cousins thought about it, the less sense anything made to anyone. Eventually, they agreed to take a break from mystery-solving for the rest of the day and devoted their energies, instead, to tidying the lawns and orchards and collecting the garbage that had washed up on the beaches during the storm.

By nightfall, they were all ready to try again. First, they devoured Mark's dinner of pasta and vegetables, which Hazel and Ned declared better than the finest meal they'd tasted in any city restaurant. Then the cousins built a giant bonfire down on the pebbly shore closest to the castle. To Hazel's surprise, they used old kindling and logs that had been stored inside instead of the brush they had piled nearby.

"Shouldn't we be burning all the branches that came down in the storm, along with the bits and pieces of the shed?" Hazel asked.

"It would still be too wet or too green," Matt replied. "But it'll make great bonfire wood later in the summer. You'll see."

There was a warm feeling in the pit of Hazel's stomach. Matt was the cousin she felt the least sure of; he was the quieter, more serious half of the twins, and out of the four cousins he was definitely the one who seemed most wary of her and Ned. Hazel had wondered whether he would blame them for bringing Clive Pritchard into their midst. But he had shown more enthusiasm than she had expected about trying to solve the mystery, and now here he was, talking as if they'd all be together for the rest of summer vacation. He even sounded happy about it.

"Right. Time to figure out what Clive Pritchard is up to," said Mark, rubbing his hands together and looking expectantly around at the group.

"Speaking of Mr. Pritchard, do you think he'll . . . come back?" Oliver asked. As he spoke, the boy glanced over his shoulder into the growing darkness that surrounded their fire pit. But there was no sign of anyone.

"Even if he did come back, we don't know for sure that he's dangerous," Deirdre said soothingly. "I mean, I guess we know he's not a *good* guy, but . . ."

"His buddy Richard C. Plevit—or whatever Big Ugly Guy's real name is—he's dangerous, though," Ned reminded her. "He hurt Frankie."

That put a damper on the conversation. For a few minutes the only sounds anyone could hear were the crackle and hiss of the fire and in the background, the gentle *shhh* of the waves lapping the shore. Hazel tore her gaze away from the leaping flames to look skyward. The stars were coming out.

"Anyway, as far as the whole anagram thing goes," Ned began, breaking the silence in a matter-of-fact voice, "I guess we know that 'Clive Pritchard' *is* actually Clive Pritchard's real name?"

"Yeah," Mark agreed. "We've lived on the island all our lives, so we know Clive Pritchard is who he says he is. He was even born here. Maybe he uses aliases when he's not on the island, but when he's here, he can't hide. I mean, everyone knows his name."

"So, I suppose that means we can assume it's the people like critic Reva L. who don't exist," Ned continued. "Unless they do exist, but they have made-up names. Like aliases or something."

"I guess that would make Clive Pritchard the evil mastermind," said Oliver, "if he gets to go around naming everyone else after himself."

"Pretty egotistical if you ask—I mean, pretty egotistical," Deirdre stammered. "Not to mention kind of weird. It's like he's *begging* people to make the connection between the websites and him . . . It's almost like Pritchard wants to get found out."

"Or maybe he just thinks he's so much smarter than anyone else that he won't get found out," Ned said. "Maybe he's like his nephew Kenny, and he thinks no one can touch him."

"I wonder what Richard C. Plevit's *real* name is?" Hazel said.

"*I* wonder what Clive Pritchard was doing here at Land's End," Matt said. "At first I thought he'd come to complain about the basketball game or something, but he seemed more like he was trying to avoid us than trying to find us."

"I thought you guys said he chased you down the tunnel," Mark said. "Which, incidentally, I took a look at myself this afternoon: freaky place. I wish I'd known it existed before. Could have come in handy when we were little enough to play hide and seek."

"I *did* think he was following us, at first," Matt admitted. "But if he had been chasing us, he would have ended up on the beach like we did. I think maybe he *wanted* us to run away."

"To scare us?" Hazel asked.

Matt just shrugged. Reliving their flight through the tunnels,

Hazel recalled the moment when she had wanted to turn right, but Matt had ordered them to go left. Hazel sat up a little straighter.

"What if he wasn't trying to scare us exactly, so much as scare us off? You know what I mean? Like, what if he was trying to keep us away from something?" Hazel asked. Her eyes glowed with excitement. "Matt, you said you never go in those tunnels, and nobody but Uncle Seamus and you even knew they were there. But Clive Pritchard obviously knew about them! What if he's been using them for something? What if he hid something there, something he didn't want us to find?"

Ned, Deirdre, and Oliver each raised one eyebrow. So did Matt.

"Oh, no way," Hazel exploded. "Can *everyone* in this family raise one eyebrow except me? That's so not fair! Matt, you're not even genetically related!"

"I can't do it either, Hazel," said Mark. "Just ignore them. They're only doing it to be annoying. Anyway, your point about the tunnels is interesting. We should go back in there and poke around a little."

"Tomorrow might be good," Oliver said in a small voice. "It's getting pretty dark now."

"Well, it's going to be dark down there no matter when we go, silly," Deirdre said. But she added: "Tomorrow sounds like a good idea, though. I'm exhausted."

Hazel suppressed a sigh of frustration. The more she thought about it, the more she was convinced there must be something in those tunnels. That pull she'd felt, like a magnet, it couldn't just be a coincidence. Did they really have to wait until morning to investigate?

"It has been a pretty long day," Matt allowed.

"Okay, it looks like tomorrow for the tunnels. But in the meantime, isn't there anything else we can do?" Ned asked.

Hazel could tell from his voice that he shared her impatience.

"We could try to reach that Inspector O'Toole," Mark suggested. "I'm not sure where Interpol is based, whether it's England or France or somewhere else in Europe. Wherever it is, it'll be in a time zone six hours or so ahead of us. If we stay up late enough, it'll be morning there and we can telephone."

"I don't know if anyone there will take a bunch of kids seriously," Matt said, "but I guess we could try."

They sat in silence for a while, staring at the flames. Looking at everyone's faces, Hazel could see they were discouraged. They had so many questions and so few answers. As before, Ned was the first to break the silence.

"So, back in the city, Clive Pritchard was driving a Ferrari," Ned commented. "That makes him a pretty rich man. How'd he make his money?"

Before anyone could answer, they heard the sound of footsteps crunching along the gravel shore. Straining her eyes to see who was approaching in the darkness, Hazel made out two figures, one taller than the other. She just had time to think that neither looked large enough to be Richard C. Plevit, when a woman's voice rang out:

"Yoo-hoo, Frumps—I came to ask if I could keep the truck another day or two!"

It was Charlotte. As she drew nearer, the bonfire cast a rosy glow over her cheerful grin. It also illuminated the embarrassed but determined face of her companion, Hank Packham.

"Hey, you're the guy who followed Hazel home after the basketball game," Ned said, his voice not altogether friendly.

Hazel felt her skin redden and hoped the others would think it was the heat of the flames. Charlotte motioned to Deirdre to move over, then plopped down on a log beside her and gestured to Hank to do the same. After a moment's hesitation, he did, carefully avoiding Hazel's eyes.

"I ran into Hank in town, and when I mentioned I was coming out to see you, he decided to come along," Charlotte said casually. "I hope that was okay?"

Without waiting for an answer, the woman reached into her purse and pulled out a bag of marshmallows. She waved them at the Frumps.

"I grabbed these from your kitchen when I saw the bonfire."

For the next several minutes, Mark and Oliver attempted to demonstrate to Ned how to select a roasting stick from the sodden pile of fallen tree branches, and prune away any unnecessary twigs. As the cousins bickered over the proper technique, Hank quietly retrieved two sticks from the pile, pulled out a pocket knife, and stripped the first one bare. He held it out to Hazel.

"Here. You can take this one," he muttered, still not meeting her eyes.

"Thanks, but I can get my own," Hazel replied, reaching toward the pile with her uninjured arm. But before she could grasp a stick, Hank's hand had closed around her good wrist. It wasn't tight enough to be uncomfortable, but it was a strong grip.

"Just take this one," the boy repeated. This time he met her gaze.

Hazel was tall for her age, but she had to tilt her head to look him in the face.

He really does have very blue eyes, she thought, and awfully long eyelashes for a boy.

"Please?" Hank said in a voice so low only Hazel could hear. She wasn't exactly sure why Hank cared what stick she used. But she was quite certain he wouldn't let go until she agreed. Or maybe he'd just forgotten he was still holding her wrist.

"Okay," she said, "I'll take the stick . . . if you're going to make a big deal out of it."

To her relief, Hank relaxed his grip. But he still didn't actually let go. A few more seconds of this and everyone would be staring at them . . . unless they were staring already. Hazel didn't look around to see; she didn't want to know.

She raised her eyebrows.

"So . . . are you planning on handing me that stick *before* the fire goes out, or after?" Hazel asked quietly. She was relieved to hear her voice sound calm and matter of fact.

"Uh, right. Sorry," Hank mumbled. He dropped her wrist as suddenly as if it had burst into flames and without saying another word, thrust the stick in her good hand.

Hazel sat down again and concentrated intently on roasting her marshmallow. After a moment or two, Matt cleared his throat.

"Charlotte, you left in such a hurry you didn't hear everything that's been going on," the older boy began. "If it's okay with Hazel and Ned, we should probably bring you up to speed."

Hazel saw Ned's eyes flicker toward Hank and back to her. She hesitated for a moment, then nodded. Somehow she sensed they could trust this boy. At least, they could trust him with this stuff.

"Wow," Charlotte said when they had finished. "So Seamus is heading to Istanbul to get Colin out of jail, and you're all sitting around here trying to figure out how Colin got there in the first place?"

"Essentially," Mark said. "I mean, we figure Clive Pritchard has got to be responsible, but we don't know exactly how or why. Got any ideas?"

Charlotte was lost in thought. Hank Packham silently shook his head.

"*You* don't seem all that surprised by any of this," Ned said to Hank. His tone was accusing.

Hazel noticed Matt and Mark shift uneasily as if they were considering coming to Hank's defence. Her older cousins obviously felt comfortable enough around Hank to talk freely in front of him . . . yet that crack Mark had made earlier suggested they weren't crazy about his older brother. Now Hank was speaking:

"Nothing about Kenny Pritchard's family would surprise me," he said in a dry voice. "And I'm not here to make excuses for him or anybody else."

He shot a sidelong glance at Hazel.

"But there is something that *does* surprise me," the boy continued, his voice warming. "I've been to that museum before. You guys *really* set off the alarm and then climbed out a second storey window? Into a tree?"

"Well it was *my* idea and it was *me* who pulled the fire alarm," Ned said, staring curiously at Hank.

"It was *I*," Deirdre began. But she caught herself and giggled.

Hazel was uncomfortably aware that Hank was still gazing at her with admiration and that Ned was looking at Hank looking at her. The longer this went on, the likelier it was that other people would join in. Soon *everyone* would be watching Hank watch her. She could feel her face turning redder at the prospect.

Charlotte poked the embers nearest her and frowned. "Of course, this wouldn't be the first time Clive Pritchard tangled with the law," she said finally.

"Really?" the twins chorused in unison.

"Yeah. You're all too young to have heard about it, but he was sort of the local bad boy when he was younger. It was a shame really, because he had so much talent."

"What kind of talent?" Hazel asked.

"Oh, he was a very gifted musician and a talented artist," Charlotte said. "But he never wanted to work at anything. I remember he was always getting into trouble for drawing these portraits—caricatures really—of the teachers at high school. They were very good. He captured their faces perfectly, but he'd always ruin a study by adding something rude or disrespectful. You'd start to laugh at first, and then you'd look more closely at the drawing and see how cruel it really was, and you'd just . . . just wish you'd never even seen it."

"Was his family rich?" Ned asked.

"No, not at all," Charlotte answered. "Why do you ask?"

"Well, if he didn't inherit money, then somewhere along the way he figured out how to make a ton of it," Ned said. "Does anyone know how he did it?"

"I don't know for sure," said Hank, after a moment's pause, "but Kenny always said it was from some telemarketing business."

Charlotte nodded. "I think it actually got into legal trouble. He had some kind of fraud or scam going on. But this was years ago. I can't remember if Clive was ever charged with anything, although I think perhaps his partner went to jail."

"Telemarketing?" Mark repeated. "Am I thinking of the right thing? You're talking about those very irritating people who phone when you're cooking or sitting down to dinner and try to get you to buy stuff you don't need?"

Charlotte laughed. The marshmallow she'd been toasting slid off her stick into the embers, leaving a gooey white mess on the end of the branch. She plucked a replacement from the bag and speared it with her stick.

"Yup. That's a telemarketer," she said. "But Clive was running something that went beyond annoying and actually broke some laws. I wish I could remember the details. I'm sorry."

"Did anything ever get published about it in the local papers?" asked Hazel.

"You mean back then? I think so," Charlotte frowned. "I think it also came up again in a magazine article a few years later . . . when the government was talking about cracking down on what they call white-collar crime—you know, when there's stealing but nobody gets hurt physically . . . non-violent crime."

"Hey! Where are you going?" Deirdre demanded, as Hazel, Ned, and Oliver jumped to their feet.

"We need to get back on the computer. Now!" Ned told the others. "All kinds of weird stuff turns up on the Internet—especially articles like that—in the strangest places! Even if the original publisher didn't put the stuff online, someone else might have. We just have to look."

"Okay, okay—but safety first," Matt insisted. "Let's put this fire out."

The embers sizzled as the children emptied buckets of lake water onto the flames. Hazel turned her head away to avoid choking on the smoke. Matt's words echoed in her head: *safety first*. Not a bad idea. Especially if they really *were* dealing with a madman.

CHAPTER FIFTEEN

It was lucky that Mark had such a big room because as tired as everyone was, nobody wanted to be left out of the search. Mark cleared off several chairs so people could sit by unceremoniously dumping piles of magazines onto the floor. As the glossy pages slid past her feet, Hazel noticed that most of their titles related to food in some way.

"*Gourmet/Gourmand,*" she read aloud. "*Eat Something! Chocolate Today.* . . . It sounds like you're already on your way to becoming a chef."

Mark grinned. "Oh, who knows?" he answered. "Maybe I'll become a detective."

Ned and Oliver had settled the question of which search engines to use between themselves and were busily experimenting with different combinations of words. Simply typing *Clive Pritchard* was too vague. There were obviously a great many people with that name. But once they started entering phrases such as *Clive Pritchard telemarketing* and *Clive Pritchard scam fraud,* the boys soon found success. The first place their nemesis popped up was on a list started by a teenager in California, who claimed her family received fifty phone calls every day from telemarketers.

"It's impossible to concentrate with everyone breathing down our necks and reading over our shoulders," Ned said as they all crowded around to read the next big discovery—a university student's analysis of telemarketers' methods. (Clive Pritchard figured prominently.)

Oliver agreed. "From now on, as soon as we get a hit, I'm printing out a copy of whatever it is and moving on," he informed the others. "You guys take turns reading the printouts, or divide them up, or whatever you want. Ned and me will just keep searching for stuff and printing it out."

"Ned and *I*," corrected Deirdre.

"No, better let Oliver handle it," Ned said kindly. "He's pretty good with this stuff."

Deirdre rolled her eyes. "Hilarious, Ned. Just give me the printout."

The next hour or so passed with Ned and Oliver at the computer while Charlotte and the five older kids spread out in a circle on the floor, reading and passing around the printouts. Hazel found a spot opposite Hank, between Deirdre and Charlotte, but it was difficult to concentrate; every time she looked up, Hank's piercing blue gaze was fixed on *her* instead of on the paper he was holding. Things didn't get any easier when Charlotte took a break to fetch snacks from the kitchen. As soon as she left, Hank crossed the room to stand behind Ned and Oliver for a few moments, watching the computer monitor. When he casually rejoined the reading circle on the floor, he took Charlotte's spot, his right knee just inches from Hazel's left.

But as Ned and Oliver became more successful in their searches and more selective about the material they chose to print, Hazel began to lose herself in the reading. So did everyone else. At least two more hours passed, the silence in the room punctuated by outbursts of "Hey, take a look at this!" or "Wait until you read this bit."

Eventually, Ned and Oliver announced that they were too tired to go on, and everyone agreed they already had more than enough information to discuss.

"Okay," Charlotte said, as she sorted the printed pages into neat stacks and laid them out across the worn Persian carpet. "Let's see what we've got."

What they had was an odd collection of pages culled from newspaper and magazine articles, academic research, chat lines, personal websites, and one or two online diaries, or blogs. Some of the earliest pages the boys had printed contained only passing references to Clive Pritchard. But as time passed, Ned and Oliver had begun printing only their most interesting findings, and they were useful indeed.

"The Internet is one strange universe," Mark observed. "There's stuff here from five or six years ago and stuff from yesterday. And who knows how much of it is true."

"Well, we can safely say we now know a *few* things for sure," Charlotte said. "For example, Clive Pritchard seems to have owned or partly owned a whole series of companies over the years and most of them have gotten in trouble with the law."

"Yeah, but he generally gets off with a slap on the wrist," Hank said in disgust. "And then he just disappears for a while and resurfaces later, with some other company."

"It looks like he scams new victims each time," Deirdre said, slowly leafing through one of the piles. "But I think he also doubles back and rips off the same people over and over—only they don't seem to catch on. Some of the names on the chat lines begin to look awfully familiar after a while. The same people who sign on to complain about being swindled by

Clive's first company, the Fazza Co.? They show up the next year complaining about being ripped off by the Opal Company, which Clive Pritchard also started."

"Some people never learn I guess," Mark said. "What's that saying? If it sounds like something's too good to be true, it probably is?"

"Or how about: There's a sucker born every minute," Matt replied, shaking his head. "Pritchard seems to run a lot of get-rich-quick scams, mostly by suggesting he has some kind of insider information. . . . He gets people to invest in businesses, in 'rare coins' that turn out to be worthless and 'rare, signed, numbered lithographs' that turn out to be cheap photocopies."

"He gets around a lot, too," Hank observed. "I mean, for somebody who's so busy starting up company after company, he spends a lot of time at parties and charity fundraisers."

"Yeah, so does his buddy. What's the guy's name?" Mark asked. "Paul something . . . Paul Fazza."

"That first company must have been named after him—the Fazza Co.," Deirdre said. "He's some kind of art collector and patron of the arts. They're always showing up at fancy dress balls together and stuff."

"With a name like Fazza . . . is he Italian?" Oliver asked.

"No, I think I read somewhere he's from Turkey," Hank replied.

"Hey. That's gotta be more than a coincidence, with Uncle Colin being in a Turkish prison," Mark said.

"Yeah, but we still don't know what it all means," Ned said with a sigh.

"And on that note, I really think we should call it quits for tonight," said Charlotte. She was half-sitting, half-lying across the end of Mark's bed, her eyes closed. "I've still got to drive home," she sighed. She opened one eye and peered at her watch. Suddenly she bolted upright. "Oh, Hank! Your parents!

It's almost one o'clock in the morning! Won't they be worried sick about you?"

"No, it's okay," Hank said. "They're out of town for a week. My brother's supposed to be keeping an eye on me, but he doesn't care what time I get home."

"Hmm," Charlotte said skeptically. "Still, I think we'd better get going. See you tomorrow, Frumps?"

Everyone nodded except Deirdre, who had fallen asleep on the Persian carpet.

"Okay, well . . ." Hank spoke reluctantly. "See you tomorrow, I guess?"

Was it her imagination or was everyone waiting for her reply, Hazel wondered. What exactly did they expect her to say?

"Sure," Hazel shrugged. "I guess."

"Later, guy," Mark said. "See you, Charlotte."

"I'll come down with you. I think I should lock up for the night," Matt said, ushering Hank and Charlotte into the hall. As their footsteps died away, Hazel could hear her cousin questioning Hank.

"So, Packham, what's up with Kenny Pritchard? You still friends with that kid, or what's the story?"

Hazel sighed. It was one thing to have acquired older cousins this summer. But Matt was beginning to sound like an older brother: a nosey, over-protective older brother.

"Listen, I know we should all go to bed, and I promise to get out of your room really soon," Hazel told Mark. "But there's one thing I want to check first."

"Sure," her cousin agreed, although he couldn't stifle a massive yawn. "Like what?"

"It's all the charity balls and parties and stuff," Hazel said. "I'm just wondering why Clive Pritchard would waste his time with them. I mean, at first I thought he was trying to rebuild his reputation. But if he cares so much what people think of him, why keep ripping them off with the telemarketing companies? He doesn't exactly act like somebody who's trying to turn over a new leaf."

"So what's your idea?" Oliver demanded.

"Can I use the computer for a few minutes?" Hazel asked. "I know it would probably go faster if somebody with two good hands did the typing, but I just want to see for myself. Okay?"

The three boys shrugged and stood back as Hazel settled herself in front of the monitor. It took her a few minutes; Hazel hadn't spent as much time searching the Internet as the younger boys, and her injury had turned her into a one-handed typist. But by the time Matt reappeared, she had printed out what she needed.

"Okay. Now, compare the names in *these* printouts to the ones we already read—about the parties and the fundraisers," Hazel ordered, handing copies of news reports to the four boys.

"These are all articles about stolen art and jewellery," Mark said in a puzzled voice, "all stuff that was taken from private homes, and sometimes museums, in cities across Canada, the United States, and Europe."

"Exactly," Hazel said. "But look at the names of the people who had their stuff stolen. Look at the names of the museums that got burgled. Now look at the names of the people who gave the parties Clive Pritchard attended, and check out the guest lists."

The boys studied the pages. Oliver rubbed his eyes as if he could barely keep them open.

"I get it," Matt said. "Anywhere from a few days to a few months after Clive shows up at one of these parties, the host or hostess is robbed. . . . Or one of the other party guests is burgled."

Hazel nodded. "And lots of times that Paul Fazza guy turns

up at those parties, too," she added. "I think they're more than business partners. I think they're partners in crime."

"Wow," Oliver said, impressed. "So they'll steal anything from anybody."

"Including our dad," Ned observed. "I'd bet money they're the ones who burgled our apartment and cleaned out Dad's study."

"I'm still confused, though," Matt said.

"Join the club!" said Mark. "The whole thing's confusing. I mean, okay, so Clive Pritchard and this guy, Paul Fazza, are ripping people off with the telemarketing businesses. And maybe robbing rich folk, too—or just organizing the burglaries. But how does that fit in with Ned's project on that artist, Paolo Cafazzo, and the websites that disappeared and the painting Hazel has and Uncle Colin going to jail?"

"You left out Richard C. Plevit, the man who threatened their neighbour and turned up at the museum and the tower," Matt added. "Where does he fit in?"

Deirdre mumbled in her sleep and rolled over. The carpet had left a red mark on her cheek.

"What did she just say?" Hazel asked.

"I think she said *anagrams*," Oliver answered.

A light switched on in Hazel's head. Reaching for one of the stacks of paper the boys had printed out, she began riffling through it furiously.

"Anyone got a pen?" she asked, "or a pencil—anything? Deirdre may be able to do this in her head, but I can't. I have to see the letters on paper."

"What are you talking about?" Mark asked, handing her a pen. But Hazel was too busy scribbling to reply right away.

"Anagrams," said Hazel after a moment. She set down the pen with a flourish. "Check this out: Clive Pritchard's first company was called the Fazza Co., after his partner, Paul Fazza."

"So?" Oliver asked.

176

"Well, Paul in Italian is Paolo, right? So that makes it the Paolo Fazza Co. If you rearrange those letters, you get Paolo Cafazzo!"

"I hate these anagrams," Matt announced. "I can't figure out why they're using them."

"I'm not sure, either," said Hazel, "except maybe to be clever. But there's more. After the Fazza Co., Clive opens something called the Opal Company and starts selling worthless 'gems' to people over the phone."

"I don't see any anagram there," Mark confessed.

"Then take another look at this gossip column," Hazel said, pointing. "The one that talks about Clive Pritchard supposedly naming the Opal Co. after a former girlfriend, someone named Opal Fazzoa."

"If you rearrange the letters in the name Opal Fazzoa Co., do you get Paolo Cafazzo?" guessed Ned.

"Bingo!" Hazel said triumphantly.

"I still don't get it, though," Mark moaned. "Do *any* of these names belong to real people? Is there really a Paolo Cafazzo, a Paul Fazza, or an Opal Fazzoa?"

"I'm pretty sure at this point that Paolo Cafazzo isn't real," Ned said grimly. He had returned to the computer and was tapping away furiously at the keyboard. "I bet Clive Pritchard is Paolo Cafazzo. I bet he took his artistic talents and put them to use creating this phoney Romantic artist. I think he's not just greedy, he's crazy! I don't even think it's about the money anymore. I think he just likes making fools out of people."

"What are you looking for?" asked Hazel.

"I'm looking for Richard C. Plevit," Ned answered. "I think all along, this has been about two men—two greedy, crazy men— who like to make up aliases out of anagrams 'cause they think they're clever. Somewhere on the Internet there's got to be a photograph and a name . . . aha!"

"Did you really just say 'aha!'?" Mark asked, shaking his head.

"I'm entitled," Ned stated. "This is an 'aha!' moment if there ever was one. Take a look!"

Hazel, Oliver, and the twins leaned forward to peer at the computer screen. A grainy photograph of a heavy-set man with a strikingly large bulbous nose swam before their exhausted eyes. Hazel could just make out the jagged scar she'd glimpsed in the gallery.

"That's him," she announced. "That's Richard C. Plevit!"

Scanning the text that accompanied it, Hazel read that he was Paul Fazza, an entrepreneur who had grown up in Turkey and now lived in Montreal. He was described as a patron of the arts and a collector of Romantic paintings.

"So Richard C. Plevit is really Paul Fazza," Matt said hesitantly, as if half-expecting someone to correct him.

"Riiiiiiiiiiiiight," Mark said, exhaling slowly.

"So that means there are two bad guys: Clive Pritchard and his accomplice, Paul Fazza, also known as Plevit," Oliver said carefully.

Hazel and Ned nodded.

"Well, that explains everything," said Mark, his voice dripping with sarcasm.

Hazel didn't know whether to laugh or cry. Mark was right; there were still so many unanswered questions.

"Look, it's one-thirty in the morning. We could stay up until dawn trying to figure out what those guys are up to and how Uncle Colin got mixed up in it," Matt said. "But I think we'd be better off getting some sleep and tackling it fresh, after breakfast."

Deirdre was sleeping so soundly, Mark had to sling her over his shoulders and carry her to her room. The others stumbled down the halls under their own steam.

At the door to his room, Ned stopped and looked at his

sister through narrowed eyes. "I'm not sure I like that Hank dude," he said.

Hazel sighed. "I'm not sure I do either, Squirt," she replied. "Goodnight."

But as she fumbled along the passageway, she heard her brother mutter, "Yeah, but he likes *you.*"

Back in her room, Hazel expected to find sleep the moment her head hit the pillow—maybe even before. Yet, tired as she was, sleep refused to come. Long after she had stopped counting yawns, she was still wide awake.

Why is it that the more you *want* to sleep the more you feel you *never* will? she wondered. She was exhausted; why couldn't she sleep? It had nothing, absolutely nothing, to do with the fact that when she closed her eyes, all she could see was the bluest pair of eyes she could imagine, staring back at her.

Tossing back the covers in frustration, she sat up and peered outside. The breeze from the open window sent a tiny shiver down her back. The moon was almost full and cast a cold, glittering path across the lake toward the island. Hazel's eyes followed the moonlight to where the Martello tower and the surrounding pines should have appeared as inky blobs.

But bright lights blazed from the tower.

CHAPTER SIXTEEN

Hazel flew down the stairs to Deirdre's room, calling her cousin's name. But Deirdre was sleeping soundly. She was in mid-snore when Hazel burst through the door.

"Wake up, wake up," Hazel implored, shaking her cousin by the shoulders. "There's someone in the tower!"

"What? What tower? *This* tower?" Deirdre asked, squinting up at Hazel.

"No, not one of the castle towers. I'm talking about the one on the little island," Hazel replied, gesturing toward the window. "The whatsit . . . the Martello tower."

"Probably just kids goofing around," Deirdre said. She yawned and lay back against the pillows. "We can report it to the police tomorrow."

"Are you crazy? You can't just go back to sleep at a time like this," Hazel scolded, yanking on Deirdre's arm. "That tower is the last place I saw Richard C. Plevit. I mean, Paul Fazza. Oh, whatever his name is—you know, Clive Pritchard's accomplice. It's got to be them."

But Deirdre had rolled onto her stomach and bunched her pillow over her head to block Hazel's voice.

"Fine, get your beauty rest," Hazel said. "I'll get the others; *they* won't want to miss this."

But as Hazel hurried along the corridors she wondered whether that was true. Everyone was exhausted. What if each of the boys was just as fast asleep as Deirdre? It would take ages to wake them all up and go through the same explanation over and over. She could just hear sober, cautious Matt decreeing that they should all go back to bed and investigate in the morning.

"I don't have time for arguments," Hazel muttered to herself. "I can't let them get away again."

Clive Pritchard had disappeared awfully quickly last time he showed up, Hazel reasoned. Paul Fazza might do the same. But how could she get over to the island? It looked close enough to swim to, but she wasn't sure she'd want to risk it, especially at night. And she didn't know how to sail. She'd have to at least wake Mark or Matt; one of them could take a boat out.

A sudden thought struck Hazel and she stopped in mid-stride, just two doors away from Ned and Oliver's room. What if there was another way to the island? What if *that* was where Clive Pritchard had gone after they left the tunnels? What if he had turned right instead of left, and ended up at the island?

The instant the thought occurred to her, Hazel knew it was true. The tunnels *must* lead to the tower. She would stake her life on it. Back at the bonfire she'd wondered aloud whether Clive Pritchard was hiding something in the tunnels, but now she knew it just had to be in the tower. Only now that he knew the Frumps had discovered the tunnels, he had come back, under cover of darkness, to clear away whatever he'd hidden in the Martello tower.

She was running now, passing Ned and Oliver's door without even noticing. Her mind was racing ahead, faster than her feet could carry her. Maybe Clive hadn't even gone as far as the island earlier. Maybe he had followed them into the tunnels just to reassure himself that the Frumps weren't headed to the tower, before hurrying back to his truck. He mustn't be planning on using the tunnels now—at least not the part that led into the castle cellar. He couldn't take the risk they'd hear him. So how had he gotten to the island? And how would he take things off the island? He must have a boat. Hadn't one of the cousins said he owned a big, fancy yacht? His partner, Paul Fazza, could have a boat, too. Either one of them could have hidden a boat around the far side of the island, where the trees towered over a high slope. They could have watched until the Frumps' bonfire was extinguished, waited even until most of the lights in the castle were switched off, then gone to work.

Hazel was in the cellar before she realized she had no flashlight. Now *that* was unfortunate. It had been one thing to enter the musty passageway before—when she was in the company of four others and a flashlight. It was quite another thing to go in alone, with nothing, not even a candle or some matches.

But as she hesitated by the door to the box room, Hazel remembered how Deirdre had spied the cigarette butt on the floor and then the lighter on the old trunk.

"Please let this thing still work," Hazel whispered aloud, as her hand closed around the metal lighter. It was blanketed by a thick layer of dust, but when she flicked it on, a tiny flame spurted out; she fumbled and almost dropped it in her excitement.

"Thank you," Hazel murmured.

Just possessing the lighter cheered Hazel immensely, even though she knew she'd have to use it sparingly; she had no way of knowing how much lighter fluid she had left. But as she began making her way down the dusty tunnel, she found her eyes slowly growing accustomed to the darkness.

It seemed to Hazel that she reached the place where the tunnel diverged a little sooner than she had when she was with the others. But then Matt hadn't been hurrying at the beginning, and tonight Hazel was determined to move as quickly as possible. She *must* reach the tower before Clive Pritchard or Paul Fazza could make their escape.

Resolutely pushing all thoughts of insects and spiders to the back of her mind, Hazel set off down the right-hand tunnel. She found herself slowing a little at first, not wanting to stumble or trip on unfamiliar ground. But this tunnel proved easier than the one that had led the children to the beach; it was wider and, within a minute or two, it was taller as well. Presently, she became aware that the gradual downhill slant of the passageway was growing steeper.

"I must be going deeper under the lake," she whispered aloud, as if the sound of her own voice would reassure her. But there were strange acoustics underground, and her whispered phrase echoed eerily back to her, growing louder before it died away. The effect was undeniably spooky, and Hazel resolved not to open her mouth again until she was above ground.

The tunnel suddenly widened again and, just ahead, Hazel could make out a thin ribbon of light running along the ground. As she grew closer, she flicked the lighter and realized the ribbon she'd glimpsed was light escaping from the bottom of a small oak door set in a stone wall. She had come to the end of the tunnel.

Hazel put a hand on the door and listened. She could hear nothing from the other side. Feeling around for a way to open it, her hands closed on a cold metal knob. No dust, Hazel observed. Someone had come through this door recently. But when she took a deep breath and turned the knob, nothing happened. She put her shoulder to the door and pushed; still, it refused to budge. She flicked the lighter again. The door was no taller than she was, and just at eye level there was an old-fashioned keyhole with a long skeleton key protruding from the lock. The key turned easily in her hands, and she heard the latch give way. Hazel turned the knob and pushed.

She was standing at the entrance to a large, round room encircled by walls of rough-hewn stone. The floor beneath her was formed from the same hard-packed earth as the tunnels, but the low ceiling above her was fashioned from wide planks of wood laid across beams the size and shape of massive tree trunks. A narrow staircase—steep enough that it could have been deemed a ladder—led to a trap door directly above her head. This had to be the Martello tower.

The room was completely empty. If anything had been hidden here, it had already been removed. Yet from the muffled sounds of voices and the creaking of the boards above her head, as feet stomped and shuffled back and forth, it was clear that several men were still hard at work upstairs. Holding her breath, Hazel crept toward the staircase and settled herself on the bottom step to listen.

"We should have cleared this place out long ago, Pritchard, as soon as we suspected Frump was on to us."

It was the voice of the man Hazel had heard threaten Frankie. The lazy voice that replied had to be Clive Pritchard.

"Relax, Fazza," Clive said. "A couple more hours and we're out of here. All the paintings will be on the boat, and we'll be headed across the border. No worries."

"I do worry," replied the other man. "You never know when to quit, that's your problem."

"Hey—the burglaries were your idea, my friend," Clive Pritchard replied, laughing. "And I have to admit, a lucrative one. Nobody ever suspected that two such upstanding citizens would attend those parties just to get a better look at the Monet over the fireplace or the safe in the study."

Hazel grinned. All those fundraisers really had been about stealing! Emboldened, she crept a little higher up the staircase.

"But you don't know when enough is enough," Paul Fazza said. "You had to invent this Paolo Cafazzo and try to fool Colin Frump."

"You're just upset because he didn't give your stupid painting back before he disappeared," Clive retorted.

He doesn't sound quite so relaxed now, Hazel thought.

"Stupid painting? You call my Caspar David Friedrich a stupid painting? Your Cafazzo fakes look pitiful beside that masterpiece and you know it—otherwise you wouldn't have needed it for bait. You and your *brilliant* plan." Paul Fazza sounded so venomous that Hazel retreated two steps before she even noticed what she was doing.

"It *was* brilliant. All you had to do was show the work to him, say it's a Cafazzo, and get him interested," Clive Pritchard said sulkily. "You weren't supposed to leave it with him. It's your fault the painting's vanished. Frump probably took it to Interpol, to show that Inspector O'Toole."

Hazel froze, her hand covering her mouth. She had assumed that her Paolo Cafazzo painting, the one her father had given her by mistake, the one hidden in her room at the castle, was a fake—a Clive Pritchard original. But if she truly understood what the men were saying, then she had Paul Fazza's precious painting by Caspar Whatshisname. A rare and valuable painting, more than a hundred years old, was lying beneath the window seat of her room right now, tucked inside her old sweatshirt. And that must have been what they were looking for in the gallery and the museum—even in her father's study.

"I just can't believe we are fleeing without my Friedrich," Paul Fazza whined, the anger in his voice replaced by self-pity.

"I said I was sorry," Clive Pritchard responded wearily. "But we've wasted enough time looking for it. If we can just get out of here before Frump shows up with the cops, you can buy another Friedrich. Or a Delacroix. Or whatever *true* Romantic artist you like."

Hazel had heard enough. The men clearly didn't know where her father was. Somehow, Colin Frump had gone from helping Interpol try to catch Fazza and Pritchard to languishing in prison in Istanbul, accused of being their accomplice. Uncle Seamus would straighten that out, but it probably wouldn't hurt if she could turn Fazza and Pritchard over to the police first.

But for that, she'd need help.

Hazel was backing down the steps as quietly as she could, when she heard Fazza ask: "What about the cellar? Did we get everything out?"

Hazel's heart skipped a beat. Maybe two.

"Yeah, I already checked," Clive Pritchard replied. "But if you want to look, be my guest."

"No, it's all right," Paul Fazza said irritably. There was a pause, and Hazel began descending the steps again. She had reached the bottom when she heard Fazza add: "Wait—is the door to the tunnel locked?"

Clive Pritchard gave a loud, theatrical groan. "That was the whole reason I drove over here this afternoon," he said. "I made sure those kids weren't around, and then went through the tunnel to the tower door and locked it myself."

"Yes, I know, but did you remember to take the key? You didn't leave it where anyone could find it?"

Hazel didn't wait for Clive Pritchard's answer. She scampered across the room and escaped through the tunnel door, pulling it shut behind her. With trembling fingers she reached up and turned the skeleton key in the lock, just as she heard the trap door to the cellar room open. Heavy footsteps thudded down the stairs she had perched on just moments ago.

Leaning against the tunnel wall, eyes fixed on the door she *hoped* she had just locked, Hazel willed herself to remain calm. She clamped her uninjured hand over her nose and mouth to stifle the sound of her breathing. The knob rattled and the door shook. Hazel didn't move until she heard the footsteps retreating up the stairs. Then she bolted, running as fast as she could in the darkness, back through the tunnels to the safety of the castle.

When Hazel emerged from the cellar, out of breath, heart pounding, she heard voices coming from the kitchen. Ned and the four Frump cousins were overjoyed to see her. Apparently, Deirdre had not gone back to sleep for long after Hazel had left her. And when she had jolted awake, wondering whether she had dreamed the whole thing, Deirdre had checked Hazel's room and found her gone. In no time, Deirdre had roused the others and they had assembled in the kitchen to discuss what to do next.

"So where *did* you go?" Deirdre demanded, her voice cracking with emotion. "Did I dream it, or did you say something about going to the tower?"

Hazel filled them in as quickly as she could: " . . . and they're still there," she finished. "But they said something about a boat, and Clive Pritchard was talking about how it wouldn't take long to clear the place out. We've got to find some way to trap them on the island or keep them here until we can get the police!"

"So Ned was right about Clive Pritchard being the real Paolo Cafazzo all along," Oliver said.

"Yeah, but I wish I'd been there to hear him admit it," Ned muttered.

"Anyway, you're *sure* that they've got stolen paintings and jewels with them right now," Matt asked, "even though you didn't actually see anything yourself?"

Hazel gritted her teeth. They were wasting time.

"That's what they said," Hazel repeated. "They've obviously been using your tower as a place to stash the loot—probably because they figured no one would go near a place that was supposedly haunted."

"Also because we're close to the American border here," Mark observed. "I'll bet they've got someplace nearby on the U.S. side where they can take the stuff by boat and stash it until they're ready to move again."

"Well, before they can do that, Hazel's right, we'd better get the cops here, so they can catch them with the goods," Matt said. "Except, while we were discussing what to do about you, Hazel, we discovered the phone lines are down again. With no phones, and our truck still over at Charlotte's, getting to the police isn't going to be easy."

Hazel felt her heart sink. They couldn't let Clive Pritchard escape, not now.

"Well, we're not totally helpless," Mark began, rubbing his hands together with a look of mischief. "For example, Matt, I seem to recall a rather mean trick you played years ago when Gordon Paige was showing off with his new boat."

Hazel didn't understand, but she could see that Matt did. He was squirming! Deirdre let out a whoop.

"Omigosh, Mark! That's brilliant," she cried. "Hazel, Matt once stranded this guy on that very island by taking a little piece out of the engine on his boat. It was so cool. He could do it again, couldn't you Matt? You could take the canoe over, and when no one's looking, climb aboard and do your stuff!"

Hazel stared at her cousin in disbelief. *Matt* had done that? It sounded more like something Mark would have done. But Matt was shaking his head.

"That trick worked because the kid couldn't swim," he said. "We want to make sure those guys stay on the island. We don't want Pritchard or Plevit—Fazza, I mean—swimming ashore and causing trouble here."

"Well, in the meantime, I'll go for help," Deirdre offered. "I did win the cross-country race for my age group this year, and even in the dark, it won't take me more than twenty minutes or so to get to Charlotte's."

"Go then," Mark said. "And tell Charlotte to get her police constable boyfriend over here as soon as possible and to alert the coast guard, too."

To Hazel's amazement, Deirdre, who had seemed impossible to rouse less than an hour ago, nodded and disappeared out the door. Mark turned to Matt.

"If you're going to sneak over there and disable their boat engine, you'll need a distraction here onshore," he said. "I'll give you ten minutes' head start, then I'll start setting off those fireworks we bought for Dad's birthday."

"I don't know . . . they still could decide to swim for it before Deirdre manages to bring help," Matt objected. But he rose from the table anyway.

"Hey, what about us?" Ned demanded.

"Uh . . . you two stay by the phones and keep checking for a dial tone," Mark said. "The instant that sucker's working, you call 911."

From their expressions, Hazel could see Ned and Oliver were unimpressed by the role assigned to them. But she was starting to get an idea herself. She turned to Mark.

"What about me?" she asked evenly.

"Kiddo, you've had enough adventures for one night," Mark said. "You're exhausted. Stay here and keep an eye on the squirts."

Without waiting for a reply, he was gone. Hazel and the boys could hear him holler to Matt as he headed down the hallway: "I'm going to set the fireworks off from the lookout tower, so they'll be sure to see 'em. Better get paddling, bro. The first one's going off in ten minutes . . . nine minutes and fifty-nine seconds . . . nine minutes and fifty-eight seconds . . ."

Matt surveyed the younger boys' glum faces.

"Sorry, kids. Take care of Hazel," was all he said before he, too, disappeared.

Hazel let silence reign in the kitchen for a few moments. Then she stood and stretched and smiled down at the two boys. With her good hand she beckoned to them.

"You didn't really think we were just going to sit here, did you?" she asked. "Matt's right. The crooks could just swim to shore . . . unless we stop them first."

"But how?" Ned asked.

"I'm thinking about the NIDS," Hazel said. She was smiling broadly now. "The Ned's Incredibly Disgusting Stinkbomb. The original one's in my room. You guys didn't happen to make another, did you?"

CHAPTER SEVENTEEN

"This is it," Hazel whispered to Ned. "This is the door to the Martello tower. Once we open it, we'll be in the cellar."

Ned's eyes were wide, but Hazel noticed he did not remove his glasses for polishing. That had to be a good sign—maybe he was feeling calmer than she'd expected. Or maybe it was because his hands were too full: the plastic bags Ned carried in each hand held the original stinkbomb as well as a new version he and Oliver had created.

"I think Oliver made the right decision, staying behind to dial 911 if the phones start working again," Ned whispered.

Hazel looked more closely at her brother. Oliver had supplied her with a flashlight, and now it was easy to see the nervousness in Ned's eyes. Tiny beads of sweat had formed on his brow, even though it was cool down here in the tunnel.

"You don't have to come in with me," Hazel said. "You can just hand me the stinkbombs and wait here by the door. You can be in charge of slamming the door shut after I get back, and locking it. Can you reach the lock?"

Ned stretched his hand up and grasped the key. But then he let go, turned to face Hazel, and squared his shoulders.

"It doesn't matter anyway because you're not leaving me here," he said. "I'm coming with you. We started this together and we're going to finish it together."

Hazel squeezed her brother's shoulder. For a little kid he was pretty brave, she reflected. Less than a year separated Ned from Oliver, and in many ways the two boys were very much alike. But Hazel had guessed Oliver would elect to stay behind even as she had no doubt Ned would remain by her side.

"I can't think of anyone else I'd rather have with me," she said. Then she cocked her head to one side. "Unless maybe I could have one of those guys from the martial arts movies that kick through stone walls with their bare feet and smash metal pipes with their hands. Or maybe, you know, a police officer. With a gun. Or maybe—"

"Maybe we should get going before we miss everything," Ned interrupted. "By my watch, Mark's probably already set off the first firework."

Hazel inserted the key in the lock and pushed open the door. The round cellar room was as empty as she'd left it, but the trap door above their heads was now open. At the sight of it, Hazel recoiled, pushing Ned back against the wall. But no sooner had she done so than Hazel realized there were no sounds coming from above. The tower was deserted. The men were gone.

"Hey! Watch it!" Ned hissed. "I told you, the NIDS is very sensitive. We don't want to set it off accidentally. We'll only have between five and ten seconds to get away before the smell overwhelms us."

"Sorry," Hazel apologized absently. She put her foot on the lowest step of the staircase and began to climb. Halfway up she turned back to address Ned again. "Just how bad are these things?" she whispered.

"Well, the smell is like rotten eggs mixed with vomit, and

it'll make the air unbearable for a good six to eight hours," Ned said in a low voice. "If it gets on your skin, it'll last even longer, and washing just seems to make it worse. Oh—and there's a particularly nasty side effect I haven't been able to get rid of. If it gets in your eyes, there's this horrible itching and pain that takes a long time to go away."

Hazel stared at her brother for a long moment.

"All I can say is, I'm glad you're on *my* side," she said finally, before turning and continuing her climb.

Hazel didn't entirely trust the silence in the tower. When the moment came to poke her head through the trap door, she found it took all her resolve not to flinch or close her eyes. What if Clive Pritchard was lying in wait?

But there was nothing on the dirty wooden floor except some scraps of cardboard and a roll of packing tape. She scrambled up the rest of the stairs, beckoning to Ned to follow.

The round stone walls that encircled this floor had clearly been whitewashed years ago, but the paint was peeling now in many places. A heavy wooden door leading to the outside was slightly ajar. Hugging the far wall, she could see a stone staircase that led to an upper floor; it traced a semi-circle around half the room as it climbed. Hazel stared at it. There was something oddly familiar about those stairs. In fact, now that she was above ground, there was something oddly familiar about this whole place.

But she had no time to think about it now. Ned was dragging her across the room to one of the tall arched windows that looked out over the lake. Showers of pink, gold, and brilliant white were raining down from the castle's lookout tower. Mark had proved as good as his word.

"I hope this is the distraction Matt needs," Ned muttered.

Just then they heard shouts from outside. Hurrying to the door, the siblings peered through the opening. They were looking out over the southwestern side of the island, the side farthest away from the castle. The fireworks were now behind them, but their bursts of light, combined with an almost full moon, were strong enough to illuminate the little clearing surrounding the tower. Where the ground sloped away toward the lake, their view was partially blocked by a stand of tall white pines. Hazel could see that just beyond the trees a large boat was moored to a dock, and at least three men were moving around on it.

There was a loud splash, and both children heard Paul Fazza yell, "Stop him! He tried to do something to my boat—don't let him get away!"

Hazel pushed the tower door open wider and stepped outside. Her brother followed. "I can't see—did they get Matt?" she asked.

Ned peered through the trees then pointed triumphantly. "I see him! I see him! He's in the canoe, paddling away from the island!"

"If only we knew whether he succeeded in sabotaging the boat before they spotted him," Hazel said.

"I don't think he would have had enough time," Ned replied dubiously. "We'd better get out of here before they spot us."

"I guess," Hazel said, frowning.

Ned was already at the bottom of the cellar stairs by the time Hazel reached the trap door. And then she heard it: the engine on the yacht was coming to life. It made a spluttering sound and then another. Hazel froze. She wished she knew enough about engines or boats to know whether the sounds were good or bad. She didn't want Clive Pritchard and his accomplices to get away. She also didn't want them using their boat to catch up to Matt's canoe.

"Ned," she said excitedly. "I need one of the NIDS."

"Technically only the first one, the prototype, is a NIDS,"

Ned said, handing up the heavier of the two bags. "The other one is a NOIDS—you know, Ned's and Oliver's Incredibly Disgusting Stinkbomb."

"Whatever. Look, here's the deal. I'm going to go back out there and throw one on the yacht," said Hazel. "That way they won't want to go near it."

"What about the other one?"

"How about we deliver that one to Clive Pritchard personally?" Hazel said.

Ned peered up at her, his eyes thoughtful.

"It's tempting," he acknowledged. "But I think this last one should be for the tower, so they won't be able to come back in here or try to follow us into the tunnel."

That made the most sense, even though the image of Clive Pritchard covered in stink held a certain emotional appeal.

"Okay, good idea," Hazel said. "We'll still lock the door behind us anyway, just to be safe."

"Lock what door, little girl?"

It was Clive Pritchard. Hazel slowly tore her eyes from Ned's frightened gaze and looked across to where the tower door was now wide open. The slender blond man was leaning nonchalantly against the door jamb, arms crossed. Moonlight streamed through the doorway, casting Pritchard's long, dark shadow across the wooden floor.

"Who are you talking to?" Clive Pritchard enquired in a silky voice. "Are you a friend of that young man out there, the one paddling so determinedly toward shore? Is there another friend hiding downstairs, perhaps?"

Hazel didn't look at Ned. She kept her gaze fixed on the man in the doorway. She wanted to be ready to run if he moved closer. But she spoke to her brother in a low, determined voice:

"You go back the way we came and don't wait for me—I think I feel like going for a swim. But what we just talked about? We're still going to do it: both of us, on my count. I'm depending on you. Do you understand?"

Hazel risked a darting glance at Ned. Barely waiting for his nod, she took a step toward Clive Pritchard and the open door.

"Who are you talking to?" demanded Pritchard, his voice amused. "Just what do you think you are up to, child?"

"On three," Hazel said quietly. "You've got a good arm, Ned. Throw hard and don't worry about me—just go. Now . . . *one!*"

Hazel was moving toward Clive Pritchard now. She could feel her palms sweating and hoped she didn't drop the bomb prematurely.

"*Two,*" she yelled. Then, as if she was on a basketball court, she feinted left. Clive Pritchard tried to block her, unfolding his arms and moving away from the door. At the last second, Hazel veered right, sped past Clive, and ran through the open door. Caught off guard by Hazel's sudden change of direction, Pritchard stumbled and almost fell.

Outside the tower, Hazel stopped abruptly and swung around to face the entrance. "*Three!*" she shouted as loudly as she could.

There was a moment's delay and then Hazel saw a small object fly up from the open trap door. It smashed on the wooden floor. She saw Clive Pritchard take a step toward the broken stinkbomb. Hazel began backing away from the tower. Pritchard howled and fell to his knees, bringing his hands to his eyes. Hazel turned and ran as fast as she could, through the trees, toward the boat.

Paul Fazza and another man were standing aboard the yacht. The noise of the still-sputtering engine masked the sound of Hazel's running feet and heavy breathing. They didn't notice her until she reached the rocky shore.

"Who are you?" Paul Fazza demanded angrily. "What are you doing here?"

Before Hazel could answer, the air was split by unearthly

howls. Even she turned to see what was making the sound. Clive Pritchard was stumbling down the hill toward them, his hands over his eyes.

"Help me, I'm dying," he screamed, before running headlong into a tree. Hazel winced.

"He's not dying," Hazel assured the two men, who were transfixed by the sight of Pritchard. He was now rolling on the ground, moaning and still clutching his eyes.

"But he does feel pretty bad," Hazel continued. "And so will you, if you try to use this boat."

With that, she hurled the remaining stinkbomb onto the deck of the yacht. It should have been a dramatic moment, and it would have been, if the bomb had burst as it was supposed to. But it lay on the gleaming deck, looking about as threatening as a jar of applesauce, Hazel noted ruefully.

"Oops," she muttered under her breath.

"What's this?" Paul Fazza asked, stooping to pick up the stinkbomb.

"Let me see," demanded the other man, in a whiny tone that reminded Hazel of the basketball-wielding bully, Kenny Pritchard.

"Get your paws off," Fazza barked, as he made a clumsy grab for the bomb.

Or maybe not oops, Hazel thought. The men were so intent on the stinkbomb they seemed to have forgotten her and the moaning Clive Pritchard. Hazel peered at the water lapping at the rocky ledge she was standing on. She knew better than to dive into strange waters; she had no way of knowing the water's depth or whether there were more rocks below the surface. With one eye on the bickering men, Hazel crouched down and began removing her shoes. She took off the sling that had been supporting her injured wrist and stuck one foot in the black water. It was cold.

"I wanna see," the whiner said, grabbing again for the bomb.

"It's *my* boat," Fazza replied. Both men had a hand on the bomb now. There was no time to worry about the water temperature. Hazel lowered herself quickly into the lake and began swimming away from the island. Several strokes later she heard a loud pop and the sound of shattering glass. She quickened her stroke, hoping the breeze would not carry the smell in her direction.

"Agh, what is this? I can't see!" Paul Fazza yelled.

They had done it. They had trapped all three men—well and truly. The smell was obviously so dreadful that they wouldn't be able to go near the boat or the tunnels for ages. It would take hours for their eyes and skin to recover, and if they tried to escape by swimming, hadn't Ned said water made it worse?

All Hazel had to worry about now was staying afloat and making it to shore. She just wished she'd remembered her injured wrist before deciding to swim to safety.

As the island receded behind her, Hazel realized the castle was much farther away than she'd thought. The waves were higher, too, and unless she was mistaken, there was a bit of a current, pulling her slightly off course. The glow of satisfaction she'd felt about capturing Pritchard and Fazza was fading fast. She couldn't feel her toes for the cold, and with her wrist injured, she couldn't use her strongest strokes. The best she could manage was an old-fashioned side stroke.

The cold combined with her fatigue to make time blur. Hazel wasn't sure how long she'd been swimming, but she'd almost given up hope of reaching shore when she felt something bump against her leg. She was disoriented enough to wonder briefly about sharks before she heard a familiar voice.

"Hazel! Grab my hand and I'll pull you up," Matt instructed.

It was easier said than done, but two long minutes later,

a shivering Hazel was slumped in the bottom of the canoe. Someone draped a moth-eaten blanket over her shoulders. It took her a few more minutes to become fully aware that the canoe was being propelled toward shore by Matt, seated in the rear, and Mark, who was in the front.

"Hey, good fireworks," she mumbled through lips numbed by cold.

"Thanks," Mark replied. "But it sounds like you and Ned put on a pretty good show yourselves."

"Ned!" Hazel said, struggling to sit upright. "Is he okay? Did he make it back?"

"He's fine," Matt answered. "He ran back through the tunnels so fast I don't think he stopped to breathe. He was worried you wouldn't make it off the island, and if you did, that you'd never manage the swim. He flagged me down from shore and sent me back to find you."

"I'd run out of firepower anyway, so I came along for the ride," Mark added.

"*And* because the current here is pretty strong, even for someone in a canoe," Matt said sternly. "We'd never try to swim it."

"Oh. I didn't know," Hazel said. She felt foolish. She knew enough never to swim in strange waters without checking for hazards like currents. Her cousins must think her such a baby.

"You're either one of the stupidest people we know," Mark added, "or one of the smartest. We can't decide. Ned told us about the stinkbombs. That was brilliant. And it seems to have worked, which is good, because Matt didn't have quite enough time to disable the engine before they spotted him."

"Yeah—the engine's hurting, but it's not dead. They'd probably have been able to fix it if you hadn't come along," Matt said. "You also probably stopped that other guy from coming after me. I couldn't be sure in the dark, but I think he was Kenny Pritchard's dad."

"Anyway, stupidest or smartest?" Mark continued. "We can't decide. We were thinking we'd hold a vote."

"I think we decided: bravest," Matt interjected. "And I think we also agreed we wouldn't give her a hard time. At least, not until we know she's okay."

"I'm okay," Hazel said. "I'm more than okay . . . we caught the bad guys. It's over."

The canoe was close enough to shore now that Hazel could see her brother and Oliver dancing up and down on the pebbly beach. But as she looked, she realized they were not alone. At least ten people, some in uniform, were gathered behind the boys. As she watched, Hazel saw Charlotte and Deirdre break away from the group and join the boys.

"I don't think I've ever seen that many police officers on Île du Loup before," Matt said with a whistle. "They must have brought over a launch from Frontenac."

"Can you guys just explain everything to them?" Hazel asked wearily. "I'm so tired and I'm so cold. I just want to go to bed."

"Too bad, little cousin," Mark said with a grin. "You're the hero of the hour. And that means you've got a lot of explaining to do."

CHAPTER EIGHTEEN

Mark was right: there *was* a great deal of explaining to do. It was now after 3:00 a.m., but her bed, Hazel soon realized, would simply have to wait. Before any serious questioning began, a kindly police officer with hair as red as Hazel's scooped her out of the canoe and carried her up to the castle. They were accompanied by Charlotte, who made sure that Hazel had dry clothes and several cleaner, softer blankets before settling her into one of the overstuffed armchairs in the kitchen. Charlotte then insisted that Hazel drink two steaming mugs of hot chocolate and nibble on some toast before she spoke to anyone.

Hazel listened as Mark and Matt did a fine job of walking several of the officers through the events of the past few days. She was so tired and the blankets felt so warm and cozy that she couldn't help closing her eyes. The swirl of voices around her soon blended into a sort of background noise; presently she could no longer tell who was talking. The soft Victorian chair Hazel was curled up in had become the calm at the eye of a storm. Maybe she *could* sleep, just for a few minutes. Maybe no one would notice.

"Hazel!"

She opened her eyes. Oliver and Ned were both kneeling at the foot of her chair. They were gazing at her with such worried faces that Hazel wondered what could have gone wrong now.

"What?" she asked, struggling to sit upright. "What is it? What's wrong?"

"Nothing," Ned said hastily, patting her arm. "You just looked really pale and sort of still. We weren't sure you were even breathing anymore."

"I'm breathing, all right," Hazel reassured him. "I think I'm hyperventilating."

She looked around the kitchen. It was empty save for the officer who had carried her from the canoe. He was keeping watch by the screen door.

"Where'd everybody go?" Hazel asked.

"Most of them—my brothers and Deirdre and Charlotte, and some detectives—went into Dad's office to call him," Oliver said. "Turns out Dad had already spoken to the Frontenac police and the Royal Canadian Mounted Police to warn them about Clive Pritchard."

"Yeah, and from what some of the officers are saying, some-body's going to be in deep trouble, because Pritchard was sup-posed to be under surveillance," Ned whispered, looking over his shoulder to see whether the officer was paying attention. "They're saying he would have gotten away if it wasn't for you, Hazel. It's like you kind of saved the police!"

"You mean *we* saved them," Hazel said. But she felt a warm glow spread through her insides at the praise.

"Aw, what did we do?" Ned shrugged.

Hazel looked at her brother, then at Oliver. They were both pale and drawn; Ned's hands were scratched and filthy. Had he fallen during his flight through the tunnels to get help for Hazel? She could see dark circles under Oliver's eyes. The boys were probably just as tired as she was, yet she couldn't recall seeing anyone fetch *them* hot chocolate or tuck them up in soft blankets. She took a deep breath and began with Oliver.

"From where I sit, you guys did nothing," she said in a dismissive tone. "Except for a few little things, like Oliver, here, being brave enough to stay all alone in a deserted castle surrounded by burglars and smugglers, just to man the phones and try to get help. Congratulations, by the way! It looks like you succeeded beyond anybody's wildest dreams!"

Oliver beamed. "I got through to 911. But I was worried they wouldn't take me seriously enough, so I told them the men on the island had guns; I figured that would make the police come fast." His face fell. "Actually, they're a bit upset about that part."

Hazel choked on a mouthful of lukewarm cocoa.

"You told them *what?*" she said. Uncle Seamus really did need to have a talk with her most innocent-looking cousin. "Well . . . you shouldn't make up stuff like that . . . but I sure was glad to see all those cops on the beach."

Hazel turned to Ned.

"And you? First of all, if you hadn't made those stinkbombs the bad guys would probably be on their way to the United States by now, along with a boatload of evidence. And if you hadn't thrown that stinkbomb when you did, Clive Pritchard might have taken me with them, as a . . . a hostage or something!"

Hazel paused and took another deep breath. Ned's face had lost its downcast look and he was listening intently now.

"And if you hadn't torn through those tunnels so fast, then Matt and Mark wouldn't have gotten to me in the canoe when they did. And, Ned, it was really cold in that water . . . I was getting so tired and the shore just kept getting farther away. . . ."

Hazel's voice trailed away at the memory of those last few minutes in the lake. She swallowed and blinked her eyes furiously. She was *not* going to cry. Not now, when it was all over.

"You know what? If I wasn't wrapped up in so many blankets, I'd . . . I'd . . . I'd hug both of you this very minute," Hazel said shakily.

"Ew, gross," squealed Oliver.

"Yeah, just try it and see what happens to your other wrist," Ned growled. But his cheeks were flushed and his shoulders were thrown back. Hazel felt satisfied. She grinned at Ned and was rewarded by a welcoming smile.

"Hazel, if you're feeling up to it now, I think the detectives would like a word with you," the police officer said from his post by the door. "And, boys, I'm told your cousin Charlotte wants a word with *you*."

Hazel sipped the last of her cocoa as the man left the room with Oliver and Ned, returning a few moments later with an older woman dressed in jeans and a leather jacket as black as her hair. Following a few steps behind was an elderly man with a grey beard and eyes to match. They introduced themselves as Detective Heather Mallard and Sergeant Steve Bridge. Hazel thought they'd want to know mostly about what she'd seen and heard in the tower that night, but they made Hazel go back and tell her story from the very beginning, all the way back to the morning she'd woken up to find her father gone.

It was slow going. The woman in particular kept stopping her to ask questions and made her repeat parts of the tale several times. Sergeant Bridge, who had a thick British accent, mostly listened. He had set up a machine at the beginning to tape their conversation, but he also kept a notepad beside him, on which he scribbled illegible words. At first Hazel felt uncomfortable, speaking into a tape recorder. But the longer she spoke, the less she noticed it, even when the greybeard had to ask her to stop while he changed the tape. The whole thing went on so long that Charlotte, Matt, Mark, and some of the other officers came and went from the room several times, stopping once to make tea and more hot chocolate for Hazel. It went on so long that another female officer (whose name, Hazel learned, was Sheelagh) had to escort Hazel to the washroom not once but twice. Several times a phone rang and Detective Mallard left the room to take it, leaving Hazel to strain to hear the clipped tones out in the hall. On those occasions the bearded sergeant would turn his soft grey eyes on Hazel and tell her she was doing splendidly, and it would be over soon.

Hazel's voice was giving out by the time the woman sat back in her chair, clasped her hands behind her head, and exhaled slowly. She gave Hazel a surprisingly warm smile.

"That was brilliant, my dear," the detective said. Her voice was far softer now that it had been for the past few hours, Hazel noted. The greybeard nodded.

"You've taken some extraordinary risks in the past few days, particularly tonight," Sergeant Bridge said, wagging a finger at her. "But you've been extraordinarily lucky, too."

"Oh, give the girl a bit more credit than that, Steve," Detective Mallard said sharply. "She's been smart and strong . . . brave, too."

"I'm not denying any of that," Sergeant Bridge said mildly. "But she has been lucky—lucky to come from a big family that knows how to back her up."

Hazel nodded. Images flitted through her exhausted mind. She pictured Deirdre running through the dark country night to fetch help; Oliver sitting alone in the castle, nervously dialing 911; Ned's face peering up at her from the tower cellar; the twins hauling her into the canoe; Charlotte insisting the police wait until she'd had cocoa. There were other images too: Monsieur Gentil escorting her and Ned onto the train; Uncle Seamus flying to Istanbul at a moment's notice; Frankie meeting him there. She *did* come from a big family. And they had all backed her up—even when what she was suggesting was so outlandish, nobody would have blamed them for not believing her.

"Look, you need to get some sleep now," the woman was saying. "But as you've answered all our questions, are there any we can answer for you?"

Hazel was so tired she could barely hold her head up as she looked at the black-haired detective. She tried to concentrate. Detective Mallard was giving her a gift and she didn't want to squander it.

"Um, yes, please. What's happening with Clive Pritchard and the other two—Richard C. Plevit . . . no, I mean Paul Fazza. I mean . . ." her voice died away. Sergeant Bridge chuckled.

"Don't worry about them. We've sent some officers to make sure they don't try to leave the island," he explained. "But your young lads warned us about trying to land too soon. So we've stationed a few boats around the island and informed your captives of their arrest by loudspeaker. The Mounties have also been kind enough to fly over with their helicopter a couple of times just to reinforce the message that they are not to move."

"Is the smell really so bad that you can't land?" Hazel asked in disbelief.

"We didn't believe your brother at first," the woman admitted. "But it only took one officer attempting to go ashore before we changed our minds. He's in quarantine now."

Hazel looked so worried, Detective Mallard had to laugh.

"Oh, he's fine, he's not sick or anything," she hastened to assure the girl. "But that man stinks to high heaven; no one will go near him."

Hazel gave silent thanks that she had not been close enough to either of the bombs to be affected.

"We'll collect them soon enough," Sergeant Bridge added. "Your brother says the worst of the smell is over now, but I think we'll wait another hour or so, just to be safe."

"What time is it now?" Hazel asked. She felt as if she had been up for days.

"Let's just say you can probably still get lunch if the kitchen is co-operative," said Charlotte, letting the screen door swing shut behind her. "Are you done with her now?"

"Yes, for now," Sergeant Bridge said, packing up his tape recorder and notebook. "But one more thing: Hazel, we've taken the painting from your room. It's evidence, I'm afraid."

"That's okay—it's not my real birthday present. My dad gave it to me by mistake," Hazel said.

"Speaking of your dad, dear, wouldn't you like to ask us anything about him?" Detective Mallard said gently.

"Oh. Yes. Please. Why is he in jail?" Hazel stammered. "And when is he getting out?"

"It is official police business, of course," the grey-haired sergeant said, smoothing his beard.

"Oh, for crying out loud, Steve, after everything this girl and her family have been through," Detective Mallard began, her voice exasperated.

"I'm just saying . . ." the older man said. But he smiled and shrugged, waiting for his partner to continue.

"Your father has been working for some time as a consultant to Interpol, helping the police investigate certain art thefts and forgeries," Detective Mallard explained. "But until recently, it was just consulting, mostly helping an old friend of his on the force—that Inspector O'Toole, whose email you stumbled upon but didn't read."

She paused and looked at Hazel to see if she remembered. Hazel nodded. If only she *had* read that email, maybe a lot of the summer's mysteries would have been solved right then.

"So how does a consultant end up in prison?" Hazel asked. "Did my dad do something wrong?"

"Oh, no," Detective Mallard reassured her. "Colin Frump

went into that prison as part of an undercover operation, a 'sting' we call it. Your father was just pretending to be a crooked art collector and criminal associate of Clive Pritchard. You see, Inspector O'Toole was going to use a police officer for the job, but at the last minute the fellow he had lined up to play the part became very ill; your father offered to fill in for him."

"But why did he have to go to prison?" Hazel asked.

"It was only supposed to be for a day or two," Detective Mallard said. Her voice, Hazel noticed, sounded awkward and unsure for the first time that day. "At Inspector O'Toole's request, your father had met with some very shady characters in Europe. The plan was for your father to then be 'arrested' with a lot of publicity and fanfare, and put in a jail cell with a certain criminal. This is a man who we suspect knows a great deal about the crime ring Pritchard and Fazza have been running—at least, the European end of things. Inspector O'Toole hoped that your father would be able to win this man's confidence and gather useful information from him while they shared the cell."

"Did it work?" Hazel asked.

"I'm told your father has succeeded beyond our wildest expectations."

"You don't sound too happy about it," Hazel remarked.

"Oh, I am, I mean, we are," the detective said. "But there was a mix-up and—I'm very sorry about this—your father has ended up spending considerably more time behind bars than anyone planned."

"What do you mean?" Hazel demanded. She felt as if something, a heavy weight, had settled on her chest; it was hard to breathe. "What kind of mix-up?"

"Inspector O'Toole was the one running the operation in Istanbul," Sergeant Bridge explained. "Apart from her, almost no one there knew your father's true identity. But O'Toole was hit by a car in a very suspicious accident, just after the Turkish police put your father in jail. She was in intensive care for a few days. She's all right now. But during that time, well, nobody was monitoring your father's situation."

"Basically, Interpol lost Colin Frump for a few days," Detective Mallard said bluntly. "His file was, uh, temporarily misplaced and he was on his own. But it's all been straightened out now, and he's fine. He's none the worse for us having . . . lost track of him."

"Lost track of him," Hazel repeated. "All this time, Clive Pritchard and Paul Fazza were walking around free as can be— nearly getting away with it—and the police were letting my dad rot in prison?"

"Well, it really was just a *few* days," Detective Mallard said with a faint smile. "He didn't have time to *rot*, exactly." When she saw the look on Hazel's face, the detective smoothed her face into a mask of polite regret. "Your father is okay, and he was well-treated by the authorities at the prison. Still, it was a very regrettable mix-up."

"You can say that again." It was Ned. He and Oliver and the twins had entered without Hazel noticing, so intently was she focused on the detective's tale.

"Okay. It was very, *very* regrettable," Detective Mallard said, turning to face the boys. "But thanks to all of you, Clive Pritchard and his brother and Paul Fazza did *not* get away."

"You're welcome," Mark said coldly.

"And thanks to your determined friend, Frankie," Detective Mallard continued, as if Mark had not spoken, "not to mention the considerable legal clout and connections of one Seamus Frump, Colin Frump's situation has been all sorted out."

"So our dad's out of jail now? He's coming home?" Ned glared at Detective Mallard.

"Yes, he's out of jail," Sergeant Bridge nodded. "It will be a few days before he can actually return home, however. There is a great deal of paperwork to complete, and although the Turkish authorities now understand that Colin Frump was indeed on our side, they are a little miffed that they were not properly briefed by Interpol in advance. They may insist your father does not actually leave the country straight away, not until they have had the chance to conduct their own interviews with him and, er, fill out their own paperwork."

"Your father has been very understanding about the need for delicacy with the Turkish government," Detective Mallard said.

"I guess Dad's a lot more understanding than I am," Ned said, shaking his head. "He must be really good friends with this O'Toole person."

"I believe they do go back a long way," Detective Mallard said briskly. "However, I think you may find your father has also developed a taste for this sort of work: the adventure, the danger. I can't think where he gets it from; clearly you kids prefer a much quieter life."

Hazel could see the twinkle in the woman's eye, but she wasn't ready yet to be friends. What kind of police force gets someone's dad to do them a favour and then forgets about him *while he's still in jail?*

"One thing I don't understand," Mark said, and Hazel could tell he was still angry, too, "is how Hazel ended up with this valuable painting of Fazza's. By the way, I presume you are giving her a receipt for it? Just in case *it* gets, ah . . . misplaced?"

Detective Mallard smothered another smile.

"Why, yes, we are giving Hazel a receipt for the Caspar David whatsit, aren't we Steve?" she said, turning to the Sergeant. He nodded.

"I know my dad meant to give me a different painting," Hazel said. "But how did they get switched?"

"Just before he left for Europe, your father posed as an interested buyer for a Cafazzo, and that's when Fazza and Pritchard lent him the Caspar David Friedrich," Detective Mallard said. "But then he got an urgent call from O'Toole to hop the first flight to Europe, to do this undercover thing. It seems your father just grabbed the wrong painting on the way out."

"So when did he realize that I had Plevit's, I mean Mr. Fazza's painting?" Hazel asked.

"He didn't, not until your uncle got to Istanbul and told him about it," Sergeant Bridge interjected. Detective Mallard nodded.

"Even now, I'm sure he assumes you just have one of the Pritchard fakes," she said. "If he'd suspected you had something truly valuable, from Fazza's own private collection, Colin Frump would have been worried indeed; he'd have known Fazza would want it back, and be willing to do almost anything to get it."

"We thought it was a Cafazzo," Ned confessed. "And we were confused, because it looks so much like this castle."

"It does," Sergeant Bridge agreed. "But not as much as the pictures Clive Pritchard painted—or rather, which his alter ego, Cafazzo painted."

"We think Pritchard was inspired by the Friedrich and its similarities to Land's End," Detective Mallard explained. "He obviously tried to imitate the Friedrich style in his own work and used Land's End as a model. His 'Cafazzo' paintings are mostly renditions of your castle or the tower."

"Maybe that's another reason they gave the Friedrich to my dad instead of one of Pritchard's own works." Hazel said. "Do you think they figured Dad would have recognized Land's End?"

"Quite likely," said Detective Mallard. "Also, of course, the Caspar David Friedrich is a much better painting than any of

Pritchard's fakes. Look, I'd like to talk more, but I'm afraid the sergeant and I really need to speak with some of the officers. Thank you for your patience, all of you. And try not to look so glum. You've done good work here, and we're all very grateful."

As the screen door swung closed behind the pair, Ned muttered something under his breath. Hazel didn't catch the words, but the tone was far from pleasant.

"Look, kids, it's well past breakfast time and I'm starving. Who wants brunch?" Charlotte asked cheerfully. She glanced at her watch. "Well, lunch?"

"That depends," said Mark warily. "*You're* not cooking it are you?"

"Just for that, I nominate you as chef," Charlotte laughed. "Come on, kids, we won't be able to rest until all the cops and robbers have cleared out, but we might as well seize the moment to take a break and eat!"

Nobody would let Hazel help, not even to set the table. She sat back in the chair and watched as everyone else bustled around the room. Ned and Oliver had obviously showered and changed their clothes while she was talking with the detectives. They looked wide awake, too—had they napped? The thought of it made Hazel close her own eyes. When she opened them again, Deirdre was tugging on her arm and gesturing toward the table, which was now laden with food.

"I can't believe Dad was working as some kind of undercover agent all along," Ned said between mouthfuls of scrambled egg, bacon, toast, and jam.

"*Almost* all along," corrected Mark as he set one last platter of bacon and sausage on the kitchen table. "It sounds like it got a little too real toward the end, when this O'Toole person dropped out of the picture, and nobody in Istanbul knew Uncle Colin was just pretending to be a criminal."

"Well, I think he could have at least told *us*," Ned said, jabbing at a sausage. "I mean we could have kept his secret. And after all, it was my project that tipped him off about Clive Pritchard being Paolo Cafazzo."

"This family has a long history of secrets," Oliver said disapprovingly.

A silence descended on the table then, and everyone concentrated on eating. After at least ten minutes, Hazel put down her fork and pushed her plate away with a sigh of satisfaction.

"That was great," she told Mark. "I had no idea how hungry I was."

"If you were anything like me, you felt like you hadn't eaten in about eighteen hours," Mark said, "which, if you're wondering, is exactly how long it *has* been since we ate a real meal."

"I'm going to go check on the police," Mattt announced, pushing back his chair.

"I'll come with you," Deirdre said.

Hazel didn't know where they found the energy to even care what the police were doing. She laid her head on the table and closed her eyes. After a few minutes, though, she opened them.

"Hey—what day is it?" she asked no one in particular.

"It's Monday," Charlotte informed her, as the screen door slammed. Matt strode in, Deirdre at his heels.

"Come outside!" he said, "Now!"

"Why?" asked Oliver, shovelling one last forkful of egg into his mouth as he spoke. "Whassup?"

"They're taking them off the island," said Deirdre excitedly, "Clive Pritchard and Kenny Pritchard's father and Paul Fazza. They're taking them to Frontenac, to the jail."

"And they're bringing them *here* first?" Hazel asked. She felt a queasy sensation that had nothing to do with the meal she'd just wolfed down. "No thanks. I don't think I want to get that close to those guys again."

"No, they're not coming here," Matt said. "They're taking them to Frontenac by boat. They'll be sailing past any second now."

"We thought we should see them go," Deirdre explained. "All of us together, you know, like an honour guard—except, I guess, more of a *dis*-honour guard—if you ask me."

"Come on, Hazel, all for one and one for all," Mark said, pushing back his chair and standing up in one fluid motion. He held out his hand. "They can't hurt you now."

Hazel nodded reluctantly. It was silly, she supposed, to feel nervous after everything she'd been through. It wasn't like they were alone either—by Mark's last count there were still at least a dozen police and Coast Guard officers roaming the castle and island.

As the children hurried toward the pebbly shore, they passed the red-haired officer.

"Come to see them being taken away?" he asked Hazel. "You should feel proud of what you've done. I hear they've ripped off thousands of people over the years with their Internet scams and the burglaries and forgeries."

"We are proud," said Hazel, linking arms with Ned and Oliver, "the whole team."

"Hmm . . . yeah, I heard about those bombs. You kids want to make sure you use your powers for good, not evil, right?" the red-haired officer said, giving the boys a stern look.

"We promise," Oliver said solemnly. Ned nodded.

"Off you go then—you don't want to miss the show," the officer said, breaking into a friendly grin.

The children fell silent as they reached the shore. The largest of the police boats was just backing away from the island and they could see many uniformed officers aboard.

"I don't see Pritchard," Ned muttered.

"I do," Deirdre replied, her voice squeaking in excitement.

"Look—Mr. Pritchard and, uh, the other Mr. Pritchard, Kenny's dad—they're sitting in the stern. That Fazza guy, he's standing a few feet away."

"Oh, and don't they look cranky," Mark observed, as the boat swung closer.

It was all Hazel could do, not to look away. Paul Fazza glared at the children, shook his fist angrily, and shouted words they were relieved they couldn't make out over the roar of the boat's engines. Kenny's father didn't even look up; he was slumped in his seat, his shoulders hunched—"the picture of self-pity," Mark said later.

But Clive Pritchard, to Hazel's astonishment, rose to his feet as the boat drew near, and met the gaze of the watching children. As his eyes met Hazel's, he gave a mocking smile and, despite his handcuffs, swept a low, graceful bow.

"Cheeky beggar," said a voice with a heavy British accent. Turning to look, Hazel realized they had been joined by Sergeant Bridge and Detective Mallard.

"That's for you, you know," Detective Mallard said, nudging Hazel. "Not us."

Confused, Hazel turned back toward the boat. All the officers on board had arrayed themselves in a line, as far away from the handcuffed captives as possible. Every officer had his or her hand raised in a salute.

CHAPTER NINETEEN

Hazel stretched, yawned, and stretched again. Sunlight was streaming through the open windows of her tower room and at least three cardinals in the tree below were vying with each other to see which could sing the loudest. She felt rested—as if she had slept for days. Her stomach felt as empty as if she hadn't eaten for that long, too. Yet her watch showed it was early in the morning—only six-thirty.

There was no point trying to go back to sleep. Hazel's stomach was growling now. She shivered as she tossed back the covers. It had been hot and sticky, without a hint of a breeze, when she'd finally been able to crawl into her bed. A cold front must have moved in overnight. Stopping first to pull a sweatshirt and track pants over the T-shirt and shorts she'd slept in, Hazel headed for the stairs.

The house was so quiet she began to wonder if everyone else had woken up before her; but as she passed Deirdre's room she could hear her cousin snoring gustily away. Stifling a grin, Hazel continued down the stairs to the kitchen, hoping to find Mark awake and preparing one of his amazing breakfast feasts. But the big room was deserted.

"I guess I'm just the first one up," she observed.

It had to have been late by the time the police had packed up and left, so it wasn't surprising that the others would still be sleeping off their big adventure. Hazel just couldn't understand why she wasn't still sleeping too. Helping herself to a sticky bun and a glass of orange juice, she stepped out onto the veranda.

Hank Packham was stretched out on one of the wicker sofas, his legs dangling over the side and a thin blanket partially covering his T-shirt, jeans, and basketball shoes.

"Yikes!" Hazel exclaimed aloud. The boy bolted upright, rubbing his eyes.

"What? What is it?" Hank said.

"What are you doing here? It's like . . . six o'clock in the morning," Hazel said in disbelief.

"Oh. Really?" Hank Packham was taken aback. "I guess I must have fallen asleep."

"No kidding. When exactly did you fall asleep?" Hazel demanded. "What did you do, get here at dawn?"

"No, I came over yesterday to see how you . . . how all you guys were," Hank explained. "But you were still sleeping."

"What are you talking about?" Hazel said. "I was here all day yesterday, and I was definitely not sleeping."

Hank gazed at her for a moment without speaking. Hazel was reminded again just how long his eyelashes were. His eyes were such a startling shade of blue. They were almost *too* blue, really. Freakishly blue. Probably lots of girls liked him just for those eyes.

"Hey!" Hank said, so abruptly that Hazel jumped. Could he read minds?

"Does your watch have a thing that shows the date, not just the time?" Hank asked.

"Yeah," Hazel answered.

"Look at it and you'll see I'm right," Hank said. "It's the day *after* the day that you think it is."

Hazel raised her eyebrows. If life were fair, only one eyebrow would have gone up, but sometimes you have to settle for what you get.

"Honest," Hank continued. "You've been asleep for, like, thirty-six hours or something. I *did* come by yesterday, after the news went through the village about what happened here. I would have come sooner, only Kenny Pritchard was freaking out about his dad being arrested, and he took off and his mum asked me to go look for him and . . . uh, anyway, I came over. But your cousins said you were still fast asleep, and even though you'd been sleeping all day, they didn't want to wake you up."

Hazel stared at her watch. Hank was telling the truth; it was Wednesday. No wonder her stomach was growling! Now that she thought about it, her injured wrist wasn't even sore anymore; all the swelling had disappeared. She flexed her wrist and waggled her fingers: good as new.

"Wow. I've never slept that long in my whole life," she said with a grin.

"I was impressed. I thought only guys like my brother could sleep that long," Hank said. "You're not like any girl I've ever met, that's for sure."

Hazel gave him what she hoped was a stern look.

"Come on, let's get some breakfast," she said. She motioned for him to follow her back into the kitchen. Over cereal Hazel asked Hank again how long he'd been out on the porch.

"I guess I spent the night out there," Hank admitted. "I didn't mean to . . . I was just hanging around. I thought you'd wake up and come downstairs eventually. The last thing I remember is talking to Charlotte. I must've fallen asleep."

"She probably put the blanket over you," Hazel said, "although I don't know why she didn't just drive you home."

"I guess she figured it would be okay for me to crash here," Hank said. "My brother's gone out of town for a couple of days and my parents are still away."

"There really *is* something going on with all the adults this summer," Hazel observed. "They just don't seem to stick around."

"Yeah. Except Charlotte," Hank said quickly. "She's been sleeping here ever since you caught those guys. She told me she's not leaving until your uncle gets back, just in case any of you have more adventures planned that she doesn't know about."

"Hmm," Hazel replied. "I think I speak for everyone when I say I've had enough adventures to last me a long, long time."

"So I heard," Hank said, his blue eyes shining with admiration. There was a girl at Hazel's school who was so proud of her blue eyes the other girls teased her about it. But Hank's eyes were bluer. Hazel stood up from the table.

"Let's go for a walk," she suggested.

As they made their way through the apple orchard toward the dunes, Hank peppered Hazel with questions about her confrontation with Clive Pritchard and Paul Fazza. With the sun shining and the police long gone, even Hazel thought her tale sounded outlandish. But Hank hung on every word. When he finally ran out of questions, he just gazed at her with such a rapt expression that Hazel snapped.

"Would you quit *looking* at me like that?" she said. "You're making me nervous."

"Looking at you like what?" Hank said. His blue eyes were wide and innocent.

"Huh. See, there's a girl I know at school who has these big blue eyes," Hazel said, picking up a stone from the beach and trying unsuccessfully to skip it across the water. "She thinks she can get away with anything because of them. I'll bet you do that. I'll bet your whole life people have told you how *beauuuuuuuuuutiful* your eyes are."

"Nope. Nobody's ever mentioned it," Hank said, "except you, of course."

Hazel glared at him, but Hank was busy selecting a pebble of his own. To her irritation, a tiny smile appeared to hover about his lips.

"So all the mysteries have been solved, then," he said, skipping the pebble across the waves. It bounced four times before disappearing from view. As Hazel watched, he skipped another and then another. Each time, the pebbles bounced effortlessly four times off the water's surface. Hazel wondered how he did that.

"Yeah, all the mysteries," Hazel agreed after a moment. "Well, all but one. I still don't know why my dad kept us away from here all our lives."

Hank shot her a puzzled look.

"What do you mean?" he asked. "Everyone knows that story."

Hazel froze. She had been in the middle of choosing between two pebbles, trying to decide which was the flattest. Now she clenched both pebbles tightly in her fist.

"What story?" she asked carefully.

"You know. The accident," Hank said impatiently.

"What accident?" Hazel whispered.

Hank stared at her for a moment. He gave a long, low whistle. Then he turned away and launched his pebble over the waves. It sank as soon as it hit the water.

"Hazel, I guess you've noticed I kind of like you," the boy said finally. "I was hoping we could be friends. So, if you don't know about your mum and all that stuff, well, I don't think I want to be the one to tell you."

"What? Why not?" Hazel pleaded. "You've *got* to tell me!"

"Because you could end up hating me," Hank said. "Or even if you don't, you'll always think of me as the guy that told you."

"I promise I won't," Hazel said quickly. "I promise I'll forget it was you who told me. But you can't *not* tell me now. Please!"

Hank sighed. He picked up another pebble and sent it flying over the lake. It skipped once, twice, three times, before disappearing.

"Okay . . . I'll tell you what I know," he said. "I grew up here so I know the same story everyone else knows. But it's probably not the *whole* story. Know what I mean? You're going to want—no, you're going to *need*—to talk to your family about it."

"Whatever," Hazel said. It was her turn to sound impatient now.

"Well, it sounds like you don't remember, but your mum used to bring you here all the time when you were little," Hank began. "Ned, too, after he was born."

"To visit Uncle Seamus?" Hazel said.

"Well, yeah, and your Aunt Julia," Hank replied. "She was your mum's sister, right?"

"What?" Hazel said.

"Oh geez," Hank sighed. "Okay, look. It's sort of like a fairy tale . . . only one with a not-so-happy ending, at least so far. Your dad and your Uncle Seamus are brothers, right? Well, the two brothers married two sisters, Jane—your mother—and Julia, your cousins' mum. I think they met through Charlotte. She's some kind of distant cousin on your mother's side of the family, and Jane and Julia used to spend summers visiting Charlotte's family here on Île du Loup. From what I hear, Charlotte really looked up to Jane and Julia, you know? They were good to her—they were much older, but they always let her tag along."

Something tugged at the corner of Hazel's mind . . . the tears she thought she'd glimpsed when Charlotte met them at the station. She'd asked the twins if Charlotte was a cousin, but they'd avoided answering. So many secrets. . . . She tried to focus on Hank's voice.

"Anyway, at some point a long, long time ago, your mum married Colin and Julia married Seamus. And they hung out together all the time. Even more after they started having kids, and that lasted for years, right up until the car accident."

"Car accident?" Hazel repeated slowly.

"Yeah," replied Hank in a reluctant voice. "I guess I can see how you wouldn't remember. You were pretty little and Ned would have been a toddler—maybe one or two? Your cousin Oliver was just a tiny baby. The story goes that there was this party in Frontenac. Your dad really wanted to go and so did your aunt. Oliver was just a few months old and your aunt hadn't been out much. Your mother wasn't big on parties, but she knew they both really wanted her to go. So your uncle stayed home with all the kids. Charlotte—she was a teenager back then—came over to help babysit. And your mum and aunt and dad drove to the ferry.

"Only they never made it."

"What happened?" Hazel whispered.

"There used to be this really bad stretch of road on the island," Hank said awkwardly. "The driver lost control and the car went off the road and your mum and your aunt were killed instantly. I'm really sorry."

"Who was driving?" Hazel asked. But even before the answer came, she knew.

"Your dad," Hank said gently.

"So it was his fault?" Hazel said. She spoke so softly Hank wasn't sure at first he'd heard correctly. But when he saw a tear slip down her cheek, he hastened to reassure her.

"No, there was nothing your father could have done. There was even an inquest and everything, and everybody agreed it wasn't his fault," Hank said. "Afterwards, it came out that some people on the town council—including Kenny Pritchard's dad—had been warned the road was really dangerous. They were supposed to have fixed it, but they hadn't. They fixed it later, of course."

Of course. Hazel was silent for a few moments, watching the waves rise and fall. Her father didn't own a car now. She had never seen him drive. She had thought he didn't know how.

"But I guess Uncle Seamus and my cousins," she began painfully, "I guess they were pretty mad at my father. I mean, I guess *they* blamed him, even if nobody else did."

"I don't know," Hank said. "Nobody does. Nobody in the village has ever talked to Seamus about it, as far as I know. I think people didn't want to upset him."

"But Dad knew, because he kept us apart," Hazel said, more to herself than to Hank. "He blamed himself. He knew they blamed him."

"You don't know that," Hank said. "Anyway, maybe they *were* angry back then, but they're not now. You can tell. And if you ask them, I'm sure they'll say so."

But Hazel didn't hear him. She was picturing her father at the scene of the crash. Had he been injured too? Did he try to go for help?

Hazel felt sick to her stomach. When someone dies instantly, is it really instant? she wondered. Did her aunt have time to realize she was dying, and know that she would never see her baby, Oliver, again? Did her mother call out for her or Ned?

"They all would have hated him," she said quietly. "And he knew they'd end up hating me and Ned too, because it was our father who killed their mother."

Hank was silent. Hazel was grateful for that. There was nothing to say, anyway. Nothing that she wanted to hear. He couldn't say he knew how she felt. *His* father hadn't accidentally killed his mother and aunt. He didn't know how she felt. Nobody knew.

Hazel had been sitting on the soft dunes, hugging her knees to her chest and staring out across the lake. Now she buried her face in her knees. It was as if the world had been turned inside out. She didn't want to believe in something so horrible. She wanted to tell Hank to take it back, to admit he'd made it all up.

But it had to be true. It explained so much, like why her father never talked about their mother and why none of the cousins would tell her the reason the families had kept apart for so long.

At first Hazel was too shocked to cry. Then she was too angry. How could her father have kept something like this from her? Letting her think their mother had died of an illness, letting her believe they had no family. It was the same thing as a lie.

But as she sat there, miserably reliving every conversation she'd ever had with Colin Frump about her family or her mother, the anger slowly ebbed away—replaced by sorrow.

Her father must have felt so guilty. Hank had said the accident wasn't Colin Frump's fault. Uncle Seamus and the cousins must believe that now, or they wouldn't have tried so hard to help him. But Hazel knew her father. She knew he blamed himself. What had he said to her, as they stood on the cliff? *The fear is not that you will fall, but that you will jump?* He must have spent years replaying the crash over and over, wondering if he could have done something differently. One tiny little thing, maybe. And then six children wouldn't have had to grow up without their mothers, and two men wouldn't have had to raise their families alone.

No wonder her father had never brought them back here.

When the tears finally came, it was almost a relief. Hazel wept for what seemed a very long time, and Hank just waited silently. He didn't try to touch her or say anything. He just sat nearby and waited.

Eventually, she ran out of tears. But now her face was swollen and she desperately needed to blow her nose. Hazel sniffed and wiped her eyes on her sleeve. She felt suddenly self-conscious. She really didn't want anyone to see her right now—especially Hank.

"Listen, Hazel," Hank said. "If it's okay with you, I should probably go let your family know where you are. They're probably up by now, and what with everything that's been going on around here lately, they might start to panic if they can't find you. Also, I could bring you back some Kleenex or a handkerchief or something."

Hazel still couldn't bring herself to look at Hank; she didn't even lift her head off her knees. But she nodded gratefully.

"Okay then. I'll be back as soon as I can," the boy said, getting to his feet.

Hazel took a deep breath and then another. She lifted her head and stared at the waves.

"Hey . . . Hank?" she called over her shoulder. She heard him pause behind her.

"Yeah?"

"Just . . . thanks," she said.

She wondered if he would reply. But when she turned to look a few moments later, Hank was gone.

The fresh breeze had turned into a wind and seagulls keened overhead. Hazel wrapped her arms around herself and tried to keep from shivering, but it was no use. After a few minutes, she had to get up and walk around a little to keep warm. Despite the chill, Hazel decided to splash some water on her tear-splotched face; she was pleasantly surprised to find that the temperature of the lake was warmer than the air around her.

It was good to have some time alone. She wasn't sure when she'd feel ready to face the cousins and Ned. Oh, Ned! Hazel felt her heart sink. How could she tell him? She would have to—it wasn't right that she knew and he didn't. She had promised him: no more secrets.

If only she had known that promise would be so hard to keep.

"I'm back," Hank called from the edge of the orchard. He was carrying something under one arm. As he drew closer, Hazel could see it was a picnic basket.

"What on earth is that?" she asked, pointing to it.

"Uh, not really my idea," he stammered, handing over the basket. As Hazel opened it, he explained. "Everybody was up and wondering where you were, and I figured I'd better tell them that we'd had . . . this conversation."

Hazel glanced up at him.

"Yeah, they were upset. But mad at me, not you. Then your brother said he was glad you knew about the accident, because he'd already found out, and he'd been trying to work up his nerve to tell you. That's when all hell broke loose, and everybody started talking and Charlotte took me aside and told me to keep you away until things had calmed down and until you were ready to face them. *She* packed the basket."

Hazel stared at the contents: fruit, cookies, sticky buns, a thermos (filled, no doubt, with more hot chocolate), an entire box of tissues, and a picnic blanket.

"Wait—my brother knows already?" she asked Hank.

"Yeah. Apparently he found some stuff about the accident when he was searching on the computer the other night—when we were all in Mark's room? He said he went on Oliver's computer later that night—probably while you were sneaking off to the tower that first time—and he dug up more stuff. Then, yesterday when you were sleeping, he had a look around your uncle's study and found some old newspaper clippings and letters from your father to Seamus."

"This detective stuff is getting out of hand," Hazel murmured. But a great weight had been lifted from her shoulders. Now, at least she wouldn't have to tell Ned how their mother had died.

"So . . . what do you want to do?" Hank asked.

Hazel blew her nose twice and pushed her unruly mop of hair out of her eyes.

"Let's eat," she said.

They were halfway through the contents of the basket when Hazel gave a small cry. Hank looked at her in alarm.

"What now?" he asked.

"I've just remembered something," she replied. "Today is my birthday!"

Hank looked horror-stricken. "Now you're *really* never going to forgive me for telling you," he said.

"No, you know what? I'm okay," Hazel said. "I mean . . . I'm *going* to be okay, anyway. All that stuff about the accident and my dad is so horrible and sad. The saddest thing I ever heard. I wish it hadn't happened, for all our sakes. But it did. So . . . I'm glad I finally know. And I'm grateful to you for telling me the story when nobody else would."

Hank stared at her. He was getting that admiring look again.

"I think you're the bravest person I ever met," he told her.

Hazel rolled her eyes. "Yeah, yeah," she said. "Go make gooey eyes at someone else. You're not getting that last cookie."

"Well . . . since it's your birthday," Hank said magnanimously. He split the cookie in two and held out one half toward her, batting his eyelashes as he did.

Hazel stared at him. From somewhere deep inside her she felt a giggle start. She tried to suppress it, but the look on Hank's face was just too much. She giggled and giggled. She couldn't stop. Her sides were aching, and once again tears were streaming down her face, but this time they were tears of laughter.

"I guess you were right," Hank said, surveying her thoughtfully. "You *are* going to be okay."

CHAPTER TWENTY

Even from thousands of miles away, Hazel could hear the anxiety in Frankie's voice. Ned, listening in on the extension, shrugged helplessly.

"Oh, Hazel, I know it should be your father wishing you a happy birthday instead of me," Frankie said. "But at least Colin is out of prison now; he's just stuck in all these debriefings with police and museum curators and government officials. Still, I know he's dying to talk to you, sweetheart—to you and Ned both."

Hazel wondered whether Frankie believed her own words. After all her father had done for the police, Hazel figured, they would *totally* let him call home to talk to his children . . . *if* he asked . . . which, she bet, he hadn't.

"It's okay, Frankie. I understand," Hazel said. It was true, she told herself, she understood perfectly. She understood that Colin Frump was avoiding them. From the look on Ned's face, she knew he understood, too. "Can you put Uncle Seamus back on, please?"

As soon as Hazel heard her uncle's voice she told him about the conversation she'd had had with Hank that morning.

"So, please tell Dad that we know all about it now," Hazel said. "And tell him that all of us—that includes *everyone* here— well . . . just tell him we're all looking forward to seeing him again, back at Land's End."

For a long time, Uncle Seamus was silent. So long, that Hazel began to wonder if her cousins were wrong. Perhaps Uncle Seamus didn't want Colin Frump at Land's End, after all. But when at last he spoke, it was clear Uncle Seamus had been crying. Yet all he said was: "Thank you, my dear. We will be home as soon as we can."

It was not a typical birthday phone call, Hazel reflected, but then this was not a typical summer. After their strange, wind-swept picnic on the beach, Hank had walked her back to the castle, not holding hands but staying so close beside her that his arm kept brushing against hers. When they reached Land's End, the cousins had squashed the breath out of her with a series of heartfelt hugs, before melting away, Hank in tow, so that Hazel and Ned could have some time alone. They had needed to talk, and they did for a long, long while. But by the time Uncle Seamus and Frankie called to wish Hazel a happy birthday, both siblings were ready for a break.

"Cake time!" Mark announced now, as he wheeled an enor-mous wooden tea trolley into the kitchen where Hazel and Ned were sitting. Perched precariously atop the trolley was the largest, weirdest cake Hazel had ever seen. Iced in a garish orange frosting, it was, of course, in the shape of a basketball. But not half a basketball, with the rounded side facing up. That would have been far too simple for her cousins, Hazel realized. No, somehow they had fashioned a cake just as round and just as wobbly as an actual basketball. If it begins to roll, Hazel told herself, I mustn't dive for it. Not unless I'm prepared to be covered in all that icing.

It may not have been a typical birthday, but it was a glorious one, Hazel decided. The cousins presented her with a hoard of presents, and later, after a dinner of all her favourite foods, there was another bonfire by the shore. When Charlotte and the twins disappeared during their singalong only to reappear minutes later, lugging an enormous crate that turned out to contain an NBA regulation-size basketball hoop, the birthday was complete.

The next few days passed in what Ned described as "action-packed slow motion." The children filled their hours with swimming, tree-climbing, exploring, and trying to teach each other the skills they envied. Mark attempted to teach Ned several recipes for what he called safe, non-smelly, non-toxic chemical creations, such as chili. Matt took Hazel out in the canoe, and gave her basic instructions for operating the small sailboat. Hazel and Ned taught basketball drills to Deirdre, Oliver, and Hank using the net Charlotte had installed for Hazel's birthday. And Charlotte took them all with her on several of her veterinary calls so they could help hold and soothe nervous horses while they received shots.

But despite all their activities, Ned was right: time did seem to move in slow motion. With no further word from Uncle Seamus and her father, the days and nights seemed to Hazel to stretch forever.

One rainy evening, nearly a week after Hazel's birthday, the children dragged out all their old family photo albums, and Hazel and Ned were given lengthy histories for everyone from distant cousins to great-grandparents. The reason for Ned and Oliver's close resemblance was explained when Hazel found a faded photograph of the maternal grandfather they shared: he was a short, slender man with light brown skin, straight brown hair and dark eyes partly obscured by a pair of spectacles. In the picture he was standing proudly beside a bizarre contraption, which resembled a hang-glider that had sprouted hundreds of tiny propellers, fashioned mostly from tin cans and rubber bands.

"Mum used to tell us her father was always inventing something," Matt told Ned, "including his own versions of what he called personal aircraft. Some of them actually flew, although not very far. Apparently your mother had to get him down out of a cherry tree once, after his flying machine crashed into it on takeoff."

Hazel didn't like the gleam of approval she detected in Ned's eyes as he studied the photograph. But her attention was distracted by the appearance of an album overflowing with pictures of her mother. To Hazel's delight, the smiling woman in the photographs had the same green eyes and pale, freckled skin that she had. In fact, all the features of her face bore a remarkable resemblance to Hazel. But where Hazel was tall and long-limbed, her mother was petite, like Ned and Oliver. Worse, her mother's long, thick hair was as sandy in colour as Deirdre's short mop. Hazel couldn't hide her disappointment.

"But you still do look a lot like Aunt Jane," Deirdre said comfortingly. "If you ask me, you look more like your mother than I look like mine."

"Really?" Hazel replied skeptically.

Deirdre grinned.

"Let me show you what I mean," she said, pulling another album from the shelf. "Check out *my* mother."

Aunt Julia's face, smiling out at Hazel from the photographs, actually did look a little like Deirdre, Hazel reflected. However, her rangy, long-limbed frame was a perfect match for Hazel's, and her unkempt mane of hair was every bit as red.

"Wow," Ned observed, peering over Hazel's shoulder. "You're like a total blend of the two sisters. It's like there isn't a speck of DNA from Dad's side of the family."

"Well, while we're on the subject of gene pools," Mark said, "I guess it may as well be our turn."

With a flourish, the teenager produced a dog-eared photograph album of his own, which included pictures of the twins' birth parents.

"But I thought you two were adopted as newborns," Hazel exclaimed in surprise. Leafing through the pages, she saw dozens of photographs that showed the boys with a beautiful Trinidadian woman Mark identified as their mother, Eleanor. The album followed them from birth through kindergarten.

"No. Our mother died when we were six," Matt said quietly. "It was cancer. But she had known for a long time that the treatments weren't working, and since she was closer to your Uncle Seamus and Aunt Julia than she was to her own family, she asked them to become our guardians."

Hazel's eyes widened in shock. Her mind was quickly doing the math, but Mark got there before she could.

"Yup. That means we lost our first mother when we were six, and our second mother—your aunt—when we were nine," he said.

"Oh boy," Ned said, shaking his head.

"No wonder our dad couldn't face you," Hazel whispered.

"Hey, that's enough of that," Matt said sharply. "We're not going to deny that it was rough. We still miss both of them— and Aunt Jane, too, for that matter. But I thought we were all agreed that it was time to move on."

"The accident really wasn't Uncle Colin's fault," Mark added. "We do know that, Hazel. Maybe that was hard for us to grasp eight years ago, but we realize it now."

"You should know that your Uncle Seamus sat down with us a few years ago and went through all the newspaper clippings and the coroner's report, just to make sure we really did understand," Matt said. "We've had a long time to come to grips with it. It must be hard for you and Ned, getting hit with everything all at once."

"But you *have* to deal with it," Deirdre said firmly. "So that when Uncle Colin gets here, you can help him. Because, if you ask me, it's time we all stopped letting the past control the present. We're a family again, and that's how it's going to stay!"

Deirdre's words reverberated in her head as Hazel climbed into bed that night. They *were* a family. They were a terrific family. So why was it that, for the first time in years, Hazel found herself missing her mother? How different things would be if she were still alive. Tears pricked at her eyelids. If only her mother were here, maybe she could help Colin Frump deal with the past. She sighed. That made no sense. If her mother *was* here, there would be no past for her father to deal with. There was no sense wishing things were different.

"I'll just have to do it myself," Hazel said aloud into the quiet of her darkened tower room. "Somehow, I'll find a way to help Dad."

CHAPTER TWENTY-ONE

Hazel opened her eyes. She was in the tower again. She could feel the cool flagstones beneath her cheek. The stars outside the gothic window were shining their cold light over the easels and canvases that filled the round room.

What was she doing here again? It was the dream, she knew that. But why? She hadn't had the dream in ages. She had begun to believe she'd never have it again. Everything was supposed to be okay now. Why was she back here, trapped in this room?

"*Get up,*" the woman's voice urged.

"I can't," Hazel replied. Then she realized it wasn't true: she could move. Her legs were no longer paralyzed. She rose and gazed around her. The tower room was filled with paintings, many of them unfinished. A long, wooden table beside her held an array of paints and brushes and rags for cleaning the brushes. The waves below the open window pounded against the rocks. She turned to the easel closest to her. It was shrouded in white canvas. Hazel stretched out a trembling hand toward it. She had to see what lay underneath.

"*It's time, Hazel,*" the woman said. "*This is where you are supposed to be.*"

"Okay, sure. Whatever—just let me look at this," Hazel replied impatiently.

"*Now, Hazel!*" the voice insisted. "*It's time. Come!*"

A sudden sense of urgency gripped Hazel and her hand fell to her side. She *was* needed. Now.

"I'm coming!" Hazel called out loud, and her eyes flew open.

She bolted out of bed. It was early. Outside her window dawn had broken, but the daylight was still weak. The only sounds were those of birds trilling in the treetops, but Hazel could still hear her own name ringing in her ears. She had to go.

Without pausing to grab a sweatshirt or dressing-gown, Hazel threw open her door and flew down the stairs. She raced silently along the corridors, her heartbeat almost drowning out the voice that echoed in her head, still calling her name. Hazel knew where she had to go, and she wasn't the least bit afraid this time. When she came to the cellar and the entrance to the tunnels, she hardly paused to let her eyes adjust to the dark. She just kept running.

When she reached the heavy oak door that connected the tunnels to the tower, Hazel found it standing open. She hesitated, but nine days after her escape from Clive Pritchard, there was no longer even a trace of the horrid stinkbomb smell. Hazel climbed the steep stairs to the trap door and heaved it open, entering the empty ground-floor room slightly out of breath. She didn't stop to gaze at the spot where she had slipped past Clive Pritchard. Her eyes were fixed on the curving stone staircase. The trap door at the top, leading to the upper storey, was open.

Hazel's fear of heights checked her stride for a fraction of a second before she began climbing. The sense of urgency she'd felt in the dream had not ebbed away. She could still hear the voice in her head, insisting she come.

As Hazel climbed toward the opening, her ears strained to pick up sounds. All she could hear were the waves outside.

When, at last, she pulled herself through the opening into the room at the top of the Martello tower, she was startled to find it almost empty. There were no easels, no brushes and paints. But Hazel knew she had finally returned to the tower of her dream. The long, wooden table was still there, near the tall, arched window. And standing behind the table, with his back to Hazel, a man was gazing out that window.

"Dad?" Hazel whispered. "Daddy?"

The tall, dark-haired man turned at the sound of her voice, just in time to be nearly knocked over, as Hazel rushed into her father's arms.

"Hazel?" he said, folding his arms around her and lifting her off the ground. "Why aren't you still in bed? How did you get here? And how did you know I was here?"

Colin Frump stepped back to look into his daughter's face, but held fast to her shoulders as if he couldn't risk letting go.

"I don't know, I just—I had this dream and I had to come," Hazel said. She was laughing and crying at the same time. "How did you get here?"

"Frankie and Seamus and I flew back together last night," her father replied. "We took Frankie home first, but Seamus and I agreed we needed to get here as soon as possible. We drove through the night to get to Frontenac and took the water taxi over—we didn't want to wait for the ferry. I thought it would be hours before any of you woke up. So I thought I would just . . . come here first."

He broke off, looking around the deserted room.

"Do you remember this place, Hazel?" he asked. The words sounded as though they hurt him.

"Just from my dreams," Hazel replied.

"Your dreams?" her father repeated. He frowned.

"Yes. I've dreamed about this room for years," Hazel explained. "What is this place, Daddy? And why did you come here?"

"This was your mother's studio," her father said. "She spent so many hours here. She loved the light in this room. I haven't been here since . . ."

"Since when?" prompted Hazel.

"I haven't been here since the day of the accident," her father answered, squaring his shoulders. "I gather you know all about that now."

"Yes," Hazel said. Her chin wobbled slightly, but she kept her voice steady. "Everybody knows. And everybody knows it wasn't your fault. And everybody agrees it's time you came home and we all started being a family again."

Her dad swallowed.

"I'm proud of you and your brother, you know. Figuring out what Clive Pritchard was up to . . . Although, I suppose I should be grounding you or something for putting yourselves at risk the way you did. . . ."

"Dad. Don't change the subject," Hazel began, but her father held up a hand to silence her.

"I'm not changing the subject," he said heavily. "I was going to say that as grateful as I am for your detecting skills, I am even more grateful that you have managed to bring me back here . . . to bring our family back."

Hazel could see that her father was struggling not to cry. She could feel a tingling in her nose warning her that her own tears weren't far off.

"Well, so long as you're not mad about missing a great birthday party," Hazel tried to joke.

Her father took a deep breath. "Yes, I'm sorry about that, too. And I understand that somehow, between Frankie's filing system and my own, er, lack of organizational skills, you received the wrong painting for a present. I have with me here the painting I intended you to have. . . ."

He turned away from Hazel and she saw a small, flat package

wrapped in brown paper leaning against the wall behind him. He placed it on the wooden table and began slowly unwrapping it.

"You may have been too young at the time to remember this," he said. "But I have been keeping it for you. I wanted to wait until you were ready . . . or perhaps, if I'm honest, until I was ready. Do you remember this?"

Hazel stared. Her father was holding a family portrait that showed Hazel as a little girl, her arms wrapped around a baby, who was clearly Ned. Both he and Hazel were laughing, their faces turned toward a younger and happier-looking image of her father. A smiling woman was holding his hand. Even without the photographs she had seen the night before, Hazel would have known it was her mother.

"You used to come here all the time to watch Janey work," her father reminisced, staring at the canvas. "She would give you fingerpaints, watercolours, markers—anything you liked— and the two of you would spend hours in this room."

"I *remember* this painting," Hazel said. She could hardly breathe.

"Your mother was working on it the day she died. She had promised you she would finish it that day, but I made her come with me and Julia to that stupid party. You were upset; she had promised to give you the painting, to hang it in your room when it was done. So your mother promised you that no matter how late we stayed out, when she got back she would come straight here and finish it.

"That night—the night of the accident—you must have crept out of bed after Uncle Seamus had tucked you in, and come back here to wait for her. How you managed it on your own, through all those dark tunnels . . . I wondered about that for years. Anyway, somehow you found your way here, and here you stayed. You waited all night. When I came home from the hospital, I found the entire household in an uproar. First, of course, because of the accident. But then because nobody could find you."

"Who found me?" Hazel whispered.

"I found you. I came here. You were curled up on the floor right over there, beside your mother's easel."

Hazel slipped her arm around her father's waist and stared at the painting. She felt sorrow for the little girl who had waited by herself, all night long, for a mother who would never come. But she didn't remember that night, not really, just the dream version.

Still—and this was odd—she remembered the painting. She remembered how happy everyone looked.

As Hazel thought about how her mother had wanted to give the painting to her, the craziest idea came to her. Maybe, in a way, her mother had finally done just that. That voice in her dreams . . . could it have been her mother's?

Hazel opened her mouth to tell her father and then closed it again. This was the sort of secret it was okay to keep, at least for now. Maybe she would tell him later. But for now, he needed her help for one last thing.

"Are you hungry?" she asked her father, "Because I am. And you probably don't know this, but they make a pretty decent breakfast here."

Her dad laughed. It was a little nervous, Hazel decided, but it wasn't an unhappy laugh.

"I don't know if I'm ready to see everybody just yet," her father began.

"Well, you don't have much of a choice because they're ready to see you," Hazel told him, pushing him toward the trap door. "Only we better stop by Ned's room before we hit the kitchen. He'll flip when he finds out I found you first."

"I hear there's a local boy I should meet soon as well.

Someone named Hank? It sounds like you and I might need to have a talk."

Hazel gasped. Who had been telling her father about Hank? And just what had they said? But as a sense of outrage began to build inside her, she noticed a mischievous smile on her father's face. This was a side of Colin Frump Hazel had not seen before.

"Dad—since you left, Ned and I have been pretty busy: fending off burglars, shutting down museums with fire alarms, finding long-lost relatives, hiding from tornados, using practically lethal stinkbombs to catch international crooks, and trying to get you out of jail. And you want to talk about a *boy*?"

"Well, when you put it like that," her dad began, "actually, yes. Yes, I do."

Hazel burst out laughing. After a moment's pause, her father joined her. As the two of them made their way down the stairs, Hazel squeezed his hand.

"I'm glad you're back," she told him.

"So am I," said her father.

ACKNOWLEDGEMENTS

Jane Lanthier (1942–2006) read every version except this last one. This book would not have been written without her support and that of Stephen Rogers, Nicola, Buzz, and James Lanthier-Rogers. This book would not have been published without the efforts of Nina Richmond, Lynne Missen, and Akka Janssen. When I was tempted to give up, Ginger Knowlton, Barbara Berson, and the brilliant Heather Mallick encouraged me to continue. The talents of Sheryl Barton, Karen Jordan, Nanci Kirkland, and Andrea Steele made it possible for me to write and edit. Kelci Gershon gave me a place to work. Carol Jupiter, Carolyn Kennedy, Jane Christ, Nicky Lanthier-Rogers, and Richard Scrimger read various versions and gave invaluable advice. Mary-Ann Roberts and her class of 2004/2005 were insightful and inspiring and earned my thanks forever. Thanks are also due to photographer Jill Goodman and to the basketball gurus: James Lanthier, Nicky L-R, Nancy, Margot, and Jill Eisenhauer. For their patience and professionalism, I am indebted to Chuck Swirsky and Kevin DiPietro of the Toronto Raptors, Paul Jones and Eric Smith, Jillian Svensson of Maple Leaf Sports and Entertainment, and Tanya Phillipps of

Canada Basketball. Sheelagh Frame, Sadie Frame, Victoria Gall, Maxine Hersch, and The Runners (Julie Cohen, Paige Cowan, Claire Cram, Gillian Cummings, Janet Deacon, Susan Doyle, Ruth Durgy, Chris Filipiuk, Heather Gardiner, Susan Gordon, Julia Holland, Katherine Lake Berz, Michelle Martin, Carrie Scace, and Carol Wildi) always had my back. Andrée-Ann Gagnon, Cybèle Lanthier, Louise Setlakwe, and Julia Holland are not responsible for any errors I may have made on behalf of Monsieur Gentil. I would also like to thank the Hart House Gallery Grill, E. Nesbit, Joss Whedon, Berry, Buck, Mills, and Stipe, and the young Alvin Williams, #20 forever.